The Way
They Lived Then

Serious Interviews, Strong Women, and
Lessons for Life in the Novels of Anthony Trollope

Taylor Prewitt

iBoo Press
London

The Way They Lived Then

Serious Interviews, Strong Women, and
Lessons for Life in the Novels of Anthony Trollope

Taylor Prewitt

Layout & Cover © Copyright 2020 iBooPress, London

Published by
iBooPress

3rd Floor
86-90 Paul Street
London, EC2A4NE UK

info@iboo.com II iBoo.com

iBooPress, iBooExport & Cagaloglu are the trademark of
F.Oncu Consulting.

ISBNs
978-1-64181-381-5 (h)
978-1-64181-382-2 (p)

iBoo Classics
http://iboo.com/en/iboo-classics

We care about the environment. This paper used in this
publication is both acid free and totally chlorine-free (TCF).
It meets the minumum requirements of ANSI / NISO z39-
49-1992 (r 1997)

Printed in the United States

Contents

INTRODUCTION

Several pleasant hosts wearing the blue and orange scarves or bow ties of the Trollope Society were circulating through the crowd on a May evening at the Knickerbocker Club in New York, making conversation and bringing the outliers among us into small groupings to join in. These board members were faithfully performing their task of "pushing the ball along," as Trollope sometimes put it, at the society's annual dinner. Comparing notes as to what Trollope novel we had last read was the default gambit. One of the books mentioned was Kept in the Dark; another was He Knew He was Right—a bit beyond the entry-level Barsetshire and Palliser series.

These reviews of all forty-seven of Trollope's novels were written somewhat in the spirit of such dinner-table chatter as one might hear at a meeting of the Trollope Society—appreciative, mostly, but not without a word of criticism here and there. The guests I met were stockbrokers, booksellers, doctors, retirees; and these reviews were written by and for such a reader as one might encounter at a cocktail party—whose interests are a bit more informal than those of grad students searching for original information and insights for their dissertations.

It so happens that my wife and I were introduced to Anthony Trollope through Simon Raven's BBC production of The Pallisers in 1974; a few subsequent television series have brought in other novels. This may qualify as a response to the public media. But if there is any common thread among the faithful readers of Trollope, it is a willingness to pick up something to read that is not on the current best seller list, hardly on a book club list, not something that everyone is talking about.

The better-known and more frequently read of his novels are pretty long. A few have told me that they have read all six of the Barsetshire series, or all six of the Palliser series. A few have stepped out beyond these familiar confines to the relatively uncharted void of his other thirty-five novels. A couple of these, the acclaimed The Way We Live Now and He Knew He Was Right, are available as video copies of television productions. Several others are sitting there on the shelf, waiting for some genius to bring them forward in similar fashion. I have entertained myself at times with generating my own candidates: among these are Orley Farm, The Claverings, and The American Senator.

Trollope sabotaged his own reputation with his disclosure of his writing habits, and it may never recover. The very idea that anyone could approach writing without appealing to the muse, just getting up every morning and doing it—two hours every morning, with a self-imposed quota of words to write! The muse was not amused, and her devotees have been unforgiving. If this confession had been well known during his years in service, I suspect that his advancement would have been significantly curtailed. The public requires its geniuses to be seized by the spirit. It's not as if just anybody could do it. An inspired author must rise from a dinner table full of guests when gripped by his muse, as did Charles Dickens, and, as if in a trance, transcribe the words dictated by the spirit.

Any respectable agent, if Trollope had had one, would surely have warned him about the risks of overexposure. Even the great and prolific Dickens wrote only about a dozen novels. Jane Austen wrote six. George Eliot and the Brontes only wrote a few.

A prodigious writer must necessarily have a little tool box, deploying and mixing different plot devices, assumptions about society, views on current issues, and references to the way they lived then—which was different in many ways from our own world, and similar in others.

One of his favorite tools was the Serious Interview, and few writers have used it to such advantage as did Trollope. He introduces this device in a chapter entitled "The Serious Interview" in Barchester Towers, one of his early novels, in which Archdeacon Grantly makes the strategic error of engaging his sister-in-law Eleanor Bold about his suspicion that she is about to accept a marriage proposal from the sly and scheming Rev. Slope. The components of the Serious Interview are present in this prototype:

The prologue, in which Trollope explains to the reader that there are some who delight in offering advice or administering rebuke, and that the archdeacon is among these.

The entry of the combatants. In this instance Eleanor's usually mild demeanor was absent, and the archdeacon "almost wished he had taken his wife's advice," i.e., not to speak to her.

The opening statements. Here he assures her that she has no sincerer friend than he.

The initial sparring. He accuses her of having received a letter from Mr. Slope, and she admits it.

The counterattack. She tells him he may read the letter, and she hands it over to him. She over-reacts, however, in claiming that Mr. Slope is an "industrious, well-meaning clergyman."

The author's commentary. In a paragraph beginning, "Here undoubtedly Eleanor put herself in the wrong," Trollope indulges in a review of the defender's tactics—her assumption of the "prejudice and conceit of the archdeacon" leading to her error of going too far. "She would neither give nor take quarter."

The attacker's final thrust, in which the archdeacon says that Mr. Arabin (who is destined to marry Eleanor in one of the last chapters) agrees with him and his wife "that it is quite impossible you should be received at Plumstead as Mrs. Slope."

The defender's final reaction. Her look was one Dr. Grantly "did not soon forget," and saying, "How dare you be so impertinent?" she hurriedly leaves the room—with the standard reaction in private: "and then, locking the door, she threw herself on her bed and sobbed as though her heart would break."

The postmortem. "By some maneuver of her brain, she attributed the origin of the accusation to Mr. Arabin," and she lay awake all night thinking of what had been said. "Nor was the archdeacon a bit better satisfied with the result of the serious interview than was Eleanor." He understood that she was angry, but it never occurred to him that Eleanor viewed the supposed union with Mr. Slope with as much disgust as did he. "He returned to his wife vexed and somewhat disconsolate."

The morning after. Eleanor sent word that she was not well enough to attend prayers. "Everyone walked about with subdued feet." The sisters (Eleanor and the Archdeacon's wife) were peeved with each other, but after a bit of diplomacy by their father Mr. Harding, they "sat down each to her crochet work as though nothing was amiss in all the world."

As noted, the author often serves as a guide to the reader, offering his own critical observations on how each of the participants played their hand. Indeed, most of his novels include at least one of these confrontations that serve primarily to entertain the reader, but also to unveil hitherto unappreciated character traits and to advance the story.

Trollope enjoyed using his stories as little Clinics in the Lessons of Life, injecting himself as an observer, critic and instructor in other everyday matters. In Ralph the Heir he explains how the beauty of Mary Bonner afforded her the Priority of Service that is the due primarily of beauty, but also of money, political position, and noble birth. A diligent worker himself, he extolled the virtues of hard work in Castle Richmond: "It is my opinion that nothing seasons the mind for endurance like hard work. Port wine should perhaps be added."

Victorians wrote letters, and they mailed them by post, and Trollope as a veteran of the postal service used letters and the service of mail delivery to advantage, again often with editorial asides as to how something may have been better phrased. In another little lesson of life in The Bertrams, he offered another too-frequently-neglected lesson: "Sit down and write your letter; write it with all the venom in your power ... and, as a matter of course, burn it before breakfast the next morning." He goes on to extol pleasant letters, concluding his advice for letter writing: "But, above all things, see that it be good-humored."

The development of character is generally one of Trollope's strengths. His observations were probing and acute; these are transformed into portrayals of certain characters who are so life-like that the reader comes to know them and their foibles as well as he knows his own friends and neighbors. Certain character traits must have particularly fascinated Trollope because they re-cur in several of his novels. Among these is the trait that might be referred to as terminal stubbornness, most obviously shown in Louis Trevelyan and Emily Rowley, who becomes Trevelyan's wife in He Knew He Was Right. Emily receives frequent visits from an older family friend, Colonel Osborne. Her husband Lou-is considers these to be inappropriate and an affront to his honor, whether they represent any misbehavior by his wife or not. She has been raised to be an independent spirit and refuses to follow his command. This difference is pursued to the end, literally, with Trevelyan finally succumbing to his madness.

Other couples demonstrating a reluctance or refusal to come to terms with each other appear in The Bertrams (Caroline Wad-dington and Arthur Wilkinson), Kept in the Dark (Cecilia Holt and George Western), and Cousin Henry (Isabel Brodrick and Reverend William Owen).

Several plots rely on a woman's determination to remain true, no matter what, to a man whom she once agreed to marry—most notoriously in the case of Lily Dale, in The Small House at Al-lington. Forsaken by a handsome rake who subsequently makes a more advantageous marriage, Lily considers herself consigned to spinsterhood, refusing to consider any other suitor, particular-ly the devoted Johnny Eames. Occasionally these self-sacrificing women can be persuaded to get a life for themselves, but it's nev-er easy and often impossible. Some of these steadfast heroines are Florence Mountjoy in Mr. Scarborough's Family and Lady Anna, Linda Tressel, Rachel Ray, and Nina Balatka in the novels bearing their names. Of these, Linda fails to survive. Emily Hotspur also succumbs after being forbidden to marry her worthless cousin George Hotspur, a somewhat ordinary rake, in Sir Harry Hotspur of Humblethwaite.

The Victorian woman suffered a number of disadvantages that no longer apply to today's woman, and Trollope explored these features of the world of his day, illustrating them so that today's reader cries out at such injustices. Trollope himself never acknowl-edged any sympathy for the feminist movement, and indeed he sometimes parodied some of its more ardent advocates, but a number of his works can be read as feminist texts for exposing the problems that women faced. Lady Laura Standish, in Phineas Finn, refuses Phineas's gallant offer of marriage, even though she loves him, because neither of them has enough money to support his political ambitions. However, she devotes herself to furthering his political career, hoping to use him as a mouthpiece for her own political interests. Caroline Waddington in The Bertrams suffers the powerless state of a married woman before the appearance in England of rather modest reforms.

Trollope's insight and skill in presenting women was such that the faithful reader is tempted to sort them into bins—not an unfair analysis of a writer who was so workmanlike in his approach to his craft that he wrote regularly and prolifically. Some of his women appear as rather one-dimensional role players, even though they may be designated as "heroines"; others are developed in such depth that the reader feels that he knows them as long-time friends. Individuals, even fictional creations, defy classification, but the all-too-conscientious reader cannot resist creating a few tentative file folders:

The Faithful Woman, exemplified by Lily Dale, has already been mentioned.

There are a few Women Who Can't Make Up Their Mind, among whom Alice Vavasor of Can You Forgive Her? is the prototype. Others include Lady Clara Desmond in Castle Richmond and Clara Amedroz of The Belton Estate.

The Husband Hunter (one is tempted to refer to her as the Gold Digger) is the woman who sets out to marry well; Arabella Trefoil of The American Senator stands out among these. Another is Lizzie Greystock of The Eustace Diamonds, who does not become Lady Eustace for love of the sickly Florian Eustace.

The Senior Dowager is well represented by Lady Lufton, who stands down the elderly Duke of Omnium in Framley Parsonage. These are some of the most entertaining of the women, who also include Lady Aylmer in The Belton Estate.

A somewhat younger variant is the Woman of Independent Means. Miss Martha Dunstable is undaunted by the Archbishop's wife in Barchester Towers, gently declines the proposal of Frank Gresham in Dr. Thorne, and eventually marries Dr. Thorne in Framley Parsonage. Others are Miss Todd of The Bertrams and the eponymous Miss Mackenzie.

Trollope seemed to have had a particular fondness for The Little Woman Who Could, exemplified by Lucy Robarts, who rose to the occasion to assert herself when challenged by Lady Lufton in Framley Parsonage. Mary Thorne in Doctor Thorne and Florence Burton of The Claverings were a few other of these courageous young women.

And then there is the American Woman, described as "exigeant" by Charles Glascock in He Knew He Was Right. (Would "high maintenance" be the current equivalent of "exigeant"?) Trollope had personal experience with the American woman in his close friendship with Kate Field and aspects of her personality must have surely appeared in some of his American women: Caroline Spalding, the woman who was tarred with the "exigeant" brush in He Knew He Was Right; Isabel Boncassen (The Duke's Children); Rachel O'Mahoney (The Landleaguers); and Lucinda Roanoke (The Eustace Diamonds).

Is there a classification for Lady Glencora Palliser, who dominates the society of the Palliser novels, even after her death, and for Mrs. Proudie, who also exerts the power of her personality throughout the Barsetshire series? I prefer to think of these women as Unclassified. And a list of memorable Trollope women must include a few who appeared in only one novel—Dorothy ("Dolly") Grey, daughter of the attorney Mr. Grey in Mr. Scarborough's Family, Lizzie Eustace of The Eustace Diamonds, and Lady Mary Mason of Orley Farm.

Trollope's own interest in politics evidenced itself in the glorification of an ambition to serve in Parliament—as in Mr. Grey and also Plantagenet Palliser in the Palliser series. However, he was disgusted by rotten boroughs and the corrupt practices of buying votes. We see these practices as a potential path to ruin for several of his characters, including George Vavasor in Can You Forgive Her?, Sir Thomas Underwood in Ralph the Heir, and Butler Cornbury in Rachel Ray.

Much depended on birth in the Victorian world. The eldest son, by right of birth, got it all. This was of such importance that there was sometimes a question as to who was the oldest son—that is, who was the oldest legitimate son. Alleged weddings on foreign soil were particularly suspect, as in Marion Fay, Lady Anna, and Is He Popenjoy? The questions of birthright could be complex in the extreme and could foster blackmail and fraud. Castle Richmond and Mr. Scarborough's Family show us how family secrets could be exploited.

The beginnings and endings of novels have been considerably streamlined since Trollope's day. Just as movies no longer show the credits before the action starts, today's writer knows to start the story as late into the action as possible, picking up background information along the way—or never at all. Trollope sometimes apologized to his readers for his lengthy introductory chapters, and today's readers do have to pay their dues by slogging through family trees and historical details before being allowed to read the story. However, this obligation is often mitigated by capsule summaries that are concise, ironic, and satirical.

Concluding chapters have also gone out of style. No one ever gets married at the end of a love story any more. The lovers may be seen gazing at a tropical sunset, or they may be the only ones left standing, but the reader has to supply the details. Trollope did his duty, though, devoting one or two chapters to wrapping up all the loose ends, sometimes apologizing for having to do so. And these do indeed provide a bit of closure for the reader who has faithfully followed the trials of the principals through eight hundred or so pages. I doubt that many of even the most modern of readers will close the book with a shrug and skip the author's conclusion.

Trollope was an ardent sportsman, and many of his stories include fox hunting episodes, given with such enthusiasm and authority that the reader welcomes these outings as much as the author obviously did. Sometimes an injury or a bit of stupidity will be an important part of the ongoing story, but the reader understands that the hunt is more for fun and sport than for business.

But if the New Criticism, which was the prevailing approach during my undergraduate years, taught us anything, it is that the work stands on its own merits. We know very little about how the great cathedrals were built—we know few names of architects or engineers. But there they are. How would our assessment of these great accomplishments be modified by greater knowledge of the details of their conception and construction? Would we rearrange our pecking order of their superiority? Sometimes we can know too much.

But in the case of Anthony Trollope, we do know that he produced forty-seven novels, and other assorted writings—another of those examples of the great energy of the Victorians. Certainly there are clunkers in the lot, particularly among his earlier works, such as The Macdermots of Ballycloran and La Vendée. And the results were mixed when he attempted to get away from the English countryside, as in The Fixed Period. But I began going through them for the sleepers—the underappreciated novels that deserve more recognition. And sure enough, there are a significant number of these. It's been fun to look—as though I were rummaging around in a trunk full of books in a dusty attic to see what's in there. This is a report of what I found.

Taylor Prewitt
Fort Smith, Arkansas

COUPLES. IT IS AN ENDOWED CHARITY

We knew all about an almshouse for twelve aged men and a warden. We had read The Warden. This is the first in the Barsetshire series, six novels dealing with the clergy in and around Barchester Cathedral. Although I have often thought the Barsetshire series should be required reading for all seminary students, The Warden is perhaps less pertinent to today's church, because it exposes the disproportionately high incomes earned by some of the clergy in the Church of England, and the disproportionately small amount of work done by some. Since this is an infrequent issue in today's churches, some appreciation of the concerns in Victorian England is gained from a tabulation of clerical incomes in the novel, converted into an approximation of 2013 currency values:

Mr. Harding's income

As Precenter	£80/yr	£6,112
As Warden	£800/yr	£61,120
As Crabtree vicar	£80/yr	£6,112
Paid to Rev. Smith		
At St. Cuthbert's	£75/yr	£5,730

Archdeacon Grantley's income

As rector of

Plumstead Episcopi	£3,000/yr	£229,200
Bishop's income	£9,000/yr	£687,600 (pretax)

As of September, 2013, the conversion rate was $1.60 per pound. This shows that the Bishop's income was more than a million dollars a year before taxes. In the absence of concern about the income and bonuses of corporate CEO's in Victorian England, it's understandable that this issue led to efforts at reform.

The test case in the story is not the Bishop, at the equivalent of over a million dollars a year, or even his son the Archdeacon at a third that amount—but Mr. Septimus Harding, precentor (music and choir director in the cathedral) and also warden of Hiram's Hospital. A gentle and kindly soul, beloved of the twelve old men in his charge in the hospital, Mr. Harding frequently plays his violoncello for them. As a more concrete gesture, he has voluntarily increased their daily pittance by two shillings, which amounted to some sixty-four pounds a year out of his own income.

Mr. Harding is father-in-law to the Archdeacon, and the Bishop appointed him to this coveted sinecure shortly after the marriage between Mr. Harding's daughter and the Bishop's son. All is harmonious until some of the citizens of Barchester begin to wonder whether John Hiram, founder of Hiram's Hospital by his will, intended the warden to live in such luxury as the estate now provided. (John Hiram died in 1434, more than a hundred years before the will of Sir William Cordbell of Melford Hall established the Hospital of the Holy and Blessed Trinity in Long Melford in 1573.) This campaign of reform is led by an idealistic young surgeon of the town, Dr. John Bold, who also happens to be a suitor for the hand of Mr. Harding's daughter Eleanor.

Caught up in such controversy, Mr. Harding emerges as one of Trollope's most memorable, and certainly most lovable, characters. The question of his excessive income is publicized in The Jupiter, a London newspaper somewhat reminiscent of The Times, by Tom Towers, a young muckraking investigative journalist. Mr. Harding begins to wonder whether he can continue to hold the position under these circumstances, but he must also deal with his son-in-law Archdeacon Grantly, an outspoken and intimidating champion of the Church, who obtains the opinion of Sir Abraham Haphazard, the Attorney-General. Sir Abraham declares that the point is "so nice" that the plaintiffs would run up fifteen thousand pounds in legal costs before having a chance to prevail.

Not only are the costs of pursuing the campaign prohibitive, but John Bold himself comes to think that his respect for the Warden and his love for the Warden's daughter Eleanor are such that he must drop the case. He finds, however, that the issue, fanned by The Jupiter, has already been decided in the court of public opinion.

So we see that the problem of Mr. Harding's generous income has few parallels in today's church. Should seminarians still be required to read it? Yes. I don't know of any other series of novels that shows the many facets of clerical personalities as they interact with one another and with the world. The Warden introduces us to this community and is thus a prerequisite to an appreciation of Barchester Towers, The Last Chronicle of Barset, and the others in the series. In The Warden we meet the old Bishop of Barchester, benign and gentle, never questioning- the right of the Church to enjoy the blessings given to it by God; Archdeacon Grantly, a formidable defender of the faith who is not to be trifled with; and of course Mr. Harding, a quiet and somewhat timid man who comes to understand that his conscience commands him to assert himself.

I grew up listening to my father and grandfather discuss the preachers of the Little Rock Conference of the Methodist Church—their gifts and their shortcomings, their ambitions, their foibles. "Preachers are the most jealous profession there is," Dad explained to me. Several I knew only by name; several I came to know when they came to town and had dinner at our house.

Not knowing about Anthony Trollope's novels, I couldn't look up anything they talked about in any book. It was apparent that church politics and the variety of clerical personalities would be a fertile field for the novelist.

No one has done it like Anthony Trollope. Individual preachers turn up here and there—Sinclair Lewis's Elmer Gantry; John Ames in Marilynne Robinson's Gilead; Father Jean Marie Latour in Death Comes for the Archbishop by Willa Cather; and Reverend Arthur Dimmesdale in Nathaniel Hawthorne's The Scarlet Letter. But these books deal with individual clergy; none get into the church and its politics as does Trollope's series.

Peter Raible writes in "Images of Protestant Clergy in American Novels" (Berry Street Essay, 1978) that the sexual activities of the clergy are represented disproportionately in fictional portrayals, at the expense of those whose achievements and shortcomings are in another realm. Surely he did not include Trollope in this generalization.

And for the sake of having a list, Kim Fabricius offers on the internet the following list of "Twenty great clergymen in novels:"

1. William Collins in Jane Austen, Pride and Prejudice (1813)

2. Arthur Dimmesdale in Nathaniel Hawthorne, The Scarlet Letter (1850)

3. Father Mapple in Herman Melville, Moby-Dick (1851)

4. Obadiah Slope in Anthony Trollope, Barchester Towers (1857)

5. Charles François-Bienvenu Myriel in Victor Hugo, Les Misérables (1862)

6. Edward Casaubon in George Eliot, Middlemarch (1871)

7. Father Zossima in Fyodor Dostoevsky, The Brothers Karamazov (1880)

8. Jean Marie Latour in Willa Cather, Death Comes for the Archbishop (1927)

9. The young curate in Georges Bernanos, The Diary of a Country Priest (1936)

10. The unnamed priest in Graham Greene, The Power and the Glory (1940)

11. Father Paneloux in Albert Camus, The Plague (1947)

12. Hazel Motes in Flannery O'Connor, Wise Blood (1952)

13. Stephen Kumalo in Alan Paton, Cry, the Beloved Country (1948)

14. Dean Jocelin in William Golding, The Spire (1964)

15. Sebastião Rodrigues in Endo Shusaku, Silence (1966)

16. William of Baskerville in Umberto Eco, The Name of the Rose (1983)

17.   Oscar Hopkins in Peter Carey, Oscar and Lucinda (1988)
18.   Clarence Wilmot in John Updike, In the Beauty of the Lilies (1996)
19.   Nathan Price in Barbara Kingsolver, The Poisonwood Bible (1998)
20.   John Ames in Marilynne Robinson, Gilead (2004)

That this is by no means an authoritative or final list is shown by the absence of the illustrious Mr. Chadband of Charles Dickens's Bleak House, not to mention several more of the Barsetshire clergy, especially the Rev. Josiah Crawley of The Last Chronicle of Barset. But Trollope is the only writer who deals with a diocese full of preachers, and who presents so many of them as three-dimensional characters in their own right—not as caricatures.

Yes, seminarians should be required to read the Barsetshire novels—one a semester, perhaps.

THE CHURCH IN PEACE AND WAR

BARCHESTER TOWERS

Two passages come to mind from my first reading of Barchester Towers over thirty years ago. The first is the Archdeacon's "Good Heavens!" upon leaving his first interview with Bishop and Mrs. Proudie; this steamy outburst occurs relatively early in the story, initiating Chapter 6, "War": as "smoke issued forth from the uplifted beaver as if it were a cloud of wrath," we find ourselves immersed in the pitched battle between the new bishop and traditional Barchester.

The second is the description of Ullathorne Hall, about midway through a fifteen-page chapter describing first Wilfred Thorne, Esq., and his sister, and then the features of the ancient house they lived in. The most tedious of these passages describes "three quadrangular windows with stone mullions, each window divided into a larger portion at the bottom, and a smaller portion at the top and each portion again divided into five by perpendicular stone supporters." I remember thinking when I stumbled onto it: Why was I made for the long and the painful passage I was subjecting myself to?

Since Barchester Towers, Trollope's best-known novel, may be the first, or even the last, of Trollope that some readers may encounter, these two passages need to be acknowledged—the first to illustrate his ability to stand far enough aside from the human drama to appreciate its occasional absurdity; and the second to recognize his tendency to indulge in sentimental reflections shared, no doubt, by a number of his countrymen, but lacking in relevance to readers of another background. And although I now consider Squire Thorne's pretensions to Saxon ancestry, and the house's "delicious tawny hue which no stone can give, unless it has on it the vegetable richness of centuries" to add charm to the book, Chapter 22 would surely be the first to go in any abridged edition of the work.

Why has Barchester Towers outpaced the other novels in popularity? First, I think, because the characters are strong, memorable, in conflict with one another, and elicit just enough sympathy for their positions that the reader smiles and even laughs. There is no sugarcoating; this is no tract intended to bring its readers to commit their lives to the service of the Church of England. The reader sees the deficiencies of even the most virtuous, such as Mr. Harding, but there is also just a touch of sympathy for the worst of the villains, such as Mr. Slope and (perhaps, on a sunny day) Mrs. Proudie.

Trollope depicts the life of the church better than anyone else has done, before or since. He shows the affairs of the clergymen of Barchester much as he also shows us those of politicians, lawyers, merchants, and idle country gentlemen. Perhaps more than any other occupational group, the clergy of the close are bound together as an inner group, almost a fraternity. And this may be why clergy and politicians, the subjects of the Barsetshire series and the Palliser series, were such ready subjects for novel after novel: their professional association involved just enough interaction and jockeying for position to entertain the reader.

Several of the characters come to us from The Warden, chiefly Mr. Septimus Harding, the Warden himself, bruised from his attack in The Jupiter, the newspaper of the day. Mr. Harding has surrendered his position as Warden of Hiram's Hospital, feeling that he could not justify the high salary attached to the position, and not caring to attempt to do so. In this matter he was in direct opposition to the advice of his son-in-law Archdeacon Grantly, aggressive warrior of the Church Militant, and one who benefits even more from the riches of the church. The author must have gloated to himself as he set up the situation with which the story begins: the saintly Bishop Grantly, dear friend of Mr. Harding and father of Archdeacon Grantly, is about to die. His successor is to be named by the prime minister, who is sufficiently friendly to the Grantlys that he would be expected to name the archdeacon to succeed his father. But the government is about to fall, and the next prime minister would be expected to look elsewhere for a successor. If the bishop dies quickly, there would be time for the present prime minister to act. The poor bishop apologizes on his deathbed for taking so long.

And he does take too long. Though the conflicted archdeacon attempts to convey the news of his father's death to the prime minister before he leaves office, he does not succeed. A new prime minister makes the appointment, and the new bishop is to be a low churchman, one Dr. Proudie.

The supreme irony in this situation is not left to implication and inference, as we read of the disappointed Archdeacon Grantly's reaction:

Many will think that he was wicked to grieve for the loss of Episcopal power, wicked to have coveted it, nay, wicked even to have thought about it, in the way and at the moments he had done so.

With such censures I cannot profess that I completely agree. The nolo episcopari, though still in use, is so directly at variance with the tendency of all human wishes, that it cannot be thought to express the true aspirations of rising priests in the Church of England.

Nolo episcopari is explained on the internet in Trollope's Apollo: A Guide to the Uses of Classics in the Novels of Anthony Trollope (www.trollope-apollo.com), a project undertaken by students at Hendrix College under Professor Rebecca Resinski:

A Latin phrase meaning "I do not wish to be bishop." This is the appropriate response with which an individual should reply if he is offered the position of bishop in the church, even if he wishes to accept it. Trollope implies here that any other person, besides Bishop Proudie, would probably not want to be the bishop if he had to deal with Mrs. Proudie and her constant meddling; and thus, this person would actually mean nolo episcopari when saying the phrase. [MD]

(It is worth noting that nolo episcopari has survived in the Methodist Church to the extent that when Dean William Cannon was elected to the episcopacy in 1968, he protested, "Why, you can't elect me bishop. I didn't even bring my robes," in gentle mockery of the aggressive campaigns conducted by candidates for the episcopacy.)

Enter Mrs. Proudie, Barchester's answer to Lady Macbeth. A 1982 BBC production of The Barchester Chronicles followed the text of The Warden and Barchester Towers quite closely, and the direction and acting were superb. Mrs. Proudie, though, gave me pause. On screen she is shown as a slender, scheming woman who narrows her eyes as she schemes. I think of her as a more straightforward champion of her own views, more given to the direct approach than to subtlety. She speaks early on the evils of

Sabbath-traveling, and on the necessity for Sabbath Day schools. We can assume that she prompted the Bishop's chaplain, the sly Obadiah Slope, to preach the sermon against Mr. Harding's beloved high church music, leading the author to the following meditation on the sermon as an art form:

There is, perhaps, no greater hardship at present inflicted on mankind in civilized and free countries, than the necessity of listening to sermons. ... We desire, nay, we are resolute, to enjoy the comfort of public worship; but we desire also that we may do so without an amount of tedium which ordinary human nature cannot endure with patience; that we may be able to leave the house of God, without that anxious longing to escape, which is the common consequence of common sermons.

I should think that this paragraph alone should justify my contention that the Barchester novels, but particularly Barchester Towers, should be required study in all seminaries.

Mr. Slope goes on to use his position as chaplain to the bishop in a power struggle with Mrs. Proudie. He loses. He learns that Mr. Harding's daughter Eleanor Bold, recently widowed in a death between novels, has an income of a thousand pounds a year. (The mortality risk of the period between novels was significant in the Barsetshire and Palliser series, leading to the deaths of John Bold, Eleanor's suitor and husband in The Warden, and Lady Glencora Palliser, who did not survive the period between The Prime Minister and The Duke's Children.) Having promised Mr. Harding's former position as Warden of Hiram's Hospital to Mr. Quiverful, whose twelve children in addition to his wife and himself provided "fourteen arguments in favour of Mr. Quiverful's claims," he then reverses his field and indicates to Mrs. Bold that through his efforts and kind services her father may yet be restored to his former position. But when Eleanor shows his subsequent letter on the subject to her father, Mr. Harding finds a reference to his daughter's "silken tresses," and Mr. Slope's scheme dies aborning.

Although Mrs. Proudie reigns triumphant throughout Barchester Towers and goes on undeterred in subsequent Barsetshire novels, the reader derives some consolation from Mr. Slope's downfall. Indeed, he is refused by three women: one of the Bishop's daughters; Eleanor Bold (with a slap on the ear); and the infamous Signora Neroni. Ah, Signora Neroni! Somehow she and her family come across with more charm in the video presentation than in my reading of the book and listening to it on tape a few years ago. As feckless foils to the saintly Mr. Harding, and as legitimate targets for reform of the church, the reader may have limited patience with them. But brought to the screen by buoyant actors, they display the charm that enabled them to get by with so much in Barchester society. Trollope tells us that their heartlessness was accompanied by such good nature as to make itself "but little noticeable to the world." This introductory comment was, of course, absent from the video presentation, leaving the viewer to draw his own conclusions. But the mind of this puritanical reader, I'm afraid, was poisoned by the author's observation.

The father, Dr. Vesey Stanhope, is summoned home from Italy by the new bishop. Dr. Stanhope, it turns out, had gone to Italy for his health; he had had a sore throat twelve years earlier and had never returned. He brings with him his wife, two daughters and a son. The card of the younger daughter is decorated with a coronet, and it reads "La Signora Madeline Vesey Neroni—Nata Stanhope." She is somewhat indifferent to her situation of having married a captain of no birth and no property, leaving her with a young daughter but no husband, and a knee injury that she attributed to ascending a ruin, leaving her to walk with "the grace of a hunchback." And so she has chosen to be carried everywhere she goes.

Her brother Bertie, the son of a man without fortune, feels no obligation to earn his own bread. Madeline and Bertie prove to be rolling cannons on the decks of Barchester. The beautiful Madeline has separate and conspicuous tête-á-têtes with the Bishop, Mr. Slope, Squire Thorne, and a newly arrived clergyman from Oxford, Francis Arabin. Bertie distinguishes himself at Mrs. Proudie's reception by remarking to the bishop that he once had thoughts of being a bishop himself. "That is, a parson—a parson first, you know, and a bishop afterwards. If I had once begun, I'd have stuck to it. But on the whole, I like the Church of Rome the best."

But one comes closest to feeling some sympathy for Mr. Slope—whom the author confesses that he himself does not like—when Signora Neroni uses an audience for the purpose of humiliating him. (This is after Mr. Slope has proposed unsuccessfully to Signora Neroni and to Eleanor Bold, and at a time when he has had his friend Tom Towers of The Jupiter write in its pages that Mr. Slope would be the best candidate to replace the lately deceased Dean of the Chapter—a position that is to be offered to Mr. Harding and eventually accepted by Mr. Arabin.) Her morning levée includes Mr. Thorne; Mr. Arabin ("It may seem strange that he should thus come dangling about Madame Neroni because he was in love with Mrs. Bold; but was nevertheless the fact"); Mr. Slope; and a couple of other young men about the city.

Bertie and Charlotte are spectators as she follows one thrust at Mr. Slope with another, saying that everybody knows that he is to be the new dean, passing over old men like her father and Archdeacon. She then taunts him with having been refused by Mrs. Bold, singing

It's gude to be off with the old love—Mr. Slope,

Before you are on with the new.

'Ha, ha, ha!'

Mr. Slope's sins were such as to merit little mercy from the court of public and private opinion. And perhaps his punishment did fit his crime. But his punishment was severe.

This meeting was no serious interview. But Trollope does give the more serious sort its name in Chapter 29, "A Serious Interview," as described in the Introduction. Suffice it to repeat here, the Archdeacon assumes falsely that his daughter Eleanor Bold is likely to accept the suit of Mr. Slope. His wife had told him he would not prevail with Eleanor, but he was so sure he was right and that it was his duty to intervene, that he could not go to bed quietly. His wife, of course, was right.

Barchester Towers is a comedy, and it has a happy ending, which required a good bit of doing by the author. Trollope self-consciously bemoaned the difficulty of pronouncing a credible happy ending to a novel; but he did it anyway.

TROLLOPE'S ALTER EGO DOCTOR THORNE

Doctor Thorne is a fairy tale. What else can one say after finishing a book in which the heroine, a poor girl of illegitimate birth but "the sweetest girl in the world," is changed at a stroke (although long anticipated) into the wealthiest heiress in the county, gaining the blessings of her lover's mother, Lady Arabella, for her marriage to the most eligible young bachelor in Barsetshire? So much for the plot. Trollope cared little, in general, for maintaining the reader's suspense and usually revealed in advance how it would turn out. But the questions are: What about the good parts? The serious interviews? The irony? The social satire? And though the general outlines of the plot are predictable, are there details that keep us going?

Few of Trollope's young lovers are very complex; the supporting characters are often the ones with interesting quirks and turns. The young may be true or false, or they may be first one and then the other (as Frank Gresham, heir to the rapidly disappearing Gresham estate, shows himself to be); and one often views such turns with the detachment of Olympian gods. What fools these mortals be! But Dr. Thorne, Roger Scatcherd, Lady Arabella: they have a history as well as a future, and there is more to learn about them as one turns the pages.

I think the book succeeds as comedy, not as romance. My second time through the story was through a reading by David Case, a genius of the spoken word, and his inflections bring out the comedy that the reader may not take the time to extract while merely gliding over the text.

One of the serious interviews, the confrontation between Doctor Thorne and Lady Arabella, is a masterpiece, as she strives to use her position as a De Courcy to separate his niece Mary Thorne from her daughter Beatrice, in order to prevent a union of Mary with her son Frank.

A student in the school of life could do worse than to use Trollope as a guide in playing this game. Dr. Thorne and Lady Arabella play their hands with skill and subtlety. And lest the student miss some of the finer points, the author provides a running commentary on how each is doing in the contest. Here Dr. Thorne responds to her suggestion that his niece has been throwing herself in the way of her son, asking, "What would my dear friend Mr. Gresham say, if some neighbor's wife should come and so speak to him? I will tell you what he would say: he would quietly beg her to go back to her own home and meddle only with her own matters." Lady Arabella cannot accept Dr. Thorne's unprecedented hint that she might be at the same level as common humanity. Declaring that it would not become her to argue with him, she ends the interview.

Dr. Thorne, we see, can take care of himself. One would expect him to perform equally well in his profession, though we see relatively little of his medical life. In contrast to a "surgeon," who would be addressed as "Mr.," Dr. Thorne was a "graduated physician," entitled to be addressed as "Doctor." There was a third class of medical practitioners in England, also descended from the medieval guilds, known as "apothecaries." They compounded and sold medications. Here also Dr. Thorne differed from his proud colleagues; he served as a dispensing apothecary as well as a physician, as did many other country doctors who were more concerned with their patients' comforts than with their own dignity. Dr. Thorne was reviled in the nearby towns of Barchester, home to a number of locally eminent physicians, and Silverbridge, home to a physician for some forty years. None of these dispensed medications.

In this arcane classification of health care providers, so strange to us today, the "general practitioner" apparently played a role similar to that of the "nurse practitioner" in a rural practice today. Dr. Thorne had been preceded at Greshemsbury by an humble general practitioner, a faithful soul who duly respected the county physicians. Though he had sometimes treated the children and servants, he "had never had the presumption to put himself on a par with his betters."

Dr. Thorne at the time of his story had been in practice in the small town of Greshamsbury for over twenty years. He is described as a proud man with a sharp tongue, but his outlook was so similar to that of the author that Trollope has been said to have poured into the character of Dr. Thorne those characteristics that he himself most admired, which comprised the ideal of the conservative English country gentleman. His integrity obliged him to be open about his fees; he had a fixed schedule of how much was to be charged for each visit, with allowance for the distance he had to travel. His colleagues considered this to be unprofessional. "A physician should take his fee without letting his left hand know what his right hand was doing; it should be taken without a thought, without a look, without a move of the facial muscles; the true physician should hardly be aware that the last friendly grasp of the hand had been made more precious by the touch of gold."

In one of our few glimpses of Dr. Thorne at work, he visits his childhood friend who has become Sir Roger Scatcherd, the wealthiest man in the county. Sir Roger refuses to accept a recommendation of abstinence from alcohol and rest from work, and he threatens to call another of the town doctors, Dr. Fillgrave. Dr. Thorne calls his bluff and dares him to call Dr. Fillgrave, requesting only that he let Lady Scatcherd remove the brandy bottle.

Of course a consultation with a childhood friend can hardly be considered a representative sample of Dr. Thorne's bedside manner. But it can be assumed that he made himself sufficiently acceptable to make a living in his country practice. We are told that he was occasionally summoned to neighboring towns to consult with colleagues on difficult cases.

The great crisis in Dr. Thorne's practice had to do with Lady Arabella Gresham. After he refused to forbid his daughter to see her son, she angrily transferred her case to the infamous Dr. Fillgrave. She still did not thrive, however, and as she became worse, the family in desperation sent to London for the great Sir Omicron Pie, who came and assessed her condition. "'You should have Thorne back here, Mr. Gresham,' said Sir Omicron, almost in a whisper, when they were quite alone. 'Dr. Fillgrave is a very good man, and so is Dr. Century; very good, I am sure. But Thorne has known her ladyship so long.'" And so Dr. Thorne was recalled to the care of Lady Arabella.

The story of Dr. Thorne himself is almost a subplot in the novel that bears his name. It is enough to say here that the author is careful to take good care of Dr. Thorne in the end. And the major plot moves along its fairy tale course. We stay with the story not so much because of the plot as because of the characters who propel it. Sir Roger's story is a rather unlikely one of a stone mason who rises to become an immensely wealthy builder and contractor, but an alcoholic (more plausible) who cannot survive long to enjoy the fruits of his labors. His son Louis succumbs a bit early to the ravages of alcohol, but this is a necessary plot device.

Frank Gresham, ordered by his mother Lady Arabella to marry money, makes a rather half-hearted effort to do so, but he is put right by Miss Dunstable, who rebukes his suit but remains a constant friend and encourages him to remain true to his love for Mary despite the prohibitions by his family. We are barely introduced to Miss Dunstable before she demonstrates her social skills by trouncing Mrs. Proudie, the ardent anti-Papist wife of the bishop, who makes a cameo appearance at Courcy Castle. Discounting Mrs. Proudie's concern that the Sabbath is hardly observed at all in Rome, Miss Dunstable agrees but says that Rome is a "delicious place" and asks the bishop's wife if she has ever been there. Of course not. It's a dangerous place—not because of malaria, as Miss Dunstable appears to assume, but because of the danger to the soul in a city with no Sabbath observations.

With that Miss Dunstable turns away abruptly and asks Mr. Gresham if he has been in Rome.

Familiar figures from the two previous Barsetshire novels, The Warden and Barchester Towers, make infrequent and brief appearances, but they make good use of them. And we meet a personage who is to be prominent in the Palliser series when Frank is invited to a dinner at Omnium Castle by the Duke of Omnium and Gatherum. Frank feels himself insulted that the Duke not only doesn't welcome him to the castle but only makes a token appearance at the dinner, sitting alone at the head of the table and making an early exit.

If some of the conventions of Victorian life appear incongruous to us in the twenty-first century, we find that Trollope, the contemporary observer of the scene, found them grist for his mill. Some of the subtleties of rank and duty were spelled out in correspondence between Miss Augusta Gresham, the once-jilted eldest daughter of the proud Lady Arabella, and Augusta's mentor in such matters, her cousin Lady Amelia de Courcy of Courcy Castle. Augusta has received a proposal of marriage from an attorney who has been assisting with family business affairs, and she would like to accept him; but even more she would like to have the blessing of such a union from Courcy Castle.

She pleads that her younger sister is to marry a clergyman, and she pleads further that some attorneys are better than others. But Lady Amelia reminds Augusta that since "it has been God's pleasure that we should be born with high blood in our veins," duty must take precedence over inclination.

Thus instructed and vanquished, Augusta refuses Mr. Gazebee. But the author cannot forbear disclosing in an immediate epilogue that some four years after this exchange of correspondence, the proud Lady Amelia succeeded so well in overcoming her scruples that she could accept her own proposal of marriage from Mr. Gazebee.

Thus we see that in theory the attorney, the physician, the wealthy businessman, and to a large extent the clergyman, are viewed with disdain from the heights of nobility, whose inherited wealth seems to come from the land. But does that mean the lord of the manor is a farmer? Frank Gresham receives a lesson in this from his father when he suggests that since his proposed marriage to a penniless woman would destroy his chance for a large estate, perhaps he could settle for a relatively small farm. Preoccupied with the ruin to the family that will result from this injudicious marriage, his father—also preoccupied with the reflection that it was his own squandering of the family fortune that has led his son to the consideration of working for a living—can hardly bring himself to think of it. He barely hears his son say that it would take so much time to become an attorney or a doctor.

"Yes: I dare say you could have a farm."

How quaint these conventions seem to our twenty-first century American sensitivities, liberated from hereditary nobility! Or are they? In Boston, "where the Lowells speak only to the Cabots, and the Cabots speak only to God?" In New Orleans, where Rex is a deity? In any city, where the names of prominent families may outlast the family fortunes and retain a meaning for those who know? What is the basis for our subliminal awareness of class snobbishness, if not from a place and time so well described for us in the novels of Trollope?

And how would this Victorian romance play out in today's world? Dr. Thorne would probably not be making house calls today. Perhaps he would be the senior partner in the family practice section of a large multi-specialty clinic. Lady Arabella would be Mrs. Gresham, but she would still find a way to run through her husband's money. Her son Frank would still marry a charming though penniless young woman; and they would succeed in some ways by virtue of their own gifts, though the measure of success would be a bit different. And with luck, some wry observer of the human comedy would tell us about it. If the observer should be blessed with a certain genius, the story would be as entertaining as Dr. Thorne.

AN ALL-STAR CAST FRAMLEY PARSONAGE

Framley Parsonage is altogether a charming piece in the Barset-shire collection. The major figures in the story are new ones, but familiar friends from previous volumes reappear in subplot roles, lending continuity for the benefit of faithful readers. Indeed, Framley Parsonage is almost an all-star game, or Old Timers' Day at the Ball Park, with brief appearances by stars of previous and future novels—the Duke of Omnium and Gatherum, Rev. Josiah Crawley, Mrs. Proudie, Miss Dunstable, and Griselda Grantly. Mark Robarts appears as a favored young parson at Framley, and one gets the impression early on that this is the story of a Pinocchio, a naive and untested cleric who falls into bad company and does a few foolish things. Specifically, he becomes one of a large company of Trollope's young men who sign their names to bills of accommodation, basically cosigning a note, with no means of paying the sum involved. Perhaps this was a frequent route of descent for the foolish in Victorian society.

Following the course of Mark's stupidity becomes a bit tedious. There are, of course, other threads of action. Mark's sister Lucy Robarts falls in love with the young lord of the manor—Lord Lufton. The familiar problem of working out a match between a deserving but poor young girl and a highly-placed lover was just addressed in Dr. Thorne, and here again we have the conflict between the young swain and his mother who feels obliged to place her son's interests above every other consideration. Lady Lufton is presented as a basically kind woman who attempts to ward off little Lucy, sister of the clergyman of the parish that was "a part of her own establishment." Lady Lufton is almost persuaded to abandon her objection by Lucy's forthright presentation.

Lucy alludes to King Cophetua, a legend about a king who saw a beggar maid from his window and went out and told her that she was to be his wife. No mention is made of King Cophetua's having had a mother or an aunt to try to dissuade him from such an unequal liaison, but the efforts of such mothers and aunts have provided a useful writer's device.

Lucy's wit emerges as she tells her brother that Lady Lufton had been civil: "You would hardly believe it, but she actually asked me to dine. She always does, you know, when she wants to show her good humour. If you'd broken your leg, and she wished to commiserate you, she'd ask you to dinner."

The story rumbles along slowly but is redeemed by the great scene in which Lucy accompanies her brother to Hogglestock Parsonage and kidnaps Mr. Crawley's four children and sends them to Framley for proper care while she stays at Hogglestock to risk her life by nursing Mrs. Crawley, who has typhus, all despite the objections of Mr. Crawley, the poor but proud parson. Humble little Lucy takes action while the men at the scene, Dean Arabin and her brother Mark, just stand around.

The patient reader is rewarded for wading through familiar machinations by a number of rollicking scenes. Mr. Harold Smith delivers a lecture on the South Sea islands to the humble citizens of Barchester in which he extols the virtues of Civilization—"'And to Christianity,' shouted Mrs. Proudie, to the great amazement of the assembled people and to the thorough wakening of the bishop."

Framley Parsonage gives us our first look into the character of a singular personage who will later be the protagonist in The Last Chronicle of Barset: the Reverend Josiah Crawley. Mr. Crawley is the impoverished parson of the parish of Hogglestock, where he serves the Lord and the parish and attempts to feed his wife and four children on ninety pounds a year. His religion and his pride are unbending and immune to compromise. He is chosen by Lady Lufton to counsel her wayward parson Mark Robarts, and the scene in which he visits Mark in his study is one in which young Mark is chastened by a prophet of old. One does not envy Mark his position under the gaze of Mr. Crawley, whose "sunken gray eyes" make his victim quail under a repetition of the question: "I now make bold to ask you, Mr. Robarts, whether you are doing your best to lead such a life as may become a parish clergyman among his parishioners?"

Besides the Serious Interview, such as the one above, Trollope revels in the Victorian party scene, two of which are presented as the conversazione of Mrs. Proudie and the subsequent conversazione of Miss Dunstable. On each occasion familiar characters are summoned to play cameo roles. Lord Dumbello is introduced as a suitor for the hand of the statuesque but silent beauty Griselda Grantly, and we are given full disclosure of the extent of the courtship. Griselda observes that it is "rather cold." Lord Dumbello replies with two words: "Deuced cold." That's it. They were subsequently married, and the reader may wonder whether their conversations ever became more substantial.

Mrs. Proudie has a little tilt with Mrs. Grantly, and Miss Dunstable reappears as the good-natured fairy godmother from the previous novel, Dr. Thorne. But the meeting of meetings is that between Lady Lufton and the personification in her eyes of all that is evil and opposed to her interests in the county, the Duke of Omnium. Aware that the crowding in the room had led the Duke to being pressed close against her, she turns quickly but with maintenance of her dignity and removes her dress from the contact. Thus face to face, the Duke begs her pardon—the only words ever to pass between them in their lives. Retreating, she makes a low and slow curtsey.

[B]ut the curtsey, though it was eloquent, did not say half so much—did not reprobate the habitual iniquities of the duke with a voice nearly as potent as that which was expressed in the gradual fall of her eyes and the gradual pressure of her lips. When she commenced her curtsey she was looking full in her foe's face. By the time that she had completed it her eyes were turned upon the ground, but there was an ineffable amount of scorn expressed in the lines of her mouth.

Lady Lufton had conquered. If one is looking for a passage that illustrates Trollope's mastery of the subtleties of human interaction, this is it. What is not said, what is not done, and what little may be said or done when the world assumes that much must have been said or done, rarely escapes Trollope's notice. Griselda Grantly and Lord Hartletop hardly speak to each other; Lady Lufton says nothing to the Duke of Omnium; and nothing much is said at Gatherum Castle when the world assumes that the political powers assembled there must be constantly discussing matters of state.

Lady Lufton does not finish the course undefeated. Her inevitable fall comes when she attempts to dismiss the "insignificant," "brown," "little" Lucy Robarts as her son's intended bride. Lucy fears a lecture when she is summoned, and she heads it off at every turn, and when she makes her little speech acknowledging her love for her son, she refuses to allow Lady Lufton to interrupt her: "I beg your pardon, Lady Lufton; I shall have done directly, and then I will hear you. ..."

Never fear: all ends happily. Indeed, the author develops the reader's good will with such memorable scenes and characters that repetitious themes and plotlines are readily forgiven.

THE SWELL, THE HOBBLEDEHOY, AND THE SMALL HOUSE THE SMALL HOUSE AT AL-LINGTON

The Small House at Allington may be, after all, what Anthony Trollope's novel of this title is about. Is it really about Lily Dale? She is a major figure and comes across as a strong, even dominating individual. But her fate as a rejected woman, determined to embrace a life of spinsterhood, is settled early in the book, so that the plot is finished in Part I. What is Part II for, if not to determine the fate of the Small House, which seems doomed to be abandoned by Lily and her sister and mother?

Of the subplots, the most amusing is the celebrated introduction of Plantagenet Palliser, whose scandalous affair with Lady Dumbello is discussed all over London. The reader knows that the outward manifestations of this affair are limited to one or two comments about the weather when he comes to stand by her chair at large parties. The climax of the affair occurs when Mr. Palliser dares to address her as "Griselda," and it concludes when she promptly responds by asking him to send for her coach. Around these modest happenings the Duke of Omnium and Gatherum feels obliged to threaten to cut off his nephew from his allowance and perhaps even cut off his status as heir by marrying and begetting a son himself, at his advanced age. With no interest in Griselda until so threatened, the young nephew feels obliged to challenge his uncle by addressing Griselda. However, the seeding of the wild oats is finished with the arranged marriage of the young Member of Parliament to the wealthy young Lady Glencora McCluskie. All these events are dramatized in the 1974 BBC television series, The Pallisers, and form the prequel to Trollope's series of six novels about the Pallisers.

Such comic relief is welcome in a rather serious novel which is destined to have no fairy tale ending. As such, it stands as a credible account of human affairs as we humans may conduct them. I suppose that sometimes women do indeed take voluntary private vows of chastity after being jilted, and sometimes keep them, and perhaps it happened more often in Victorian society over a hundred years ago than in our seemingly more open society today, but it takes a strong woman to do it; and the unusual occurrence of the phenomenon is emphasized by the author in the refusal of any of Lily's family or friends to acknowledge her statement of purpose. John Eames, faithful in his unrequited love for Lily, seems to understand it better than any of them, but he sympathizes with her position in his own profession never to love anyone else.

One could make a case for the novel's being a story about the hobbledehoy, the author's term for awkward late bloomers like John Eames. Johnny progresses toward manhood and is considered to have succeeded in this by the end of Part II; he "thrashes" Adolphus Crosbie by punching him in the eye at a railway station; he is promoted to be the private secretary to Sir Raffle Baffle in the bureaucracy, and he never allows himself to be demeaned by fetching Sir Raffle's boots; he earns the friendship and patronage of the Earl de Guest by saving him from a bull in his pasture; he escapes a foolish liaison with Amelia Roper, the designing daughter of his landlady; and he receives encouragement from the Earl and from Lily's mother in his suit. But he doesn't get the girl.

Lilian Dale is one of Trollope's acclaimed heroines, and for good reason. She dominates every encounter from first to last, from proclaiming that Adolphus Crosbie is a swell when we first meet her, to her compulsive interruptions of her mother at the last as Mrs. Dale endeavors to tell her daughter of the Squire's conversion from being an old grump to being a generous old grump. She rather quickly falls in love with the swell from London and accepts his proposal of marriage, expressing her love without qualification and making generous concessions to the prospect of marrying a relatively poor London clerk. Her loving attentions to Adolphus leave the reader in no doubt as to Mr. Crosbie's good fortune in winning her hand. No scene in the book is better presented than that in which Mrs. Dale tells Lily that her letter from Mr. Crosbie puts a definite end to their engagement. Lily had expected it, and she assumes the fortitude of a Joan of Arc as she hears it, astonishing her mother with her presence of mind and astonishing the reader when she does not resort to the universal ploy of Trollope's women, who routinely retire to their room and weep on the bed after a crucial development.

The author succeeds in showing us Adolphus Crosbie as a cad and a scoundrel in the eyes of the world. But we also see the world through the eyes of Mr. Crosbie; and from his own perspective he is shown rather non-judgmentally to be stupid and lacking in a sense of purpose that would reward him with happiness. The torments of Mr. Crosbie as the son-in-law to the Earl de Courcy constitute the just punishment that his sins deserve.

And what of the Small House? It succeeds where Johnny Eames had failed: it gets the girl. We are left with the prospect of Lily and her mother permanently in residence in the Small House, which Mrs. Dale had announced that she would leave, at the behest of her daughters, in rebellion against the authority and interference of their uncle the Squire, who allowed them the use of the house rent-free. The title of the book is indeed appropriate; the Dale women's residence in the house indicates harmony and stability in their little world in Allington. In the end, communication overcomes pride, and peace returns, even though in Lily's case it is a peace of resignation and acceptance.

One accepts certain conditions in reading Trollope, and in this instance the conditions are a bit heavier than usual. Plot concludes in Part I; Part II is one of the longer epilogues in literature. The pace is leisurely; there is a bit of repetition. But the conditions, though heavy, are not without reward. Lilly is well presented, and the reader, like her friends and family, love and admire her but wish she could be a bit more flexible. Lady Dumbello is shown in a masterpiece of irony and caricature, just closely enough that one suspects that the portrait is plausible and not far from true. The phenomenon of the hobbledehoy is given its definitive representation in John Eames. In Adolphus Crosbie's disillusionment with the noble family into which he marries, we see the difference between perception and reality in how the "quality" sometimes live. One might wish for a bit of a story; but the reader is grateful for a kindly but ironic and amusing guide to the gentle country life.

THE VICTORY OF THE RIGHTEOUS THE LAST CHRONICLE OF BARSET

Is there a more memorable scene in all Trollope's novels than the image of the Rev. Josiah Crawley walking miles through the mud to answer the summons of the Bishop of Barchester? Mrs. Crawley had arranged for a local farmer to offer him a ride, but the ruse only took him part of the way, and Mr. Crawley forgot his suspicions of his wife as he thought of how, with his dirty boots and pants, he would crush the sleek and clean bishop in his own study—"crush him—crush him—crush him!" And the subsequent interview with Bishop and Mrs. Proudie stands as one of Trollope's great set pieces. Mr. Crawley, the underdog, the Perpetual Curate of Hogglestock, ignores the interruptions of the bishop's wife as he argues against the bishop's illegal request (which the reader knows originated with Mrs. Proudie) that Mr. Crawley vacate his pulpit at Hogglestock until his trial for theft of twenty pounds is concluded. And two more memorable words are not uttered in the Barsetshire series than "Peace, woman," when he finally acknowledges her presence. After further admonishing her that she was debasing her husband's high office by interfering, he wishes the bishop good morning and is out the door. "Yes, he had, he thought, in truth crushed the bishop."

One can hardly quarrel with Trollope's assertion that he considered Plantagenet and Lady Glencora Palliser and Josiah Crawley to be his best creations. Although The Last Chronicle serves as a grand summation of the Barsetshire series and reprise for its characters, it is around Mr. Crawley and the mystery of how he got the twenty pound check that everything revolves. The stubborn Perpetual Curate whom we met in Framley Parsonage continues to cling to his principles in spite of every adversity. He doubts himself to the extent that he concedes he may have absent-mindedly taken the check in question, but when roused to defend whatever position he stakes out, he does so with boldness and authority that none can withstand. And this list includes such formidable opponents as Archdeacon Grantly of the thundering "Good Heavens!", Mr. Crawley's loving wife and daughters, and the heretofore undefeated Mrs. Proudie, ruler of the episcopal palace.

Is Mr. Crawley mad? Well we may wonder: his wife thinks he sometimes is; his daughter thinks so. And he even suspects it himself. Mr. Crawley is an articulate victim of the inequalities within the Church. He knows many of the Odes of Pindar and Horace by heart, in Greek, and teaches them to his daughters. His friend from school days, Dean Arabin, dean of the Close, had not done so well in class as he had. But Mr. Arabin is Dean, wealthy enough to be traveling to Jerusalem at the time of the story, and Mr. Crawley's family can barely find enough food for the table with his meager stipend in Hogglestock. We have previously seen Mr. Crawley descending as the Voice of God on the worldly Mr. Robarts, vicar of Framley, in Framley Parsonage. And now we see him as the long-suffering servant of the brick makers of Hogglestock. He resigns his curacy (and his minuscule income) after being accused of theft, as a matter of principle. Several of his esteemed colleagues attempt to reason with him, but none can contend with him in his determination.

Trollope claimed to have avoided theological issues and to have limited himself to the personal lives of the people of the church in the Barsetshire series. Perhaps so. Few sermons are quoted. But political issues of the church rear their head at every turn: Archdeacon Grantly is twice denied the bishopric. Mr. Arabin becomes a dean. The bishop's authority is challenged. High Church contends with Low Church. Bishop Proudie and his wife come into Barsetshire opposed to its high church tendencies, and Mrs. Proudie preaches the importance of keeping the Sabbath Day holy according to her standards. No railway trips on Sunday. No games. Services twice on Sunday. The old ways of the Church are battered. Even the saintly Mr. Harding had been known to chant in Evensong, but no more.

Yet Mr. Crawley cares not for either faction. He resents the bishop's wife's interference in his right and obligation to his parish, but he cites the importance of obedience to the bishop within the limits of legality. He stands down the bishop when challenged, but he is also an uncomfortable member of the family of the bishop's chief antagonist, Archdeacon Grantly. Mr. Crawley is not comfortable with the riches of the world and conducts himself as if convinced of the literal truth of the difficulty of a rich man's entering the kingdom of heaven.

Archdeacon Grantly is not the protagonist in any of the Barsetshire novels, but he makes his appearance in the first of the series, The Warden, and appears so prominently in the others as to become one of the most memorable of Trollope's men of the cloth. Rector of Plumstead Episcopi, Archdeacon of Barsetshire, son of the Bishop, and son-in-law of Mr. Harding (the Warden), the Archdeacon is a wealthy and worldly churchman who defends the church energetically throughout the series. A wealthy clergyman? Surely a contraindication in terms. After all, this was only a little over a hundred years ago. But so it was. He inherited his wealth from his saintly father the Bishop, who possessed his wealth in connection with his position in the church. Those blessed by the material riches of the church alluded to their position with the same euphemisms employed by the nobility—those whom God has endowed, and so forth.

But not all clergymen were so endowed, as we are continually reminded by Mr. Crawley. We are not accustomed to thinking of Trollope as a social crusader, and he probably was not, certainly not in the tradition that Charles Dickens established. Trollope had his psychological baggage resulting from his impoverished childhood and a certain amount of rough treatment as a town boy among the more privileged classmates in school. But although he had no connection and little experience with the church, there is no reason to think that he didn't tell it like it was.

In The Last Chronicle Trollope was careful to conclude several of the lives. Even Mrs. Proudie meets a somewhat untimely death. If we are to believe Trollope's own account in his autobiography, he overheard some men in his club saying how tired of her they had become, and he announced to them that he was going home right away to kill her off. Her demise of a sudden cardiac death is epidemiologically correct, in that 250,000 Americans die in this way every year now. Few, however, have such a dramatic end as does Mrs. Proudie, found standing up, leaning against her bedpost. Mrs. Proudie was a great comic creation, personifying the conflict between low church and high church—yet another of the women in Victorian society who were forced to achieve their goals through the agency of their lord and master. Several others come to mind—Alice Vavasor, Glencora Palliser, Lady Laura Standish.

Mr. Septimus Harding meets a more orthodox end, dying quietly in his old age. Mr. Harding was a gentler saint than Mr. Crawley; he had also faced the humiliation of displacement from his post of service, in The Warden, accepting his fate with quietness and resignation. There are few more sympathetic portraits of the loneliness of the aged than that of Mr. Harding finishing his days wandering about the rooms of his daughter's house, "ashamed when the servants found him ever on the move."

While Mr. Crawley is facing the judgment of his community for a crime he suspects he may have actually committed, his daughter Grace finds herself in love with Major Henry Grantly, son of the Archdeacon, who violently opposes a proposed union of his son with an impoverished woman, however worthy she may be. We follow every opportunity the father and son miss in their stubborn refusal to concede any of their pride and independence in their relationship with each other. Here Trollope's persistence in showing every nuance of each character's thoughts is effective in presenting each of the men as understandable and even likeable, even though we follow each mistaken turn that each of them takes. Thank goodness they had a little help. Conflict resolution occurs only when the women in their lives lead the two men into agreement without suffering the embarrassment of losing face.

The subplot in which John Eames becomes involved in a flirtation with Madalina Desmolines through his friendship with the painter Conway Dalrymple tries the reader's patience at times; here, however, the author spins out the story of how Dalrymple mocks the impassive Clara Van Siever by offering to paint her portrait as Jael driving a peg through the head of Sisera, a story from Judges often portrayed by painters who devoutly chose Biblical themes but selected the bloodiest. This subplot concludes with a farcical scene that could be played on the stage with few alterations, in which John is entrapped by Madalina's mother. Threatened with a shotgun wedding, he only manages his escape after opening the window and calling to a policeman on the street.

And although one may have supposed that the story of Lily Dale and Johnny Eames was concluded in The Small House at Allington, both reappear to provide yet another identical conclusion to his courtship. And as another part of the epilogue to The Small House, we see Adolphus Crosbie suffering still more punishment in consequence of courting and jilting Lily. Dr. Thorne briefly appears as a magistrate considering the case of Mr. Crawley, and his wife the former Miss Dunstable also reappears to give counsel to Lily Dale. Mark Robarts of Framley Parsonage also sits with the magistrates.

Few bases remain untouched. Mr. Toogood, a London attorney and a relation of Mrs. Crawley, appears as a sleuth to dig out a few details of Mr. Crawley's mystery. Johnny Eames makes a heroic trip to Europe to help solve it. But when Mrs. Arabin (Mr. Harding's daughter) is finally notified of the problem, she sorts it out, as she would have done without any assistance.

And so the Barsetshire series is concluded. The Last Chronicle rewards the faithful reader of the previous five novels in the series with reunions with familiar friends. But it stands on its own as an outstanding novel of the nineteenth century, following the dogged Mr. Crawley as he gives his own witness to the less rigid world around him.

CAN YOU FORGIVE A FEW ADDITIONS TO THE TEXT? CAN YOU FORGIVE HER?

I met Glencora and Plantagenet Palliser when we were in England in 1974. They lived in their own television series, The Pallisers, Simon Raven's BBC television serial based on six Anthony Trollope novels. The Times published a supplement describing the Palliser series as "the finest sequence of fiction ever to be based on British Parliamentary life." Susan Hampshire played Glencora, and not only she, but the entire cast now represent those characters in my mind. And so, although I can be appropriately dispassionate and critical about Anthony Trollope and his novels, loyalty makes it difficult in regard to Plantagenet and Glencora. They are old friends.

Episodes 1-6 of The Pallisers are based on the first novel in the series, Can You Forgive Her? First, the reader and the viewer must understand that the woman we are asked to forgive is not Lady Glencora M'Cluskie, the true heroine, but Alice Vavasor, a distant cousin of Glencora's. Alice's story is indeed the main plot of the book, but Simon Raven apparently realized that Glencora's story would be more appealing to the television audience, and he focused the first episodes on her, starting with events that Trollope had described in a novel of the Barsetshire series, The Small House at Allington. The spectacular set piece in the television presentation is the first scene, a garden party given by the Duke of Omnium and Gatherum. (Trollope was shameless in the selection of names for his characters and places; other favorites include the Marquis of Auld Reekie in Scotland, the law firm of Slow and Bideawhile, and Dr. Fillgrave, who was the competitor of Dr. Thorne.) At this party Glencora flirts with Burgo Fitzgerald, a handsome rake, little knowing that her fate is being decided from on high. Her guardian, the Marchioness of Auld Reekie, is observing all from her chair beside a little Greek temple above the lake. There she negotiates with the Duke of Omnium for a marital alliance between Glencora and the Duke's heir, Plantagenet Palliser. The Duke replies, "I find the thing will suit me well enough."

The innocent reader goes from the television series to the text and immediately finds himself reading about Alice Vavasor, a young woman engaged to a young country gentleman, "John Grey, The Worthy Man." She had been previously engaged to her first cousin "George Vavasor, The Wild Man." We then stumble into subplot number one, in which George's sister goes to spend three weeks with her Aunt Greenow, a well-to-do widow who must deal with two suitors: Mr. Cheesacre, a "fat Norfolk farmer," and the rather disreputable Captain Bellfield.

Where is Glencora? Not yet to be found. By the time we reach Chapter Seventeen, the standard Trollope fox-hunting chapter, we find Burgo Fitzgerald first among the riders—

Burgo Fitzgerald, whom no man had ever known to crane at a fence, or to hug a road, or to spare his own neck or his horse's. And yet poor Burgo seldom finished well—coming to repeated grief in this matter of his hunting, as he did so constantly in other matters of his life.

In the next chapter we learn that Burgo, eighteen months earlier, had almost won the hand, as he had already won the heart, of the Lady Glencora M'Cluskie. Finally. This is page 162. But what about the garden party? About the garden party, the text is silent. That this memorable scene appears nowhere in Trollope's novel is almost beside the point. The dialogue of the BBC production is as Trollopian as any of the rest, which adheres closely to the text. Raven has the Duke later admonish Plantagenet, who has been rumored to be having an affair with Lady Dumbello (another of Trollope's apt names), that he should not pursue such an affair until after he has become respectably married and produced an heir. "After that, you may suit yourself. Only see to it that there's no open scandal. When I was a boy it didn't matter much, but for some reason it does now."

And the grand wedding that we saw at Westminster Abbey? "She had married Mr. Palliser at St. George's Square." So we, and the author, have missed the most memorable scenes in the whole series. If we go back to a few pages of The Small House at Allington, we find the story of Plantaget Palliser's flirtation with Lady Dumbello, and we find the interview between Plantagenet and Mr. Fothergill, the "man of business" for the Duke of Omnium, in which Mr. Fothergill passed the word to the rebellious young buck that he must abandon his friendship with Lady Dumbello, who happened to be the daughter-in-law of an old friend (and former mistress) of the Duke. We find no description of the scene in which the Duke brings Lady Hartletop and Lady Dumbello to Plantagenet's drawing room for Lady Dumbello to declare to Plantagenet, in a choked voice, that their association is at an end.

What we do find in Can You Forgive Her? is a brief reference to Glencora's having attempted unsuccessfully to persuade her distant cousin Alice to allow her to use her house in London for a tryst with Burgo, to arrange an elopement. Alice barely knows Glencora, and she refuses. All things conspire against Glencora, and she finds herself engaged, by arrangement of "sagacious heads," to Mr. Palliser.

And now, finally, Glencora and Alice have a chance to become acquainted with each other. Alice receives an invitation from Glencora to come to Matching Priory for a visit before Christmas.

Important conversations in Trollope sometimes occur on carriage rides, and a chapter entitled "Dandy and Flirt" is ample warning that Dandy and Flirt are the horses pulling the "light stylish-looking cart" driven by Lady Glencora, who conveys Alice from the station to Matching Priory, and demonstrates in her breathless exposition of her situation that she is, in fact, a lonely little rich girl, way out in the country, who needs a friend. (In the television production, she is often shown carrying and holding a doll in her first months of marriage.)

My wife and I saw "Matching Priory," the stately home that was used in the BBC television series, when we visited Sudely Castle one afternoon in the course of a short stay in the Cotswolds. This castle's greatest historical significance was having been the last home, and the burial place, of Katherine Parr, last wife and widow of Henry VIII. Matching Priory, though, had a somewhat different history, as described by Lady Glencora, who shows Alice the "Matching oak, under which Coeur de Lion or Edward the Third, I forget, was met by Sir Guy de Palisere as he came from the war, or from hunting, or something of that kind." Sir Guy offered the king some brandy, the king responded with a generous bequest of real estate, and the rest was history. "As Jeffrey Palliser says, it was a great deal of money for a pull at his flask."

And so we have the history of England according to Lady Glencora. And having finally arrived at subplot two, the story of the Pallisers, we can follow the development of their marriage, which is the real story of Can You Forgive Her? Trollope summarizes the contrasting personalities of Glencora and Plantagenet as he describes Glencora's reaction when she realizes that Mrs. Marsham has actually come to their house to be her duenna. Though Glencora knew little about the British Constitution, she "was much quicker, much more clever, than her husband." Though he had a keen intelligence, he could be easily deceived. "And, to a certain extent, she looked down upon him for this obtusity." This contrast in their personalities is played out in the book's production number, Lady Monk's ball. Lady Glencora begs her husband to be excused from attending because she knows Burgo, Lady Monk's nephew, will be there. But Plantagenet, saying that "it does not signify," insists that she attend. After Glencora arrives (separately), he excuses himself and takes his leave; she dances "recklessly" with Burgo, watched by her "nemesis" Mr. Bott (a political disciple of her husband) and her "duenna" Mrs. Marsham, who leaves to fetch Mr. Palliser. He arrives in the nick of time, Glencora gives him her hand, and they depart. In their carriage she says, "If you did not wish me to see Mr. Fitzgerald you should not have sent me to Lady Monk's. But, Plantagenet, I hope you will forgive me if I say that no consideration shall induce me to receive again as a guest, in my own house, either Mrs. Marsham or Mr. Bott."

There was more to be said. The night before must be followed by the morning after; Plantagenet invited his wife to breakfast with him after he had "slept on it." In these interviews the woman does not always win. But she usually does. In this case, though, it may be said that if Glencora won the battle, Plantagenet won the war. Glencora's wit and spirit posed a challenge to her husband. "'I am very serious,' she replied, as she settled herself in her chair with an air of mockery, while her eyes and mouth were bright and eloquent with a spirit which her husband did not love to see."

Plantagenet turned the tide, after her accusation that he had planted spies, with his admission: "If it were ever to come to that, that I thought spies necessary, it would be all over with me."

This changes the tone; she abandons her raillery and declares that she cannot make him happy, confesses that she loves Burgo Fitzgerald, and that she and Plantagenet do not love each other. Here Plantagenet does his duty, tells her he does love her, puts his arms around her, and decides on the spur of the moment to abandon politics for a while and take her to Europe. At this very moment the Duke of St. Bungay is announced, and he enters to offer Plantagenet the position of Chancellor of the Exchequer, the office that Plantagenet has coveted. But Plantagenet declines, pleading family reasons, and the conversation is over. No English gentleman would inquire or disclose anything further.

This is the turning point, and the rest all works itself out in subplot number two. As for the main plot, Alice Vavasor proves herself to be as contrary a heroine as Glencora is attractive, as she deals with successive engagements to George Vavasor, John Grey, back to George Vavasor, and back to John Grey, whose sainthood is assured by the persistence of his suit.

At this point we find Glencora's and Alice's personalities summarized as Glencora congratulates her friend on her fourth engagement: "I know that it is quite a misery to you that you should be made a happy woman at last. I understand it all, my dear, and my heart bleeds for you."

As for subplot number one: Simon Raven properly omitted it from his television presentation. It is a third variation on the theme of a woman torn between a dashing scoundrel and a boring steady gentleman. In this one, as it turns out, Aunt Greenow selects the impecunious Captain Bellfield, and we leave her beginning to get him housebroken.

Trollope's great achievement in this novel is the creation of Glencora and Plantagenet. They have not become household words in our time, but they had enough in them for elaboration of their stories in another medium, and they carried a series of six political novels in which they played sometimes major and sometimes quite minor roles. Political figures in England have cited these novels as the best fictional presentation of parliamentary process, and wives of great men have cited Lady Glencora as the model of all that a political wife should be and do.

It is Glencora's sense of fun and play that makes her an endearing figure to her friends, and also to the reader. At Baden she takes Alice with her to the casino to play "one little Napoleon," with which she wins a little pile and finally loses it. Plantagenet finds her, scolds her, and takes her away. Alice feels wrongly scowled upon by Mr. Palliser and follows them to their room, where Glencora affects laughter. "Here's a piece of work about a little accident."

Plantagenet fails to see the humor and admonishes her for sitting at a common gambling table amid heaps of gold. "You wrong me," Glencora replies. "There was only one heap, and that did not remain long. Did it, Alice?"

Alice, with her own agenda of being wronged, takes her candle and takes her leave. This was the set of family and friends that Simon Raven brought us on BBC. Glencora, pert and pretty, sometimes strayed, and she sometimes strayed further than to the tables of Baden; but she was a lot more fun than Alice. She was more fun than any of them.

And the inevitable question: Was the television series more fun than the book? And the required qualifying query: What did you do first—see it on television or read the book? In my case, the television series came first, and yes, the portrayal on television was more fun. But it was so much fun that the text is required reading.

ENGLISH POLITICS 101 PHINEAS FINN

Phineas Finn is a political novel. Others in Anthony Trollope's Palliser series stray here and there from the political scene in Victorian England, but this one is rooted in the pursuit of political ambition. A chapter is allocated to a cabinet meeting in which the members of the cabinet are named, described, and seated at the table. The furnishings of the "large dingy room" in Downing Street are enumerated, and rituals are observed. Political strategy is discussed and determined. The author obviously puts politics right up there with fox hunting among his passions.

Phineas Finn is the focal point of the story as he embarks on a career in the service of the nation as a Member of Parliament. Phineas appears as an impressionable young Irishman, whose charm and gift for pleasant conversation bring him opportunities that push his capacity for maintaining focus. He is several grades advanced beyond the stage of the hobbledehoy portrayed by Trollope in Johnny Eames of the Barsetshire series, but he is still learning the ways of the world. And so we learn the ways of Phineas's world as he endures the inconveniences and embarrassments of the learning process.

One could do worse than to use this novel as a textbook on the English Constitution. We follow Phineas through election to Parliament from two different boroughs, we observe the protocols and courtesies in the House of Commons, we see his landlord participate in a riot, we meet with the Cabinet, and we see governments formed, dissolved, and replaced.

Through all this Phineas pursues his career with ambition and charm. The men like him, and the women love him. He makes love to four of the women, including his childhood sweetheart, with varying results. A clandestine duel on a beach in Belgium, ending as happily as any duel can, is the central event of the story, after which our hero shrugs and marches on.

The first to refuse Phineas is Lady Laura Standish. One of Trollope's strong women, she sublimates her political interests and ambitions into a vicarious interest in Phineas's career. Though she is in love with him, they are both poor, and she decides to accept marriage to a wealthy Scot with a large home place in the country and a promising career in Parliament. Unfortunately for Laura, his unbending religious scruples destroy the marriage, affording us insights into the institution of marriage in Victorian times. Eventually she flees to Dresden to escape his lawful demand that she live in the same house with him.

Violet Effingham, beautiful and witty, also refuses a later offer of marriage. She rebels against the oppressive guardianship of her aunt, Lady Baldock, and she is too strong-willed to go along with marriage to Lord Chiltern at the first attempt, having the audacity to propose to him that he pursue a gainful occupation. Violet was shortchanged in the BBC production of The Pallisers, in which the strength of her character is sacrificed to the abbreviating demands of film making.

Madame Max Goesler figures in several of the novels as a friend to Lady Glencora and to the Duke of Omnium. Representing the foreign element in the story (and one of the few foreigners whom he presents in a favorable light), she is a wealthy young widow from Vienna, given to making innocent observations about some of the curious English customs. She attracts the elderly Duke of Omnium, who offers to marry her. Lady Glencora fears that this could lead to the birth of a son to the Duke, knocking her little son out of the line of succession to the Duke, and her interview with Madame Max is rather one-sided. Lady Glencora protests that a seventy year old Duke of Omnium "may not do as he pleases, as may another man."

Madame Max replies that his Grace should be allowed to try that question, but she puts this matter aside to assert that she would not degrade any man whom she should marry. On the other hand, she would not willingly do him any injury, and she assures Lady Glencora that her fears for her son are premature—unless Lady Glencora's arguments should drive her to marrying the Duke just to prove she is wrong. "But you had better leave me to settle the matter in my own bosom. You had indeed."

Madame Max bears the burden of offering wise observations on the world around her, acceptable to the reader who pictures her as a beautiful dark-haired young woman. Though she refuses the offer of marriage to the Duke, she remains his friend and offers this assessment of his role in society in refuting Phineas's claim that he is useless to society:

"You believe only in motion, Mr. Finn;—and not at all in quiescence. An express train at full speed is grander to you than a mountain with heaps of snow. I own that to me there is something glorious in the dignity of a man too high to do anything,—if only he knows how to carry that dignity with a proper grace. I think that there should be breasts made to carry stars."

Conversational virtuosity of this order leaves the reader with jaw agape. The English are better at this than we Americans are, as can be seen by tuning in to the prime minister's question and answer sessions on BBC-TV. And the Victorians were better at it than we are. In any event, Madame Max holds her ground with poise and polish, justifying Shirley Robin Letwin's description of her in The Gentleman in Trollope: Individuality and Moral Conduct (The Akadine Press, originally published 1982) as "the most perfect gentleman in Trollope's novels."

This is a picaresque novel that hangs together pretty well, following the hero from one adventure to the next. He meets fair damsels and does battle with dragons, also encountering mentors and would-be mentors who instruct him in le monde comme il faut. Surely the author was already planning a sequel, Phineas Redux, to rescue the young hero from the oblivion in which this story leaves him. This textbook on politics concludes with the reader waiting for one more lesson: Politicians may retire, but not for long.

A CUNNING WOMAN THE EUSTACE DIAMONDS

Lizzie Eustace is beautiful and clever, and she has no intention of parting with her late husband's gift to her, the Eustace Diamonds. But does she really have them? And where are they? This well constructed mystery is one of those Trollope novels which deserves to be better known and more widely read. (Others in this list include The Last Chronicle of Barset, The Duke's Children, and Orley Farm.) Lizzie has been compared to Becky Sharp, the prime mover in William Makepeace Thackeray's Vanity Fair; Trollope actually invites such comparison, describing her early in the book as an "opulent and aristocratic Becky Sharp."

Like Becky, Lizzie attracts admirers. "Sometimes I think her the most beautiful woman I ever saw in the world," says the obviously smitten Frank Greystock in describing Lizzie Eustace.

But Becky casts a wider net, as described by a servant: "'Miss B., they are all infatyated about that young woman,' Firkin replied. ... 'I can't tell for where nor for why; and I think somethink has bewidged everybody.' "

Lizzie does not succeed so widely, and she shows that she doesn't really understand everyone, as when she overplays her hand on first meeting her prospective mother-in-law, Lady Fawn. Lizzie had heard that a sermon was read every Sunday evening at Fawn Court, and that therefore Lady Fawn must be very religious. So it was quite natural for her to stretch her hand toward a book on Lady Fawn's table, claiming it as her guide to remind her of her duty to her noble husband. Lady Fawn, finding the book to be the Bible, replied that she could hardly do better—"but there was more of censure than of eulogy in the tone of her voice." We are told later that Lady Fawn was left with not a word to say in behalf of her future daughter-in-law, saying nothing about the little scene with the Bible, but never forgetting it.

As described above, however, Becky Sharp was capable of sweeping through a household. A governess in Crawley Hall (which she refers to as Humdrum Hall), she assists elderly Sir Pitt Crawley so effectively that he later proposes marriage to her. She is in love with Sir Pitt's second son, Rawdon Crawley, and she makes it a point to attend faithfully upon Sir Pitt's spinster sister, supplanting her dame de compagnie, Miss Briggs, so completely that her imitations of Briggs's weeping snuffle and her manner of using her handkerchief are performed so well that Miss Crawley "became quite cheerful."

Becky Sharp shows herself as a mistress of all she surveys, whereas Lizzie succeeds only with the men whom she targets. Lady Fawn and her daughters were not so easily taken in. On the other hand, Thackeray shows Becky to have an easier field—the "Vanity Fair" of foolish mortals, trusting and benighted souls, easily duped. Thackeray, like Dickens, entertains us much like Becky entertained Miss Crawley, by mockery; and their mockery spared very few. Trollope, on the other hand, may have had more respect for people in general; his portraits, though they did include "warts and all," were less caricatures than realistic renderings.

Lizzie stars in one of Trollope's memorable scenes, "The Diamonds are Seen in Public." Her fiancé Lord Fawn, troubled about the diamonds, has written a letter forbidding her to keep the diamonds, saying they belong rightfully to her late husband's family. They arrive separately at a party given by Lady Glencora, not having communicated in the three weeks since Lord Fawn's letter. She wears the diamonds, which "seemed to outshine all the jewellery in the room. ... The only doubt might be whether paste diamonds might not better suit her character." Lord Fawn confronts her as soon as he sees her, but no ears hear the inconsequential words they speak to each other. Lady Eustace joins Lord Fawn in a quadrille, dances with no one else, and very soon asks him to get her carriage for her. Taking her seat, she tells him, "You had better come to me soon." And thus does Lady Eustace savor her triumph of displaying the diamonds at Lady Glencora's house.

This may have been the high point for Lizzie. Her one goal in life was to keep the diamonds, and all else was sacrificed to this goal. It is not so much that she has an overall strategy; rather, she constantly improvises from one point to the next, keeping (supposedly) the diamonds locked up in an iron box.

Of course the diamonds are at risk—not only from Mr. Camperdown, the Eustace family lawyer who is as determined to recover the diamonds for the family as Lizzie is to keep them, but also from thieves in the night. When Lizzie goes to her late husband's ancestral castle in Scotland, she surrounds herself with unscrupulous friends, runs through her potential suitors, and loses her diamonds. On the first attempt at the diamonds, the thieves get an empty iron box, while Lady Eustace retains the jewels "in her own keeping." Not being one to blurt out the truth at the first opportunity, however, Lizzie does not tell the police that she still has the diamonds, and she digs herself deeper and deeper into her deception until it carries the name of perjury.

As Lizzie sins, so is she punished, not by the law, but by the irony of fate, receiving a proposal of marriage by Mr. Joseph Emilius, described in words which we now find difficult to forgive: "a nasty, greasy, lying, squinting Jew preacher." This follows his assertions that he is the greatest preacher of the day and can move masses. Lizzie knows he is grossly exaggerating his assets, but "A man, to be a man in her eyes, should be able to swear that all his geese are swans." When he demands an answer to his proposal of marriage, Lizzie answers him in kind, making a speech that matches his in length, protesting that after losing "the dearest husband that a woman had ever worshipped," she had once thought of matrimony with a man of high rank for the sake of her child. But he had proved unworthy of her, she discloses with a scornful expression as she declares that she can no longer be willing to consider another marriage. "Upon hearing this, Mr. Emilius bowed low, and before the street-door was closed against him had begun to calculate how much a journey to Scotland would cost him."

All these events did not go unnoticed by the gods on Mount Olympus—in this case, the Pallisers and their friends at Matching Priory. The Pallisers were less involved in this story than in any of the other five novels in the Palliser series. Lady Glencora had intervened a bit, and she had not been wise in choosing sides (a tendency which was to recur in her favoritism of the villain Lopez in The Prime Minister), and she had called on Lady Eustace to offer her support. But none of the other gods and goddesses challenged her. "It was understood that Lady Glencora was not to be snubbed, though she was very much given to snubbing others. She had attained this position for herself by a mixture of beauty, rank, wealth, and courage;—but the courage had, of the four, been her greatest mainstay." None at Matching were more entertained, however, than the greatest god of all, the old Duke of Omnium. The old duke was in his last days, and "It was admitted by them all that the robbery had been a godsend in the way of amusing the duke."

The Duke was not alone in his enjoyment of the adventures of Lizzie Eustace. The little vixen has provided pleasant diversion for many readers; she continues to amuse.

HOW THE WOMEN TOOK CARE OF PHINEAS *PHINEAS REDUX*

Perhaps the story of Phineas Finn just wouldn't fit into one novel, at least not within the limits of Trollope Standard Time, in which no nuance of thought or motive is left unexplored. Hence, *Phineas Redux*. Phineas (as he was known to many of his acquaintances even under the formal conventions of Victorian England) is no more heroic in the second novel than in the first. Would these two novels rank higher in our consciousness if the protagonist had been less flawed? Perhaps. But Phineas's penchant for muddling through without much in the way of strength or resolution is essential to the story. And even though the reader may lose patience with Phineas at times, his foibles and fallibility provide the necessary pinch of charm to this story of political gamesmanship and matrimonial maneuvering.

The familiar characters of *Phineas Finn* carry on for us. Mary Flood Jones Finn is missing, her early death having freed Phineas to return to London as a widower and resume his career and his old friendships—especially those with women. The page brightens whenever the Duchess of Omnium or Madame Max Goesler appear.

Why are these women so delightful? Bright, irreverent, saucy, the Duchess uses her lofty position in society as a springboard for making things happen. She appears and reappears in several novels in the Palliser series, sometimes as the prime mover and always as a breath of fresh air. (She even makes a cameo appearance in *Miss Mackenzie*, an unrelated story.) In *Phineas Redux* she adopts Phineas as a favorite and meddles in his fate, most prominently when she promotes his candidacy for office in opposition to the ambitions of Mr. Bonteen, whom she lures into exposing himself as a boor when her wine prompts him to make some inappropriate speeches at a dinner party. How did the author pass up the opportunity to give us the details of this dialogue? (Simon Raven's screenplay for the BBC television series remedies this omission, showing the viewer exactly how Mr. Bonteen destroyed his career.)

We see the Duchess at work when she initiates her project of promoting the status of Mr. Finn, telling the Duke of St. Bungay that he must find some place for him. In vain does he protest that he never interferes. "Why, Duke, you've made more cabinets than any man living."

She undertakes to promote the marriage prospects of her husband's cousin Adelaide Palliser by making imaginative use of an unclaimed legacy that can be used to remedy the young couple's poverty. She volunteers to intervene in Lord Chiltern's irate assertion that foxes are being poisoned at the Duke's behest. When she offers her money to get Phineas acquitted of the accusation of murdering Mr. Bonteen, the attorney, Mr. Low, is unsuccessful in persuading her that this would be immoral, illegal, and ineffective. "The more money you spend," she says, "the more fuss you make. And the longer a trial is about and the greater the interest, the more chance a man has to escape. If a man is tried for three days you always think he'll get off, but if it lasts ten minutes he is sure to be convicted and hung. I'd have Mr. Finn's trial made so long that they never could convict him."

And what if he should be convicted?

"I'd buy up the Home Secretary. It's very horrid to say so, of course, Mr. Low; and I dare say there is nothing wrong ever done in Chancery. But I know what Cabinet Ministers are. If they could get a majority by granting a pardon they'd do it quick enough."

She also provides opportunities for her friend Marie Goesler to put herself in the way of Phineas Finn in another match-making venture. And in all these projects she succeeds.

How much help does Madame Max (Marie) Goesler need? Not much, though she accepts the assistance. We have already seen Madame Goesler outface Lady Glencora (before she became Duchess), mocking Glencora when she makes a clumsy effort to dissuade Marie from pursuing a marriage with the old Duke, which would potentially disinherit her oldest son. And in this novel she again takes the high ground with Glencora, winning the love and another proposal from the dying Duke but turning him down, and then refusing the fortune and jewels bequeathed her by the old Duke (except for one little ring she says she will always wear).

Is Madame Goesler too good to be true? She is presented as a young woman, about thirty-two years of age, the same age as Phineas Finn. But she is miles beyond Phineas in maturity and capability. And not only that. Wisdom. Her utterances come across as the wisdom of the ages. In urging Phineas to accept an appointment to the cabinet, she says, "Your foot must be on the ladder before you can get to the top of it."

Madame Max never seems to make a mistake. She handles the

attentions of the Duke impeccably, and she manages her relationship with Lady Glencora with wit and consummate skill. Maybe our greatest reservation about her judgment has to do with her steadfast preference for Phineas Finn. But one can hardly doubt the happiness of the favored couple. There is little reason to doubt that Phineas can handle prosperity.

And Phineas Finn: not exactly a hobbledehoy. His gift of gab permits him to sail through social challenges. Perhaps his success with the ladies gives him self confidence. But the reader grits his teeth as Phineas allows himself to be sucked into a foolish quarrel with Mr. Bonteen. And we share Madame Max's counsel to him at the end when he is offered office and cannot bring himself to accept. His density is more believable than Madame Max's wisdom. But here the critic is at odds with the enthusiastic reader who cheers her on.

And what of poor Lady Laura, the other woman who loves Phineas? None of Trollope's women appear more true to life. She pays a long and bitter price for having sacrificed herself to bring financial solvency to her family by a marriage to a lord who ultimately proves himself to be crazy. She bares her soul to Phineas, who gamely attempts to bring temporary solace to a grieving woman. But how can she ever be comforted? Poor Phineas. Many readers may conclude that he does as well as a kind-hearted Irishman can do.

The climax of the story is Phineas's trial for murder, a device that lends pace and urgency to the story. In some respects the case is handled like that of Mr. Crawley in The Last Chronicle of Barset, in which a trip to the continent is heroically taken by an advocate for the accused, bringing back evidence that breaks open the case—though it is not necessarily essential.

One more thing: Trollope's touch in portraying the professional lawyer is as entertaining a presentation of the creed of the Law as one can hope for. Mr. Chaffanbrass, who is to defend Phineas Finn, has no interest in knowing the truth about the murderer, despite being told that the public wants to know. "[T]he public is ignorant." The public should want to know the truth about the evidence about the murder. "Now the last man to give us any useful insight into the evidence is the prisoner himself. In nineteen cases out of twenty a man tried for murder in this country committed the murder for which he is tried."

After meeting Phineas Finn, Chaffanbrass maintains that he never expresses an opinion of guilt or innocence of a client until the trial is over. In a four-hour speech he argues persuasively for Phineas's innocence, though he reflects over a pint of port wine in a small room afterward that he privately believes him to be guilty.

"But to no human being had he expressed this opinion; nor would he express it—unless his client should be hung."

Though perhaps not among the best few of Trollope's novels, why should Phineas Redux not be rated among the very good ones? The difficulty of such a judgment lies in the even quality of many of the contenders. I would give this one a "very good" rating.

"ARE NOT POLITICS ODD?" THE PRIME MINISTER

Religion and politics—the two spheres of human activity to be approached with caution, if not to be avoided, in polite conversation—are the subjects forming the basis of Anthony Trollope's two series of novels, the Barsetshire series and the Palliser series. No other writer of his stature has touched these areas on such a scale. Perhaps others have avoided them simply because they haven't been interested. Trollope was certainly interested in politics; he even ran for the House for Commons once, was defeated and was disillusioned. His interest in church affairs and church politics was less personal, though he did maintain his own personal theology.

His abiding interest in politics is evident in The Prime Minister, fifth in the series of the six Palliser novels. My recollection of the story from twenty-five years ago is mainly of Ferdinand Lopez, so that when he threw himself under a train at the Tenway Junction, I assumed that the book must be over. But no, we had the loose ends of the fate of his widow, Emily Wharton Lopez, to dispose of; and the main plot thread, that of the prime minister, the Duke of Omnium, to be concluded.

Lopez sticks in the memory as one who creates himself on a basis of audacity, charm, and freedom from any moral restraints. We meet him as a suitor for the hand of Emily Wharton, daughter of a wealthy barrister; he preys on her brother Everett and through him finds entrée to dinner at the Whartons' house. Both his social and financial careers are leveraged on slender bases that eventually collapse but support him long enough to make a sensational run. He is similar in many ways to Augustus Melmotte, who makes a larger run through the established circles of Victorian England in The Way We Live Now, Trollope's larger portrayal of contemporary mores written a year earlier in 1874.

A case might be made that the House of Commons is the major

character in the novel. We are told that although the House is sometimes led and influenced by one of its members, the House during the ministry of the Duke of Omnium had no Prime Minister sitting among its members and was essentially on its own. Plantagenet Palliser had been obliged to leave the House of Commons for the House of Lords when his uncle's death made him the new Duke of Omnium, and we can hardly doubt the new Duke when he says that he would rather be a Member of the House of Commons than Duke of Omnium. It is not that the Duke was a charismatic leader of his fellows in the House. On the contrary, he was a patient workman, doing his homework and presenting lengthy accounts of the state of the Treasury. But without even that presence, the House first labored under the leadership of Sir Orlando Drought, whom the Prime Minister offended by his lack of interest in Sir Orlando's opinions. After the resignation of Sir Orlando, the Prime Minister was represented by Mr. Monk, a more congenial colleague. But the House grew restless under a Prime Minister who made no attempt to be friendly to any of its members and eventually shucked him off. All this was foreseen and observed by the Duke of St. Bungay, old and wise, whose counsel the younger Duke could not always bring himself to heed.

But although the House plays its anthropomorphic role by default in the absence of a powerful and ambitious Prime Minister, this Prime Minister is Plantagenet Palliser, Duke of Omnium. Trollope considered him one of his three greatest characters, and in this story he reaches the peak of his political career. Another of Trollope's trio of favorites, Lady Glencora, Duchess of Omnium, reaches the height of her own ambition as wife of the Prime Minister. (The third was Mr. Crawly in The Last Chronicle of Barset.) How would this portrayal fare as an isolated novel rather than as the linchpin in a series of six lengthy works? Perhaps an experiment should be conducted in which a class reads The Prime Minister with no previous exposure to the Pallisers and another class reads the series straight through. Would there be enough unpaid volunteers for such an experiment? I think that those already familiar with the Pallisers would have keener appreciation for their portrayal in power. Here we see the Duke accept the position of Prime Minister with reluctance, suffer through the slings and arrows of criticism, and then face the issue of whether he should resign. And Lady Glencora pitches in with enthusiasm to the project of entertaining those who are of any importance to her husband's success, despite his objections and refusal to participate in the effort. She encourages the villain Lopez, who becomes a thorn in their sides, and she pulls back from her adopted role as the Hostess with the Mostest.

Robert Caro has been compared to Trollope for his delineation of men and politics in a recent multivolume biography of Lyndon Johnson. This similarity is particularly apparent in Caro's description of Coke Stevenson, Lyndon Johnson's opponent in the race for the US Senate in Texas in 1948. Stevenson had served as governor of Texas and despite his disdain for politics, he had received record majorities in his gubernatiorial campaigns. He was a scrupulously honest public servant, but he was also a proud man, too proud to stoop to indulging in a personal attack on a political opponent. Johnson knew this, and he capitalized on it.

Reading this, I thought to myself: I know about proud men in politics. I know about Plantagenet Palliser. Perhaps one of the most telling portraits is that painted by his wife as she tells her friend Mrs. Finn that if he should hear treason being plotted against him, he would stop up his ears with his fingers. "He is all trust, even when he knows that he is being deceived. He is honor complete from head to foot."

This is not to say that Coke Stevenson was a latter day Plantagenet Palliser. But the similarities between the detailed portrayals of the historical Coke Stevenson and the fictional Plantagenet Palliser serve to validate the authenticity of the fictional predecessor. Both even had similar political wives.

Fay Stevenson was outgoing and friendly, but in contrast to Lady Glencora, she did not establish friendships for political purposes.

Glencora undoubtedly had her political reasons. But Susan Hampshire, in an interview about the television series in which she played Glencora, said that politicians' wives told her they considered Glencora to be the model of the political wife. Lady Glen was a woman who could flatter Sir Orlando Drought during his visit to Gatherum, even though she disliked him and knew that her husband had not been gracious to him.

An advantage of the novelist is the absolute freedom to reveal the inner workings of the mind, and our understanding of Plantagenet Palliser, who says so little, is enhanced by such direct disclosures as his reflection that he had not had a happy day since he took office, that he had had no gratification, and that he was unconvinced that he was doing the country any good.

Glencora, on the other hand, is so articulate that she reveals the inner workings of her mind herself. Some of the last words we hear from her constitute a quick little aside to her young friend Emily Wharton:

"Are not politics odd? A few years ago I only barely knew what the word meant. ... I suppose it's wrong, but a state of pugnacity seems to me the greatest bliss we can reach here on earth."

"I shouldn't like to be always fighting."

"That's because you haven't known Sir Timothy Beeswax and two or three other gentlemen whom I could name. The day will come, I dare say, when you will care about politics."

In The Prime Minister we reach the culmination of the political career of two of Trollope's favorite characters, and we learn how they handled the acquisition and the loss of power. And yet the memorable part of the book is not the political drama but the occurrence at the Tenway Junction, when Ferdinand Lopez finishes his meteoric career by throwing himself under the wheels of the morning express from Euston to Inverness. As in some of his other works (such as Can You Forgive Her? in which Plantagenet and Glencora steal the scenes from the protagonists of the primary plot), the subplot upstages the primary story line. Lopez preys on the weaknesses of others (as does Lyndon Johnson in Caro's biography) and shrewdly makes a place for himself. But it is a place that will not last. Emily sees the real man she has married after the wedding ceremony (as Lady Bird Johnson learned that she was to be humiliated in front of their friends by her husband's peremptory and petty orders). Perhaps the most unpalatable of Lopez's commands to his wife is his telling her to "get round" her father in order to satisfy Lopez's urgent desire for money to cover his losses in speculation in guano.

Lopez's initial conquests include not only the Whartons but even the Duchess of Omnium, who, still somewhat aggrieved after years of marriage that she was not allowed to marry the beautiful scoundrel Burgo Fitzgerald, has a weakness for charming and beautiful young scoundrels. There are no bounds to Lopez's ambition and effrontery: having lost an election in the Duke's home borough of Silverbridge and having had his campaign expenses reimbursed by his father-in-law Mr. Wharton, he writes the Duke and demands that the five hundred pounds expenses be paid by the Duke, since his wife had encouraged him to run for the office and the Duke had compelled her to withdraw the endorsement of "the Castle." Somewhat to his surprise, Lopez's letter hits a vulnerable target, and the Duke sends five hundred pounds.

Nemesis stalks Lopez in the form of the market for guano, which fails to meet his expectations and requirements, and the steadfast refusal of Mr. Wharton to send good money after bad. And so to the Tenway Junction. Like so many others, he thought he could walk on water.

So maybe this is why Trollope has a virtual monopoly on the political novel (and also the church novel). Scoundrels are more interesting. But wait; are there scoundrels in politics? Of course there are. This is where the biographer comes in with the life of Lyndon Johnson. For better or worse, that story wasn't fiction. One wishes for a latter-day Anthony Trollope to give us a story of such a towering figure, unencumbered by the requirements of nonfiction.

THE OLD ORDER PASSETH THE DUKE'S CHILDREN

Do I identify more with the Duke of Omnium, or with Lord Silverbridge, as the Duke tells Isabelle Boncassen, "My boy's wife shall be my daughter in very deed"? Would I be so close to tears when he gives her his late wife's ring, if I had not known Glencora through the previous five novels of the Palliser series? The Duke's Children stands up very well on its own, but its force is clearly enhanced by its predecessors. While the characters from previous novels may be received as old friends in new stages of their lives, their children may be presented as various mixtures of their parents' personalities. The reader greets the children in the process of making the transition to adulthood with the pleasure of recognition of the character traits of the parents.

Lady Glencora, Duchess of Omnium, has died in the interval between The Prime Minister and The Duke's Children, but her influence persists. She has sanctioned the suit of Francis Tregear, an impoverished commoner, for the hand of her daughter Lady Mary without the Duke's knowledge. So here is a variation on the theme of Glencora's love for the worthless Burgo Fitzgerald, which she never pretended to give up after her arranged marriage to Plantagenet Palliser. We find her daughter Lady Mary perhaps less reckless but even more persistent, and successful, in her chosen love. Tregear has apparently gotten over his previous love for Lady Mabel Grex, whom the Duke favors for his son's wife, and Tregear shows himself to be a more worthy individual than the dissolute Burgo.

Lord Silverbridge sows his wild oats as one would expect of Glencora's son, but like Prince Hal, he grows appropriately into recognition of his responsibilities. The reader sees, before the Duke brings himself to acknowledge it, that Silverbridge makes a wise choice in his selection of the American Isabelle Boncassen as the object of his affections.

Gerald, the younger son, plays a lesser role but manages to repent of some relatively minor offenses: he manages to continue with college studies, and his gambling debts do not compare in magnitude to those of his older and more richly endowed brother.

New blood is brought into the family, new faces appear in the story. The woman who brings a bit of spice is Lady Mabel Grex. She has loved her childhood friend, Francis Tregear, but she decided that since they were both penniless, each had better marry for money. (Shades of Lady Laura Standish!) Tregear goes on to better things, as bees flit from flower to flower, but Lady Mabel never loses her love. She reveals herself when she confides to her older companion Miss Cassewary that Lord Silverbridge would have proposed to her if she had given him any encouragement, but "I spared him;—out of sheer downright Christian charity! I said to myself, 'Love your neighbours.' 'Don't be selfish.' 'Do unto him as you would he should do unto you,'—that is, think of his welfare. Though I had him in my net, I let him go. Shall I go to heaven for doing that?"

Isabel Boncassen, her successor in the Duchess of Omnium sweepstakes, faces different challenges from those that confront Lady Mabel. Frankly in love with Silverbridge, her disadvantage is one not readily appreciated on this side of the Atlantic: she is American. As Lady Mabel is revealed in the above passage, so we see Isabel as she walks with Silverbridge among the old graves at Matching and hears him tell her how Sir Guy ran away with half a dozen heiresses.

"Nobody should have run away with me. I have no idea of going on such a journey except on terms of equality,—just step and step alike." Then she took hold of his arm and put out one foot. "Are you ready?"

The action of the story is all carried out by the young people. They gamble and lose, they fall in love, they run for office, they scheme and dally, they sin and reform. But the story is really about the one person who doesn't do anything: the Duke of Omnium. Grieved by the sudden loss of his wife and forced to deal with issues she would have addressed—basically, the children—he is forced to learn that where the children are concerned, even the Duke is far from omnipotent. One who had stated that he would prefer the House of Commons to the House of Lords, he is found defending the order and telling his children of their obligation to marry within their rank. He instructs Miss Boncassen on the opportunity that the poorest man in England has to rise by merit to the highest office in the land, and he has long conversations with Isabel on the advantages of a decimal coinage system, but it never occurs to him that her wit and beauty should outweigh the rank of Lady Mabel Grex as qualifications for becoming his son's wife.

Lest the reader miss the irony, Trollope spells it out in telling the reader that in his heart of hearts the Duke kept his own family and his own self entirely apart from his grand theories. "That one and the same man should have been in one part of himself so unlike the other part,—that he should have one set of opinions so contrary to another set,—poor Isabel Boncassen did not understand."

The Duke must decide whether to give his blessing to two marriages to which he has been unalterably opposed. And his guide and counselor in these issues is his late wife's best friend, Mrs. Phineas Finn, the former Madame Max Goesler. Stubborn and taciturn, he is not an easy pupil. And she must first overcome his anger when he discovers that she had not come immediately to him when Lady Mary told her of her engagement to Mr. Tregear. Of course his late wife had first sinned in this way, but Marie Goesler Finn is the scapegoat for Glencora just as Alice Vavasor had been when Glencora insisted on walking in the priory ruins on a cold night, despite Alice's objections, and caught cold. Mrs. Finn refuses to be shunned by the Duke, becomes his confidante, and she continues in her role as the only character in the entire Palliser series who is always right. Married to Phineas Finn, who had once refused her own proposal of marriage to him, we see very little of their interaction in married life. But in her role as best friend to Glencora, we saw her as a voice of reason when Glencora was flighty, and later as one who would rouse the phlegmatic Duke to deal appropriately with Silverbridge's and Lady Mary's choices.

This interview occurs near the midway point of the novel, and with this the reader can guess that in the end the Duke will permit the marriage and even ask Mr. Tregear what his Christian name is. But this is a political novel. Back to business. After all, entire chapters are devoted to the maneuvers by which Sir Timothy Beeswax attempts to maintain his power with the Conservative government. Again we see politics as it is. The moves are not too complex for a Trollope novel, but they are too complex for a brief review. Suffice it to say that no government lasts forever, and the Duke is obliged to deal with political adversity. It isn't easy for him; but it is not for nothing that the Duke is one of Trollope's favorite creations.

A pleasant book. England moves on. A segment of the Liberal Party finds itself obliged to become more liberal than had been anticipated. The Palliser series comes to an end, and the readers (especially those of us who have developed a sentimental attachment to this seemingly aloof family) are entertained.

RUINS, RUIN, AND RUINED THE MACDER-MOTS OF BALLYCLORAN

I've never cared very much for junkyard photography. By this I mean rusty plows, abandoned automobiles, houses falling in, storefronts with broken glass. Of course ruins always have a certain appeal; the remains of an old well can be seen beside a trail leading down toward the river from my house. Who knows what happened around that old site? But rust and ruin have a limited appeal. Anthony Trollope encountered the ruins of an old country house on a visit to Drumsna, Ireland, in 1843, while working for the Post Office. As recorded in his autobiography, "It was one of the most melancholy spots I ever visited ... and while I was still among the ruined walls and decayed beams I fabricated the plot of The Macdermots of Ballycloran." The story that resulted from this visit might do very well to pass away a dull afternoon riding through the country; but I found the leisurely pace of the six hundred page novel tedious. Ruins, ruin, and ruined.

This was Trollope's first novel. He was twenty-eight years old, and he had been in Ireland five years, traveling through the countryside as a clerk to a postal surveyor. One of the primary rules for writers is to write about what one knows about, and he did that. But he would have never survived as an author on forty-six more such novels. Over the next decade he was to write two more rather indifferent novels and then begin The Warden, the first of the Barsetshire novels and predecessor to Barchester Towers, his best known work. It's one thing for a writer to have the requisite skills; it's another thing—whether by chance or design—to hit upon a subject or a character that will "take off." Writers are sometimes surprised by what the public likes and what it doesn't. Sir Arthur Conan Doyle looked upon Sherlock Holmes as a distraction from his higher calling as a writer of historical novels, until he realized that Holmes was his meal ticket. Few readers know anything about his historical novels. And for Trollope, the worlds of Barchester Towers and the Pallisers secured his place in English literature.

But back to the dreary world of the Macdermots. First, be warned that their story, which doesn't start very well, doesn't end well, either, as a visitor to the ruins of their country house might suspect. Larry Macdermot, reigning patriarch, is on the verge of losing his house, his property and his mind. His daughter Feemy is seduced by the English revenue agent. Larry's son Thady, the central focus of the story, has a violent encounter with Feemy's lover when she is reluctant to elope with him. It's an unhappy time for the clan.

It wasn't a happy time for Ireland, either, and the great potato famine hadn't even started yet. The English of that day were not very interested in reading about the details of daily life of the people whom they were oppressing. Trollope, on the other hand, was a young man just beginning to achieve some success and self-confidence in his voluntary exile to serve among these impoverished people. He used his skills to portray them with accuracy and even with sympathy, even though he was a loyal son of England and man of his times and felt no obligation to accord them any more than token respect. Describing Father Cullen, he writes, "He felt towards Keegan all the abhorrence which a very bigoted and ignorant Roman Catholic could feel towards a Protestant convert." An accurate account, perhaps, but could such a frank sentence be written today?

The plot is well laid out, and the story is well told, but the reader is required to plow through the Irish dialect—"'Yer honer won't be afther taking an innocent boy like me,' began Tim, 'that knows nothing at all at all about it.'" This is fair enough—the reader knows he's reading about a different country in a different century—but it does take a bit of adjustment.

Trollope loved sporting scenes, usually fox hunting, and in this one we have a horse race scene, described in the words of the spectators much like the scene at Ascot Opening Day in My Fair Lady: "There they go—Hurroo! They're off. Faix, there's Playful at her tricks already—by dad she'll be over the ropes!"

The pace of the book is leisurely, a common feature of Victorian novels. On the morning after a wedding, the reader is wondering whether any mischief came to Captain Ussher, and whether he survived the night after "the boys" had threatened to put him under the sod. But such concerns must be suspended for an account of how several of the characters felt about things. After four and a half pages of Thady's reflections, he happens to meet Ussher in the road, and the reader surmises that Ussher was not killed. We can see where minimalist fiction came from.

Another source of tedium is that the three Macdermots have hardly any redeeming features—a sleazy lot, with whom it is difficult to sympathize.

But one does find evidence of Trollope's facility to entertain. He excels in introductory summaries of his characters. About Feemy, whose mother and grandmother had died early, we are told:

Whatever her feelings were,—and for her mother they were strong,—the real effect of this was, that she was freed from the restraint and constant scolding of two stupid women at a very early age; consequently she was left alone with her father and

her brother, neither of whom were at all fitting guides for so wayward a pupil. … Her father had become almost like the tables and
chairs in the parlour, only much less useful and more difficult to
move.

The trial scene near the end of the book is well done; Trollope
excelled in trial scenes, particularly in Orley Farm and Phineas
Redux. When he introduces Mr. Allewinde, he shows us his frustration in attempting to examine Pat Brady, a reluctant witness
whose literal responses remind today's reader of "Who's on First?"

The most successful comic interlude is that of the duel between
Jonas Brown and Counsellor Webb, two of the three magistrates
who hear the case of Thady Macdermot and differ on the question of his guilt. When he receives a response to his challenge, Mr.
Brown's two sons comfort him by telling him not to worry about
his legs because Webb will fire high. "The shoulder's the spot,"
unless he takes him on the head—"which wouldn't be so pleasant," and he'd rather take his chances with a chap that fired low.
The other brother disagrees.

"The low shot's the death-shot. Why, man, if you did catch a ball
in the head, you'd get over it—if it was in the mouth, or cheek, or
neck, or anywhere but the temple; but your body's all over tender
bits. May heaven always keep lead out of my bowels—I'd sooner
have it in my brains."

As luck would have it, Brown catches a ball in the seat of his
pants, causing a bloody and inconvenient wound about an eighth
of an inch deep.

This is the closest thing to a happy ending in the book. This re-
viewer's recommendation: Read the review. Skip the book.

THE IRISH AS OTHERS SEE THEM THE KEL-
LYS AND THE O'KELLYS

If you live in an age of political incorrectness, you may as well
take advantage of it. So Anthony Trollope might have told himself, had he enjoyed the advantage of looking into the future to
our present age of political correctness. The Kellys and the O'Kellys would not survive the scrutiny of present standards. "Faix, I
b'lieve his chief failing at present's fur sthrong dhrink!" Transcrip-
tion of the Irish forms of speech warns the present day reader to
be wary; this is something that may be unfair to the Irish. Uncle
Remus fell victim to such concerns and disappeared from view in
1986 when Disney removed Song of the South from circulation,

and the glimpses of the subservient blacks that we have in older films indicate that those who use language in a distinctive way can be vulnerable to being presented in a demeaning fashion.

Of course these were not the concerns of a fledgling nineteenth century English writer who had spent five years in Ireland with the postal service. One would suspect that the intended target audience resided in England, not in Ireland. (This, his second novel, did not sell well anywhere.) Features of Irish life are described to inform the reading public in England, and those who did read it were surely entertained as well. The description of an Irish kitchen is accompanied, in the Folio Edition, by a full-page pen-and-ink drawing which features a pig, two chickens, and two ragged old men sitting on the floor, all of whom are described in detail.

Here we see Trollope discovering his comic gift. The tone of the story is that of a cartoon comedy, Looney Tunes perhaps, with rascally villains and seemingly inept heroes who seem destined to be taken in by dastardly schemers. Lord Cashel, for instance, is shown in the role of the wicked lord of the manor who only dimly suspects how unlikely it is that any of his plots and plans will succeed. He seizes an opportunity to refuse to allow one of the heroes of the story, Lord Ballindine (Frank O'Kelly), to see Fanny Wyndham, the object of his affection, who happens to be Lord Cashel's ward. Lord Cashel has other plans for Fanny, who has come into an inheritance that would wipe out the debts incurred by Lord Cashel's prodigal son Lord Kilcullen. Fanny must marry his son! He is only slightly bothered by Fanny's spirited vow to see her lover Frank O'Kelly anyway, but despite his concern about her determination, he remains confident in his own powers. As his plot unravels, one expects the standard melodramatic line, "Curses! Foiled again!"

The most evil villain, though, is Barry Lynch, limited by his sister's existence to only half of his late father's estate. He daydreams about how his worries would all be washed away if his sister should only be in some way detached from her worldly cares. The English reader might view with detached amusement the schemes of a profligate drunken young Irish lord who is staggered to learn that his sister's acute illness might not be fatal, after all, and that she might rise again to displace him.

There can be no sympathy for the dehumanized arch villain of this dark comedy, described as having no residual feelings of human kindness. Surely he can bribe the doctor to see to it that she succumbs. And the reader can only smile as he calculates further what payment he must offer, and then how he can get out of paying it.

On the other side of the moral ledger, the two heroes of the story—Martin Kelly and Frank O'Kelly—are shown as young men with good hearts. Martin is a young farmer who rents from several landlords, including Lord Ballindine (Frank O'Kelly). At one point in the story Lord Ballindine, a recovering prodigal in his own right, is in need of three hundred pounds and thinks that his renter Martin Kelly would be able to lend it to him. Martin hesitates, saying that he has the money but had been thinking of using it in another way, which would clear the way for him to marry Anty Lynch, sister of the infamous Barry. Frank backs off, saying that he had forgotten about Martin's "matrimonial speculation," and he advises him that though he needs the cash, Martin had better keep it. But Martin says that his mother could let him have the money on the security of the house, in order that his Lordship should not be short of cash.

Thank goodness these two young Irishmen have good hearts; they need them for redemption. Both of them make no bones about their plans to marry for money. Though each maintains that he really loves the lady of his choice, they both freely admit that it was the money that first attracted them. Would Trollope have granted such a blot on the escutcheon of one of his young English heroes?

Trollope's previous work, which was also his debut novel, told of the fall of an old Irish family, The Macdermots of Ballycloran, with little levity to relieve it. The Kellys and the O'Kellys, on the other hand, is a comic novel. One may wonder whether Trollope is laughing with the Irish or at them. The general impression is one of affection, with a sharp eye for entertaining foibles. We must follow a knotty skein of debts and obligations in a discussion of how Jerry Blake got a pair of breeches to wear for Lord Ballindine's hunt. The leather had to be purchased in Tuam, and an assistant tailor had to leave his mother's wake and stay up all night sewing. The tailor, however, had a long-standing debt for his garden, and the landlord was a distant relation of Jerry Blake. So the long and tangled circle is closed, and Jerry gets his breeches.

Lord Cashel appears as an earl whose cardinal virtues were negative ones. He had learned that silence is sometimes mistaken for wisdom; he had avoided intemperance, and he had not done too many stupid things. He had avoided adultery, and since his marriage, he had not seduced any of his neighbors' daughters. He was therefore "considered a moral man."

Lady Selina is the first of Trollope's high-born old maids, too proud to marry—unless someone asks her. Other examples were to include Miss Sarah Marrable in The Vicar of Bullhampton and Lady Amelia De Courcy in Dr. Thorne. The rest of the family at

Grey Abbey was "dull, solemn, slow, and respectable," but Lady Selina, daughter of the earl, exceeded them all. The "specific gravity of Lady Selina could not be calculated. It was beyond the power of figures, even in algebraic denominations, to describe her moral weight."

Cares can be put aside when one comes upon one of Trollope's fox-hunting episodes. All is given up to the pleasure of the chase, and of its anticipation, and of its recollection. Indeed one of the markers of the successful huntsman is that his experience and his horsemanship allow him to be a witness to the end of the fox so that he can recount the details afterward. Character is revealed in the field. In this case, the Protestant clergyman Reverend Armstrong (whose only parishioner is Mrs. O'Kelly) is one of those who knows every road and which way the wind is blowing, and how unlikely it is that the fox would run against it. He shows himself to be a master huntsman. Like experienced golfers who "putt for dough" while the young men "drive for show," Mr. Armstrong spares his horse, takes short-cuts, and is always at the scene of the kill before the hard-riding gallants come galloping up a minute or two late.

Barry Lynch, on the other hand, cuts his horse in front of the hounds as they approach a small stone wall, fatally injuring one of them. Frank O'Kelly is obliged to send him home in disgrace.

(The bloody end to the fox hunt is no longer to be seen within the restriction of English laws. The sport was banned in England in 2004. Hunting enthusiasts, however, claim that the number of foxes killed each year has actually increased since the ban.)

Lessons in the conduct of human affairs are to be found in Trollope's work, another feature that The Kellys and the O'Kellys shares with some of his later and better-known works. For instance, doctors, lawyers, and others who are paid to give advice learn sooner or later that one can only advise; one cannot coerce. Professionals will sometimes tell the recipient that they have given their best advice; and it is up to them to decide whether to take it. We find the young lawyer Mr. Daly resorting to this ploy as he finds that Barry Lynch is disappointed not to have prospects for a more lucrative settlement in a deal with Martin Kelly: "I've now given you my best advice; if your mind's not yet made up, perhaps you'll have the goodness to let me hear from you when it is?"

The story is a symmetrical one in which each of the two young heroes finds his reward, virtue emerges triumphant, and the wicked are vanquished. It's a warm-hearted romp in which young Anthony Trollope showed that he had the tools to keep readers entertained for years. My guess is that an Irishman can enjoy it as much as an Englishman.

A TALE OF NO CITY LA VENDÉE

False starts are usually forgotten in the early phases of an athlete's development. Young boys and girls may try their hand at several different sports and then gravitate toward the best opportunities for "showcasing their talents." Writers presumably conduct their own trials and errors, too, with the misbegotten products left buried in desk drawers, if not destroyed. Anthony Trollope's false start, La Vendée, a historical romance, was published, but it's fair to say that it has not been remembered. It was his third novel, following two Irish novels, The Macdermots of Ballycloran and The Kellys and the O'Kellys, and it was followed four years later by the first of his Barsetshire novels, The Warden, which was a great success. By then Trollope knew where his strength lay; he followed with Barchester Towers and thereafter he stuck to the world (mostly England) of his own day. He did not attempt any more historical novels.

The worst thing about La Vendée is the dialogue. Here's a conversation between husband and wife as he prepares to leave for war:

"I know, Victorine," said he, when they were alone together in the evening, when not even his own dear sister Marie was there to mar the sacred sweetness of their conference, "I know that I am doing right, and that gives me strength to leave you, and our darling child."

He goes on for another paragraph or two.

Except for the stilted, wordy dialogue, the story is not so bad. It follows a lost cause, that of the citizens of La Vendée, an agricultural region in the west of France that my wife and I drove through on our way from Normandy to Bordeaux several years ago. These faithful servants of the king opposed the republican forces of the French Revolution, and they were annihilated. We follow the men and women of the doomed faction: Jacques Cathelineau, the humble postilion who is elected first military leader of the royalists, and who is loved by the noble and lovely Agatha Larochejaquelin; Agatha's brother Henri, who succeeds Cathelineau as general of the royalist forces, and who loves Marie de Lescure; and Marie's brother Charles and his wife Victorine. That makes three couples. There is also a little comic relief of sorts with Jacques Chapeau, Henri Larochejacquelin's servant, who woos Annot Stein, daughter of the blacksmith Michael Stein. A saucy wench, Annot teases Jacques by praising Cathelineau the general.

There is also Adolphe Denot, Henri's proud friend who loves Adolphe's sister Agatha and is rejected in a dramatic proposal scene, so prolonged that "Agatha began to fear that at this rate the interview would have no end. If Adolphe remained with his arm on the marble slab, and his head on one side, making sentimental speeches till she should give him encouragement to fall at her feet, it certainly would not be ended by bedtime." Adolphe is a strange case. Stung by Agatha's refusal, he goes forth to battle determined to die, but he disgraces himself by failing to support M. de Lescure in storming a breach in the wall. He then disappears, switches sides, and leads the republican forces into battle. Finally he reappears as the "Mad Captain," leading the royalist forces in suicidal charges.

The battle scenes are well described, detained only by a few lengthy speeches by the heroes as they swing their swords.

Fictional characters mingle with the historical ones, and even Robespierre appears in two consecutive chapters unto himself. The upper classes of England were horrified by the French Revolution, and the author's judgment of Robespierre is an example:

Honesty, moral conduct, industry, constancy of purpose, temperance in power, courage, and love of country: these virtues all belonged to Robespierre; … Why, instead of the Messiah of freedom, which he believed himself to be, has his name become a byword, a reproach, and an enormity? Because he wanted faith! He believed in nothing but himself, and the reasoning faculty with which he felt himself to be endowed. He thought himself perfect in his own human nature, and wishing to make others perfect as he was, he fell into the lowest abyss of crime and misery in which a poor human creature ever wallowed. He seems almost to have been sent into the world to prove the inefficacy of human reason to effect human happiness.

We see Robespierre directly only in these two chapters toward the end of the book. Trollope was not above passing judgment on his characters, but I don't recall another exclamation like, "Because he wanted faith!" These two didactic chapters are not necessary to the story line, but the horrors of the French Revolution are hardly amenable to understatement. Though they would be the first to go in any abridgement, they do help put the whole story into historical perspective.

Trollope never visited La Vendée. His story is based primarily on the memoirs of Madame de la Rochejacquelin, who appears in the book with the name of her first husband, M. de Lescure. She subsequently married the younger brother of Henri de Larochejacquelin and bore him eight children before he was killed in a second Vendean revolt in 1815. Among the fictional characters were Marie Larochejacquelin and Adolphe Denot. How would Trollope end his story of this disaster? He created a happy interlude, and he made the best of it.

Dickens was more comfortable with the French Revolution in A Tale of Two Cities, written ten years later when he was at the peak of his powers. Its dialogue was almost as stilted, and Dickens was no stranger to a bit of purple prose. But his energy and passion allowed him to carry it off. (And it is reported to be the all-time best seller of books written originally in English.) Such a story was not Anthony Trollope's cup of tea, particularly when he was a novice still searching for his métier. Perhaps this clumsy attempt at historical fiction helps us appreciate the facility with which he later portrayed contemporary English folk. If there is a rule that allows us to discard one of an author's efforts before passing judgment on his work, let this be it for Trollope. Let us pass on to Barsetshire.

THE OFFICE THE THREE CLERKS

The Three Clerks is an inside book, written about the Civil Service by one who had himself begun his Postal Service career as a clerk. It holds up to gentle fun its little ways, its principles of management, and the ingrained habits of thought held by its faithful servants. (The present day reader may conclude that bureaucracies don't change much.) Office politics, infighting, and intrigues provide grist for the author's mill, and he makes good use of it. The story deals with three young Postal Service clerks and the family of a widow with three fair young daughters. Here, too, the author has something to work on: Will they pair off? If so, how? And how will the pairings turn out? And what of the young men and their careers in the Service? Who will advance, who will waste his talents? How will they deal with Temptation?

Henry Norman appears first, the second son of a gentleman of small property, one who plods through his duties and his courtship. Alaric Tudor was raised in Brussels, became an orphan, and finds himself at a desk adjacent to Henry Norman, with whom he subsequently shares lodgings. Alaric is street smart, knows how to advance himself, and opts for expediency over principle. Charley Tudor, son of a clergyman and a young cousin of Alaric, proves himself susceptible to the temptations offered by street life in London.

And the widow in the cottage near Hampton Court? Her late husband was a cousin of Harry Norman's father, so naturally Mrs. Woodward invites young Harry and his friends to visit on weekends.

Although the reader is entertained by the portrayal of the Departments of Internal Navigation and Weights and Measures, the book hangs mainly on the plot, and the story is basically that of the six young people. Harry falls in love with the eldest sister Gertrude, but Alaric wins her away from him and earns his sustained hatred. Harry subsequently settles for the second sister Linda, who initially thought she was in love with Alaric, who was false with her as well as with Harry. In the course of the story the youngest sister Katie grows up from thirteen to seventeen and falls in love with Charley, who saves her life by pulling her from the water.

Three brides for three friends: perhaps this wasn't so unusual in Victorian times when meetings, much less friendships, among eligible young people weren't always so easy to obtain. But then the results: the first two couplings are plausible enough, but Katie, the youngest, becomes chronically ill with unrequited love, and although the reader is reassured that the doctors who listen to her chest through wooden tubes find no evidence of consumption, the anxious reader fears that the author will let her die. Trollope became known as a skeptic of Shakespeare's dictum: "Men will die and worms will eat them, but not of love."

We are reminded how Australia was populated as Alaric takes his family there for a fresh start after serving six months in jail for betraying the trust of a young woman for whom he was named trustee. And we see how Victorians did their insider trading, as Alaric is persuaded by the villain of the story, Undy Scott, to buy shares in mines that he is evaluating for the Department of Weights and Measures.

And Trollope indulges in certain liberties. He satirizes the publishing world with Charley Tudor's writing serial novels, and here we find Mrs. Woodward reading Crinoline and Macassar aloud to the young people: "The lovely Crinoline was sitting alone at a lattice window on a summer morning, and as she sat she sang with melancholy cadence the first part of the now celebrated song which had then lately appeared. ..."

Thirteen pages of Chapter XXVIII are devoted entirely to an impassioned defense of the Civil Service, particularly of the young men who work there. This chapter is absent from my small leather-bound edition published in 1878 but is restored in the Trollope Society edition of 1992, which follows the text of the first edition, published in 1858. The chapter is irrelevant to the story; it does, however, reveal where the author is coming from. He is coming from the Civil Service, which was his ticket to self-respect and financial independence.

Finally, the first three pages of Chapter XLV, "The Criminal Population is Disposed of," are given to a comparison of this novel's villain, Undecimus Scott, with Bill Sikes. Was Charles Dickens flattered that his villain of Oliver Twist was so honored by his colleague Anthony Trollope, who apologized in the text that he could not give Undy Scott so "decent an end" as that given to Bill Sikes?

It must be added that Trollope considered The Three Clerks to be his best work yet, better than The Warden and Barchester Towers. Contemporary critics agreed with him, including Robert and Elizabeth Barrett Browning. What were they thinking? Perhaps Trollope overestimated his portrayal of Charley Tudor, who may well have been a self-portrait of the hobbledehoy who aspired to write novels but found female companionship in a social class beneath his own—indeed, having to withstand an attack in his office by the mother of a young woman who considered herself to be ill used.

Today's reader may well wonder why The Three Clerks was ever rated higher than The Warden and Barchester Towers. Posterity has certainly not concurred. In the case of Trollope's novels, religion, like politics, has trumped bureaucracy.

The book, however, primarily tells the story of six young people. I must confess that I found myself tiring of them before the author did.

THE PROUD YOUNG LOVERS THE BERTRAMS

"For the first fortnight she did not leave the house." This sentence, in Chapter XXXVII of The Bertrams by Anthony Trollope, epitomizes the difficulty for the present day reader in understanding a Victorian novel. Things have changed a great deal since then, but surely the place of women is fundamental. Did not leave her house!

Lady Harcourt was in great distress. She had left her husband (she had virtually fled), and he had the legal right to apprehend her and force her to return to his home. Divorce was not an option for her. The action of the book takes place in 1845-1848. Only in 1857 (a year before the book was written) did the Matrimonial Causes Act give women limited access to divorce. Under this act the husband only had to prove his wife's adultery to obtain a divorce, but a woman had not only to prove her husband's having committed adultery; she also had to prove incest, bigamy, cruelty, or desertion. And so she was legally and permanently bound to a husband who owned their home. The law regarded a married couple as one person; the husband had a legal obligation to protect his wife; she was bound to obey him. Personal property brought to the marriage by the wife then belonged to the husband, even after a divorce if one could be obtained. Her income belonged completely to her husband. A man's home was his castle, and the wife was part of the deal.

One has to understand these givens in order to follow the implications of the story. The wedding of Caroline Waddington to Sir Henry Harcourt created a significant problem for the central lovers of the story, Miss Waddington and George Bertram. As the enormity of her mistake became apparent to her, Caroline (now Lady Harcourt) realized that there was no good way out. These days, she would do as a senior friend of mine, a professed atheist, said he would do if, to his surprise, he should find himself standing at the Pearly Gates after his death. "I would say, 'Gentlemen, it appears that I have made a horrible mistake.'" And then she would get a divorce and marry her true love with no questions asked. But her options were few and unattractive: She could flee abroad, as Lady Laura Standish did with her father, to escape her crazed husband, in Trollope's Phineas Finn. She could (if the husband would permit it) live openly with her lover, as did George Eliot. But just as Hollywood movies follow an apparently tacit code of audience acceptability, so Trollope was unwilling to send his central figures to Europe to live together, as Glencora Palliser had contemplated doing with her lover Burgo Fitzgerald in Can You Forgive Her? (Glencora couldn't bring herself to do this, and she learned to love her husband Plantagenet Palliser, after a certain acceptable fashion.) Lady Harcourt's husband could die of illness or injury, or someone could murder him, or he could commit suicide. Trollope was not scrupulous about revealing the outcome in advance. The reader is warned, and suicide is chosen. (This was also the means of exit and retribution for Ferdinand Lopez in The Prime Minister and of Augustus Melmotte in The Way We Live Now.)

Trollope did not consider himself a feminist; he professed a conservative view of society. But he was a realist who described the world as he found it. And his findings speak for themselves. The constraints placed upon women turn up again and again, in almost every novel he wrote.

Some of the action takes place in the Middle East, and this glimpse of the experience of touring there a century and a half ago provides a virtual visit to Jerusalem as it was then: a walled city with no suburbs, appearing as "a fortress of cards built craftily on a table," where one enters and suddenly realizes "that you are beyond the region of passports."

And the description of the environs provides an uncensored and not necessarily tactful view of "all the absurdity" of the "dark un-furnished gloomy cave in which the Syrian Christians worship, so dark that the eye cannot at first discover its only ornament—a small ill-made figure of the crucified Redeemer."

The author would probably be the object of a fatwah today for his description of the Moslem washerwomen as "ape-like" and the Jewish washerwomen as "glorious specimens of feminine cre-ation."

Alexandria—"that most detestable of cities"—does not fare well. Nor do the pyramids, though they must be visited. "But let no man, and, above all, no woman, assume that the excursion will be in any way pleasurable. ... And let this also be remembered, that nothing is to be gained by entering the pyramid except dirt, noise, stench, vermin, abuse, and want of air."

A twenty-first century editor might cringe at Trollope's assertion that "as a rule, a Mahomedan hates a Christian. ... But in Egypt we have caused ourselves to be better respected: we thrash the Arabs and pay them, and therefore they are very glad to see us anywhere."

And yet in the next four pages Trollope gives us as vivid a pic-ture of the performance of whirling dervishes as we are likely to find.

But the lowly place of women in society was an obvious part of the landscape, and the travelers' observations were only window dressing; the business of the novel has to do primarily with the relationship between George Herbert and Caroline Waddington, and secondarily, between Arthur Wilkinson and Adela Gauntlet. George Herbert is a proud young man, and Miss Waddington is a proud young woman. David Skilton's pen-and-ink drawing opposite page 110 in the Folio Society edition of 1993 tells it all: With the walled city of Jerusalem represented in the background, George sits on the barren ground looking away, unhappily, to his right. Miss Waddington, parasol over her head to protect her from the sun, stands looking away in the opposite direction. He has just told her of his newly formed resolution to become a clergyman, and she has poured cold water on his enthusiasm, reminding him that he is eligible for a noble position that would be preferable to a country parsonage.

When he protests that a vicar's career can be noble, she replies, "I judge by what I see. They are generally fond of eating, very cautious about their money, untidy in their own houses, and apt to go to sleep after dinner."

These two young people, both with strong personalities, are clearly in love with each other. He gives up his idea of being a clergyman; he decides to study law. He proposes, and she accepts. He presses for an early wedding date; she demurs, saying that they must wait until he has been called to the bar, which will take two or three years. She is afraid that a small income would fray their love for each other. Neither will compromise. The engagement is broken, and she marries his friend, a rising star in the legal and political world.

Behind all this is the possible legacy of his rich uncle. George, however, refuses to humor his uncle for the sake of becoming his heir.

Such lovers' stories occur all the time. Family relationships still matter, and they still require cultivation. But as the inner thinking of each of the lovers was revealed in great detail throughout the story, I found myself protesting that these weren't real people like any the author had known. They were characters set up in a plot, and the turns of the story were just that: turns for the sake of the story, not turns that a real person would make.

Trollope summarizes the story of the progressively colder nature of their engagement with this retrospective view: "Each was too proud to make the first concession to the other, and therefore no concession was made by either."

No one can read this sentence and wonder what the book is about. But the reader may feel that it's all a fable. This is where the story starts, and the details are just filled in.

Perhaps the author's style accounted for my reaction: Raymond Carver or Ernest Hemingway might have presented the same story in a more convincing fashion, leaving out all the details of the thinking and giving us only a few scraps of dialogue to explain the action. In this instance, I failed to overcome being accustomed to the fast pace of "the way we live now," and I could not immerse myself in the more leisurely pace of the nineteenth century world. As I followed their thoughts through each turn of the story, I became so impatient with the stubbornness of George Herbert and Caroline Waddington that I lost my sympathy for them. It's hard to be a good fan when your team is losing.

Little bright spots appear throughout the book. The dialogue between Caroline, as Lady Harcourt, and her husband strikes a note of detachment reminiscent of the dialogue in Noel Coward's Private Lives. One can almost hear Carol Lawrence saying Lady Harcourt's lines in response to her husband's question:

"I hope you are happy, Caroline?" said Sir Henry, as he gently squeezed the hand that was so gently laid upon his arm.

"Happy! Oh yes—I am happy. I don't believe, you know, in a great deal of very ecstatic happiness. I never did."

Trollope shamelessly introduces some welcome comic relief in the form of a deaf lady and her ear trumpet when Miss Todd, an outspoken woman who travels in society, takes her young charge Adela Gauntlet on a social call to one of the grand dames of Littlebath (obviously a pseudonym for Bath). Miss Todd proposes that they take turns of five minutes each in talking to her and then leave after three turns.

Miss Todd is a slightly older Miss Dunstable from *Dr. Thorne*. Having enough money to speak her mind, she does so with relish, as in her defense of playing cards in a conversation with a clergyman of Littlebath:

"What are old women like us to do? We haven't eyes to read at night, even if we had minds fit for it. We can't always be saying our prayers. We have nothing to talk about except scandal. It's better than drinking; and we should come to that if we hadn't cards."

A carriage ride is one of Trollope's favorite settings for intimate conversation, with the horse sometimes getting the worst of it, as in Chapter XXI of *Framley Parsonage*, "Why Puck, the Pony, Was Beaten." In this story, it is Dumpling who catches a few impatient words as Arthur Wilkinson, the timid and browbeaten parson, speaks his mind (partially) to Adela Gauntlet, almost but not quite proposing. She patiently waits for him to grow up a bit. Dumpling bears the brunt of Wilkinson's timidity.

George's father, Sir Lionel Bertram, squanders his paternal capital by sponging on his son for money. He fails to insert himself into his brother's will, and he fails in two successive attempts to marry money: "That utterance of the verbiage of love is a disagreeable task for a gentleman of his years. He had tried it, and found it very disagreeable. He would save himself a repetition of the nuisance and write to her."

But back to the central story of Caroline Waddington: Chapter XXXVI, "A Matrimonial Dialogue," closes the marriage between her and Lord Harcourt. It is a classic Trollopian serious interview, in which Lady Harcourt routs her proud husband. She tells him that she did not invite Mr. Herbert to their house because she loved him so much that she was afraid to meet him. "As she said this she still looked into his face fearlessly—we may almost say boldly; so much so that Sir Henry's eyes almost quailed before hers. On this she had at any rate resolved, that she would never quail before him."

When Bertram writes an angry letter to Caroline, Trollope inserts instruction about writing such letters which could be included among the little lessons of life to be gleaned from reading his novels: "Sit down and write your letter; write it with all the venom in your power … and, as a matter of course, burn it before breakfast the next morning." He goes on to extol pleasant letters, concluding his advice for letter writing: "But, above all things, see that it be good-humored."

A modern novel would omit Trollope's last chapter, and he himself issues an apology for it: "Methinks it is almost unnecessary to write this last chapter. The story, as I have had to tell it, is all told. The object has been made plain—or, if not, can certainly not be made plainer in these last six or seven pages. ... But, nevertheless, custom, and the desire of making an end of the undertaken work, and in some sort completing it, compel me to this concluding chapter." Things work themselves out within the conventions of the day. A guiltless ending such as might be implied today could not be allowed, and the lovers whose course we have followed with a bit of impatience must accept the scraps of happiness that their world could accept.

I love Trollope's good-humored novels; the grim ones, like He Knew He was Right and parts of this one, are a bit like unpleasant letters. The Bertrams has enough good humor to carry us through. The proud young lovers, however, are hard to love.

COPING WITH STARVATION CASTLE RICHMOND

People of Irish descent, I recently learned, comprise thirteen percent of the population of the county where I live, matched only by those of German descent, also thirteen percent. (Other leading ancestry groups are English, ten percent; black, six percent; and Mexican, five percent.) Irish are also the most numerous ancestry group in the counties where my Arkansas children live; and in the county where I grew up, they are the most numerous white ancestry group. (Irish are six percent, blacks forty-six percent.)

That I was surprised to learn this probably indicates that I haven't been paying attention. My wife's grandfather came directly from County Cavan, in Ireland; and the family of one of my sons-in-law came from Ireland. Perhaps Irish names aren't as obvious as some of the German names. And of course the English got a head start in Virginia and New England. The big reason for the Irish numbers is the Irish potato famine, which began in 1845, when an estimated one and a half million people died and one million emigrated.

Anthony Trollope said that before he decided on "Castle Richmond" as the title for the book, he considered a title which would mention the famine. Such a title would have been more descriptive, though it might perhaps have discouraged a number of readers, including me. This would have been unfortunate, because in stumbling into the unknown territory of one of his lesser known novels, I found myself immersed in the most powerful chapter I have found in Trollope. One would have to survey Holocaust and other war stories for chapters of similar impact. Young Herbert Fitzgerald sets out to ride across the countryside to Desmond Court, the home of his fiancée, to determine whether their marriage is to take place, and in so doing he encounters a rainstorm, forcing him to seek shelter. He enters a cabin without knocking; he even rides his horse inside, which, the author assures us, was customary there. The interior is so dark he at first cannot tell whether anyone is at home. The floor is sod, the walls are bare, and there is only a very little furniture, very plain. As his eyes become accustomed to the dark, he sees a woman sitting cross-legged on the floor with a baby in her arms. He later discovers the body of a four-year-old daughter in the corner.

In those days there was a form of face which came upon the sufferers when their state of misery was far advanced, and which was a sure sign that their last stage of misery was nearly run. The mouth would fall and seem to hang, the lips at the two ends of the mouth would be dragged down, and the lower parts of the cheeks would fall as though they had been dragged and pulled. There were no signs of acute agony when this phasis of countenance was to be seen, none of the horrid symptoms of gnawing hunger by which one generally supposes that famine is accompanied. The look is one of apathy, desolation, and death. When custom had made these signs easily legible, the poor doomed wretch was known with certainty.

Sir William Osler could hardly have written a more informative description of the clinical signs of starvation in The Principles and Practice of Medicine. Trollope knew the signs; he had gone to Ireland in 1841 as a clerk to a postal surveyor, traveling about the country under orders from the surveyors. He was promoted to surveyor fifteen years later, and he did not return to England until 1859, the year he began Castle Richmond.

Mike, the starving woman's husband, had become a cripple through rheumatism and could not do the public work on the roads. This would have qualified him and his family for the poorhouse, but he may not have known this. He had found someone who would hire him to do a little work in return for a little food, and he had stolen from his employer a small amount of "Indian corn-flour"—the yellow meal made from corn sent from America—but it had failed to sustain her and the children.

Although Herbert tried to send help, no one was in a hurry to answer the call. "But had they flown to the spot on the wings of love, it would not have sufficed to prolong her life one day. Her doom had been spoken before Herbert had entered the cabin."

Trollope indulges in a little Victorian eloquence to conclude his story, which otherwise could be a case history. What would Dickens have done with such a story? The poor woman would have been borne to Heaven in the arms of angels. And if this had been a chapter in a book by Dickens, we might all know this story from the Irish Potato Famine.

The book isn't really about the potato famine. It just took place at the time of the famine. The story is one of those stories of a question of birth, which are so common in the novels from the period. In this case, we find Sir Thomas Fitzgerald of Castle Richmond being blackmailed by Mr. Matthew Mollett, who tells him that he was Lady Fitzgerald's first husband, and that he was not dead, as he had been assumed to be, when she married Sir Thomas. This would mean that her marriage to Sir Thomas is null and void, and that Sir Thomas's children are illegitimate—and that his son Herbert will not inherit the estate, which would then fall to a cousin, Owen Fitzgerald. All this leaves Sir Thomas in a state of nervous collapse, from which he does not recover.

We also have the story of a young woman, Lady Clara Desmond, who proceeds, in the fullness of time, from one engagement to another. As a young girl she pledged herself to Owen Fitzgerald, but her mother, the Countess of Desmond, reminded her that she must marry money, and she later accepted the proposal of Herbert Fitzgerald. And then, when the news of Lady Fitzgerald's first husband becomes known, young Lady Clara is seen by her mother to be left holding the bag with a second affianced lover, now become poor. Owen is presented as the mercurial Irishman whom women love: romantic and generous, fun-loving and extravagant—qualities we also see in Trollope's most well-known Irish figure, Phineas Finn. Herbert, on the other hand, is slow and methodical, serious and conscientious, reminiscent of Plantagenet Palliser. Owen makes the extravagant and rather naive offer to let Herbert have Castle Richmond and all its property if he will surrender the love of Clara. Herbert, of course, cannot understand this and refuses.

So how will all this be resolved? Very conveniently, as it turns out. A family secret is discovered. What about this and so many other stories of birth secrets, with the resolution of the plot in the revelation of some unknown bit of family history—as when Buttercup announces in the final act of HMS Pinafore that, as a nursemaid, she switched babies years ago? Was this just a convenient plot device, or was it a reflection of reality?

Trollope used variations of this theme in several of his novels. George Roden, in Marion Fay, is found to be the eldest son of an

Italian duke. Is He Popenjoy? is all about whether an unprincipled English Marquis, living in Italy, was legitimately married to an Italian duchessa and whether their son was Lord Popenjoy.

Esther Summerson, in Charles Dickens's Bleak House, does not know who her real mother is until late in the story. Oscar Wilde's The Importance of Being Earnest revolves about two babies in large handbags who were unwittingly swapped at a railway station. When this is announced in the last act, Jack throws himself on Miss Prism with a cry of "Mother!"

One actual case involved the "Tichbourne claimant," who in 1875 returned from Australia and claimed to be the rightful heir to a family fortune; the courts ruled against him. Surely this story itself could provide material for a doctoral dissertation; lacking such research, however, one would suppose that such events occurred infrequently and stirred imaginations each time, prompting fictional and comic variations on the theme.

Among the insights into Irish life are the sketches of Protestant and Catholics, preachers and priests. We find Father Bernard being petted by his sister-in-law and niece at Mick O'Dwyer's public house, where the women offer him another cup of tea, a hot muffin, or "a morsel of buttered toast" if he will only say the word.

Protestants and Catholics are obliged to work together in public assistance efforts to aid famine victims, but when it is suggested to the Protestant parson that Father Barney may be right in a certain matter, he categorically denies it. "He's altogether wrong. I never knew one of them right in my life yet in anything. How can they be right?"

On the other hand, the Catholic bias appears when Father Columb is told that men will work anywhere to keep from starving. He only replies, "Some men will," implying that Protestants would work anywhere because of their devotion to the flesh, but that Roman Catholics are under the dominion of the Spirit and would perish first.

The story moves toward its conclusion in London, where Herbert has gone to study law after leaving Castle Richmond. Here we see two lawyers at work. The first is Mr. Prendergast, the family attorney, who receives a letter revealing the family secret. Mr. Prendergast anticipates Sherlock Holmes in his powers of observation as he enters the house and searches for his quarry: "But the armchair was placed idly away from any accommodation for work, and had, as Mr. Prendergast thought, been recently filled by some idle person."

We also encounter the barrister, Mr. Die, still working hard at age seventy. Men who retire at age sixty, the author tells us, are those who have always been idle. "It is my opinion that nothing seasons the mind for endurance like hard work. Port wine should perhaps be added."

But back to the Irish famine: When one learns that during its four worst years, the English landlords in Ireland exported more food, in the form of beef, wheat, and other grains, than the country imported, one begins to understand the reasons for deep and strong feelings about the English in Ireland. From his travels in southwest Ireland from 1841 to 1859, Trollope surely knew and understood the Irish from the ground up. His fictional account bears as much authority as a journalistic one would have, and it is reinforced in the Folio Society edition with a pen-and-ink drawing opposite page 185 showing a woman dressed in rags, on her knees, surrounded by four small children, pulling at someone's cloak as she begs. She is more attractive in the drawing than in the description—"squat, uncouth, and in no way attractive to the eye."

This begging scene is rural, not on a city street. The woman who is begging is not a nameless beggar; she knows Mister Herbert and Clara by face and name. Other accounts in the book—dealing with the deliberations of the ad hoc council to establish policies about distribution of such food as is available to those without food, managing a gang of men given make-work duties leveling a hill for a roadway, and the details of a recipe for making bread from bad flour—all bear witness to a human tragedy that brought thousands of its victims to America.

Castle Richmond is a good story; it starts slowly, but it moves along, and it proceeds with dispatch in the final chapters. Trollope has given us some sobering glimpses of people, ancestors to many Americans, starving in time of famine; otherwise we are diverted by entertaining views and stories. It's unfortunate that a book so well written is doomed to the oblivion of being just one of forty-seven novels by the same author.

THE LADY FACES THEM DOWN ORLEY FARM

I can see Barbara Stanwyck playing Lady Mason in a film noir version of Orley Farm. Oh, there was no murder—only a bit of forgery. But remember, forgery could be punished with hanging in England only a few years before Orley Farm was written. The story is a bit complicated: Lady Mason forged a codicil to her late husband's will, leaving a small portion of his land holdings to their only child, taking this small home place away from his older son by a previous marriage.

Now we know that in England at that time all inheritance was to go to the eldest son as a matter of course, unless other provision was made. And we in this age are accustomed to the "pre-nup," the prenuptial agreement designed to deal with the anxieties of prospective heirs when an aged parent takes a wife—especially if the wife be of childbearing age.

In our world, therefore, few would have much difficulty in accepting the propriety of a small portion of a large estate being left to a younger son, when the elder son is well provided for. Nor, we learn, did a jury of her peers find any problem with this arrangement. Lady Mason, who had been a loyal, faithful, and attractive wife to old Sir Joseph, was acquitted of the crime of forgery, and she continued to live in the home place and raise their son to the age of majority when he might assume control of it.

We only learn the truth about the forgery about halfway through the book, some twenty years after the crime and acquittal. And then we find ourselves sympathizing with the guilty woman as she fights through a second trial.

The older son, who was now the young Sir Joseph, lived on the extensive Yorkshire holdings, under the rule of a wife too stingy to put adequate food on the table, either for her lord or for their guests when they should have any. And he nursed his grudge against the widow, whom he considered to have cheated him of his rightful inheritance.

Some of Trollope's most effective humor is sometimes inserted into an unlikely place. The first chapters, the ones that set the scene, are often so long, detailed, and tedious that they have almost disappeared in today's writing. One has to read opening chapters carefully, however, and sometimes reread them, in order to understand the setting. This is made easier in the case of the Masons of Groby Park, the large holding in Yorkshire, as Trollope continues with his introduction of the characters:

He was severe to his children, and was not loved by them; but nevertheless they were dear to him, and he endeavored to do his duty by them. The wife of his bosom was not a pleasant woman, but nevertheless he did his duty by her; that is, he neither deserted her, nor beat her, nor locked her up. I am not sure that he would not have been justified in doing one of these three things, or even all the three; for Mrs. Mason of Groby Park was not a pleasant woman.

The old quarrel resurfaces when an old tenant is dispossessed by Lady Mason's son, now old enough to begin managing the home place and aspiring to farm it in a scientific, though expensive, fashion.

With energy and perseverance the tenant discovers another paper signed by old Sir Joseph on the same day as the codicil was dated, and he finds a witness to the signature, Bridget Bolster, who will testify that she only witnessed the signing of one document.

How can Lady Mason defend herself against this attack? We see that her primary motive is to shield her proud young son from disgrace, and in this effort she deploys all the resources available to her. A small but not unattractive woman (think of Barbara Stanwyck in this role), she consults the barrister, Mr. Furnival, who defended her in the first trial, and she wraps him around her finger so effectively that Mrs. Furnival is driven by jealousy to leave home in one of the great comic episodes of the book.

Mr. Furnival sees that unusual skill will be required to defend Lady Mason successfully, and she consents to his employment of that famous defense attorney, Mr. Chaffanbrass, and another clever defense attorney, Mr. Solomon Aram. Lucius, convinced of his mother's innocence, is offended by the retaining of these sharp attorneys, and he objects that a simple portrayal of the truth of the matter will be more than sufficient. But his mother, whom we often see sitting alone in her room brooding over these matters (we can only conclude from this and other novels of the period that people spent more time sitting and brooding than is done now) quietly declines her son's advice and, much to his frustration, excludes him from the decision-making process. Here the reader begins to suspect that since she knows what she really did, she realizes she had better have some sharp legal assistance.

She also cultivates the friendship of a noble neighbor, Sir Peregrine Orme, father of her son Lucius's friend young Peregrine Orme. Sir Peregrine is an old man, but he responds to her presence in his house by falling in love with her. He rashly makes her an offer of marriage, which is opposed by his son, her son, and a brother nobleman, all of whom attempt to dissuade him.

Lady Mason had hoped to obtain maximum support from Mr. Furnival and Sir Peregrine without being forced to choose between these two champions. She accepts Sir Peregrine's proposal, but it becomes apparent that she is sacrificing the sympathy of Mr. Furnival and everyone else. So here we have the crisis of the whole story, just at the start of Book Two, in which she confesses her guilt to Sir Peregrine and subsequently to his daughter-in-law, who has also become her great friend. So the reader learns that she did indeed forge the signature to the will twenty years earlier. Sir Peregrine cancels the engagement, but both he and his daughter-in-law maintain their friendship, support, and the secret.

John Everett Millais drew the forty illustrations for the book, and the cover of the Dover Publications edition shows Lady Mason in court. Her companion Mrs. Orme sits with head down and veil in place. But Lady Mason has lifted her veil and raised her eyes. She will face them down. "She was perfect mistress of herself, and as she looked round the court, not with defiant gaze, but with eyes half raised, and a look of modest but yet conscious intelligence, those around her hardly dared to think that she could be guilty."

Trollope shows us the infatuation of two older men with Lady Mason in great detail. Mr. Furnival, who has a wife (dowdy) and a daughter (clever, like he is) and a position in the London legal establishment, cannot consider a compromising liaison, but he enjoys the company of Lady Mason and schemes to meet her. He begins to perceive rather early the strong probability that she is actually guilty, but he has a strong desire to defend her successfully. Sir Peregrine Orme is an older man and a widower, and as she remains in his house as a guest, he begins to ask, "Why should I not?"

We are not denied the drama of the courtroom, and here we see the renowned Mr. Chaffanbrass taking a witness apart. Mr. Chaffanbrass is a recurrent player in several Trollope novels—most notably in Phineas Redux, when he undertakes the defense of Phineas Finn, who is accused of murder. Again we see this wily attorney as a role player in the adversarial system of justice: "To him it was a matter of course that Lady Mason should be guilty. Had she not been guilty, he, Mr. Chaffanbrass would not have been required. Mr. Chaffanbrass well understood that the defense of injured innocence was no part of his mission."

The subplots and ancillary characters fill out the space requirements of a proper Victorian novel and are generally done well. Sophia Furnival is a more interesting character than her friend Madeline Stavely, who is practically perfect in every way. In Mr. Furnival's closing speech to the court we finally see the brilliance of his work, and we see that Sophia comes by her wit naturally, since it's apparent that she doesn't inherit it from her mother. Sophia doesn't do much better than Lady Mason does in attempting to handle two admirers.

Felix Graham, a young lawyer who falls in love with Madeline Stavely, finally begins to come through as understandable, but only partially. The story of his earlier attachment to Mary Snow as a protégé whom he had intended to train to become his bride seems a bit far-fetched; perhaps it was not so far-fetched at the time. In any event, this little story is never wrapped up. We see Felix being pressed for more money by Mary's drunken father, by her keeper Mrs. Thomas, and by the apothecary who increases the price of a partnership for Mary's new lover, Albert Fitzallen.

Felix has attempted to transfer Mary to Mr. Fitzallen, which appears to be agreeable to all parties, but the negotiations are left in limbo.

Trollope treats us to another fox hunt. A great lover of the chase, he was always on firm ground here. Thrown off almost in passing is a little comic masterpiece, the depiction of two fox hunting sisters: "But when the time for riding did come, when the hounds were really running—when other young ladies had begun to go home—then the Miss Tristams were always there;—there or thereabouts, as their admirers would warmly boast."

Julia Tristam plays a pivotal role in the major subplot as she makes a difficult jump; Felix Graham and his friend Augustus Stavely, who have been following her in an effort to participate in the best of the hunt, attempt to follow, and Felix does not make it, falling off his horse and finding that he cannot raise his arm and can hardly breathe—an accurate portrayal of the symptoms of a broken collarbone and fractured ribs. "Both Peregrine and Miss Tristam looked back. 'There's nothing wrong I hope,' said the lady; and then she rode on."

This injury results in Felix's confinement in the Stavely house, where he and Madeline Stavely fall in love.

Barchester Towers and Mrs. Proudie stand as evidence that Trollope's greatest gift was comic, and we find some humor in Orley Farm, even though a courtroom case doesn't allow for much levity. Mrs. Furnival's quarrel with her husband supplies comic relief, and Mr. Kantwise's sale of a metal table and chairs to Mr. Dockwrath and to Squire Mason is appropriately memorialized in Millais's drawing of Mr. Kantwise standing on the metal table: "There is nothing like iron, Sir; nothing."

To attempt to place a value on Orley Farm: it is good enough to be fairly compared to Bleak House, generally regarded as one of Dicken's masterpieces, and one that has been successfully presented as a television series. Nothing in Orley Farm matches the opening paragraphs of Bleak House, in which the description of the rain and mud of London sends us to turn up the heat, even if the room is warm. Dickens manages the pace of Bleak House very well, with the tempo galloping toward a conclusion in the last hundred pages or so. But Lady Mason is a more interesting woman than Lady Dedlock. Mr. Tulkinghorn is a lawyer of great power and mystery in Bleak House, but Mr. Furnival is shown in greater depth, and in his concluding speech to the court we see him at the peak of his powers. The spontaneous combustion that Dickens invokes to carry off Mr. Krook is so improbable that one doubts if even any of his readers believed it; but the proceedings of Orley Farm, if not so violent, are so true to life that the events might have been lifted from the newspapers.

The major plot is a carefully constructed story of crime and punishment; the reader is led to follow the uncertainty and the sympathy with which the community views a woman accused of a crime that only a few decades earlier could have sent her to the gallows. In presenting this story Trollope has shown his skill in presenting female characters—primarily Lady Mason, but also Sophia Furnival. Our humanity is shown sometimes with sympathy, sometimes with irony, sometimes with condemnation—but always as it is. Too bad we never got to see Barbara Stanwyck play the title role. Who would have played Sophia Furnival?

LEAR REVISITED THE STRUGGLES OF BROWN, JONES, AND ROBINSON

By One of the Firm

Graduate students in business administration routinely bury themselves in case studies, which have become a standard hurdle on the way to attaining an MBA. In doing so, they learn to insist on reliable data. However, should the students in the Stanford Graduate School of Business find themselves analyzing the failure of the London mercantile firm of Brown, Jones, and Robinson, they would surely hope to have more objective information than that found in the account of George Robinson, one of the three partners, as given in The Struggles of Brown, Jones, and Robinson, by One of the Firm. The reader begins to suspect early on that the firm failed at least in part because of expensive and misleading advertising promoted by Robinson, who himself never concedes as much. The dealings of the firm were hardly transparent, even among the three partners; and the senior partner, Mr. Brown, kept the books to himself. Meanwhile the other partner, Mr. Jones, was taking funds from the till without letting Mr. Robinson know.

Among the curious features of genius is its uneven nature. After searching unsuccessfully for his métier with a few novels about Ireland, a historical novel of the French Revolution, and a play, Trollope found his way with The Warden and Barchester Towers, which may be his best known and most loved works. Still experimenting, however, he used his personal experience in the civil service to write The Three Clerks, a critical success at the time but not well known today. And then he continued his portrayal of the world of mundane office work by venturing into a picture of the entrepreneurial spirit as shown by Brown, Jones, and Robinson. He broke off from it after two weeks and came back to it four years later, but the result was an attempt to satirize the business world. It failed, however, to match his success with the Church, the landed gentry, and the political world of the ruling class.

True, one of his most acclaimed works, The Way We Live Now, dealt with the business world; but it did so in a rough rather than a gentle way, in a later period of his life when he had begun to develop somewhat more jaundiced views of society as it had evolved. The satire of Brown, Jones, and Robinson is too clever by half. George Robinson is the young pup who defends himself after the bankruptcy of the firm with an unrepentant statement of his faith in advertising, and he presents himself as the unreliable narrator with a self-serving view of his stewardship. Demonstrating the creative imagination that led him to ruin, he compares his senior partner to King Lear. "Think what it must be to be papa to a Goneril and a Regan—without the Cordelia. I have always looked on Mrs. Jones as a regular Goneril; and as for the Regan, why it seems to me that Miss Brown is likely to be Miss Regan to the end of the chapter."

Sarah Jane, the elder sister and the "Goneril," marries Mr. Jones; and Robinson himself aspires to the hand of Maryanne, the "Regan" who joins her sister in turning on their father and attempting to secure his small fortune for themselves. Robinson's dedication to the doctrines of Credit and Advertising, rather than to those of Capital, leads him to run through that part of the four thousand pounds that Brown provided to start their haberdashery business. Brown and Jones stand agog as Robinson hires four men in armour to ride draft horses through the streets announcing the opening of Magenta House. And Mr. Brown cannot understand why Robinson should advertise four hundred dozen white cotton hose. "We haven't got 'em. ... I did want to do a genuine trade in stockings."

"And so you shall, sir. But how will you begin unless you attract your customers?" Robinson retorts, and he goes on to advertise "English-sewn Worcester gloves, made of French kid," which actually came from the wholesale houses in St. Paul's churchyard.

The inevitable downfall of the overextended firm can surely provide a number of cautionary tales for future students of the success and failure of businesses, but these lessons are lost on George Robinson, who reacts by transferring his devotion from Maryanne Brown, who abandons him in the end, to the goddess of Commerce. "Oh sweet Commerce, teach me thy lessons! Let me ever buy in the cheapest market and sell in the dearest."

What is it that made the foibles of the Church so humorous in

Trollope's hands, while the schemes of the business world merely led to a ho-hum reaction at its cupidity and stupidity? Is it that the men of the cloth retained a few cloaks of honor and respectability yet to be stripped away, while the businessmen may never have had any such cloaks? In any event, the reading public and the critics helped Trollope to find his way, which was not along the way of Commerce and Advertising.

BRINGING GOOD BEER TO DEVON RACHEL RAY

Bad beer is being brewed in East Devon. This is cider country, where apple trees grow and "men drink cider by the gallon." The bad beer comes from the firm of Messrs. Bungall and Tappitt, which is managed by the latter after the death of the former. Thus Anthony Trollope has given us a novel about beer.

But of course it's not primarily about beer. Rachel Ray is mainly a love story with plot lines familiar to readers of Trollope. The heir to the late Mr. Bungall's interest in the brewery, Luke Rowan, comes to town to assert his interests, meets a friend of the Tappitt sisters, Rachel Ray, and falls in love with her. Rachel is a rather typical Trollope heroine—spirited and bright, dwelling in an humble cottage with her timid widowed mother and a domineering older sister, also a widow. Rachel is attracted to Luke when he sits alone with her on a churchyard stile and gazes at the clouds, but she consents only by a silent nod to his proposal of marriage that comes soon after. Once having given her silent nod, however, she vows lifelong faithfulness, even though her mercurial fiancé may desert her.

Luke Rowan is no paragon. His faults are declared to the reader in a rather desultory fashion, showing him to be only slightly more interesting than a stock representation of a young lover, which he really is. It is enough to raise the reader's concern that Rachel may be doomed to a fate similar to that of Lily Dale, the tragic, faithful heroine of The Small House at Allington.

The story of Cinderella is retold with a few modifications, as the three Tappitt sisters invite Rachel, not unanimously, to a little party for the Rowans, which soon comes to be regarded as a ball. Rachel is persuaded to attend the ball only after the fairy godmother, in the form of Mrs. Butler Cornbury, invites Rachel to accompany her in her coach. Mrs. Tappitt is scandalized that Luke selects Rachel as his dancing partner of choice, and Cinderella is so overcome by it all that she persuades her fairy godmother to take her home two hours early. But to the amazement of all, the prince makes a visit to the humble cottage to see Rachel the next day.

So here we have the love story. Now back to the beer:

It was a sour and muddy stream that flowed from their vats; a beverage disagreeable to the palate, and very cold and uncomfortable to the stomach. Who drank it I could never learn. It was to be found at no respectable inn. ... Nevertheless the brewery of Messrs. Bungall and Tappitt was kept going, and the large ugly square brick house in which the Tappitt family lived was warm and comfortable. There is something in the very name of beer that makes money.

Mr. Tappitt's determination to brew bad beer is reinforced by the appearance of Luke Rowan, who aspires to participate in the management of the brewery and brew good beer. But Mr. Tappitt knows that would require capital investment. The brewery has been managing to make money under his direction, and he wants neither to concede any of his power nor to risk the profitability of the business with newfangled ideas. This divergence of views comes to a climax when Rowan offers to join the firm as an active partner, to allow Tappit to retire with an annual pension, or to sell his share of the business to Tappitt and then build his own competing brewery. Mr. Tappitt's response is to brandish a poker, and at the conclusion of this dramatic encounter Rowan departs, declaring that the matter will be turned over to his lawyer.

Having been accepted by Rachel, he now leaves town, and Rachel is left to the pernicious influence of community opinion, which is against the young man in his apparent effort to unseat a longstanding citizen of the community, even though he does brew bad beer. Rachel is influenced by her mother, who is in turn influenced by her spiritual advisor, the vicar Mr. Comfort, who in turn is influenced by community opinion conveyed by a disaffected colleague. And so Rachel's letter in response to her fiancé's first letter is so much less than passionate that she fears she has terminated their engagement.

So how will the matter be resolved? Here we see a second issue: a political contest. Politics fascinated Trollope, and he even entered an election himself. In this instance Tappitt supports a Jew from out of town, Mr. Hart, against young Butler Cornbury, eldest son of the neighboring squire. The author revels in the details of the campaign: slurs against the Jew by his opponents who probably know better, the raising of money, and the buying of votes. Luke Rowan reappears in town after having purchased property from Rachel's mother for the apparent purpose of building his own brewery. And Luke enters the political contest, even though he is not an elector in Baslehurst, supporting Butler Cornbury with fiery speeches. Luke is found to be a radical—that is, "he desires, expects, works for, and believes in, the gradual progress of the people," and he "will own no inferiority to the manhood of another."

The outcome of the election is determined by one vote. Cornbury is the winner, but Tappitt dreams of revenge. He is invited to a dinner of Hart supporters and chairs their meeting. He meets the unscrupulous lawyer Mr. Sharpit there and asks him to take his case against Mr. Rowan because his own lawyer Mr. Honyman has recommended capitulation and retirement.

But Mr. Tappitt has been ill, and his wife, who wants him to retire so she and her daughters can enjoy the delights of Torquay, has threatened to have him committed "under fitting restraint" if he goes to the meeting. This is the red pepper program: "There may be those who think that a wife goes too far in threatening a husband with a commission of lunacy, and frightening him with a prospect of various fatal diseases; but the dose must be adapted to the constitution, and the palate that is accustomed to large quantities of red pepper must have quantities larger than usual whenever some special culinary effect is to be achieved."

Tappitt comes home from the dinner drunk, and his wife finds him vulnerable the next morning. She refuses to let him out of bed until he agrees to invite Honeyman the lawyer back to the brewery, thus achieving a compromise that allows Mr. Tappitt to sell out and retire.

So everything works out. The author has also used our story to indulge his fondness for church affairs. Rachel's widowed sister has been attracted to the less formal side of the Church of England, and in particular to a rather unsavory clerical representative of this school of thought, one Mr. Prong, whose pride in his sermons exceeds the results. But in the end Rachel's sister Dorothea shrugs off Mr. Prong, who denies any interest in Dorothea's money but is unwilling to forgo the husband's legal right to her money.

It's all a good story. We share the author's fun with the radicals, the politics, the churchmen, the fairy godmother, and particularly with Mr. Tappitt. Rachel's romance works itself out, but perhaps more to the point, the men of Baslehurst will get better beer.

"HE COMETH NOT; I AM AWEARY" MISS MACKENZIE

Garish images are the ones that stick. Miss Mackenzie is a beautiful story of a deserving young woman who finally achieves love and fortune after years of service to the poor and the sick and the dying, but the image that sticks in the mind is that of Rev. Jeremiah Maguire, who was possessed "of the most terrible squint in his right eye which ever disfigured a face that in all other respects was fitted for an Apollo." In this case, as was usually the case in Trollope's novels, the physical deformity was a ready clue to the individual's character. Rev. Maguire ranks as one of the more iniquitous of the sinners in the ranks of Trollope's clergymen. It may not have been so bad that he tried to marry Margaret Mackenzie for her money, but he did so with a devious scheme to establish his own church and use the pew rents as security for the money that he would say he was giving but would then take back as payment of a loan. And when he learned that he had no chance of winning her for himself, he embarrassed her by writing several "Lion and Lamb" articles for a religious newspaper, saying that she was being cheated of her inheritance by the man whom she wished to marry. He doesn't match the villainy of Joseph Emilius, the preacher who only had a "slight defect in his left eye" and a "hooky nose," and who murdered Lizzie Eustace's protector Mr. Bonteen in The Eustace Diamonds; it is apparent, however, that not all Trollope's clergymen went to heaven.

But back to Miss Mackenzie: if one of the great pleasures in life is watching someone start out with a pleasant set of gifts and then develop a few more to become a joyous credit to the human race, then the literary proxy is reading about such a one. We are introduced to Miss Mackenzie as a Cinderella-type woman (Trollope had a weakness for Cinderellas) who devotes herself to the care of her brother for fifteen years until he dies. She is a generous but self-abasing humble woman, but we see that she can stand up for herself. Finally she appears to gain some conception of her own worth.

There has been some money in the family, but we see it slipping away due to unfortunate business decisions, and none of it appears to be destined for poor Margaret, who has little to show for the years of her young womanhood. But then she is named the beneficiary of her late brother's will! Suddenly she is a woman of independent means, if not indeed wealthy.

And now we see her deal with the friends, relatives, and suitors who flock to her. Her sense of self worth is hardly enhanced as she fends them off, comprehending pretty quickly that they are interested in her money, not so much in her. She longs to have a life. She's only thirty-six. Her "time for withering" has not yet arrived. But she feels that she should not live for herself alone, and there are numerous opportunities for doing good deeds. The death of her brother has left her sister-in-law with a house full of children, and Margaret selects one of them, a fourteen year old girl, to live with her. She will leave London, where the neighborhood just down the streets to the Thames from the Strand is pretty dull, and she will go to Littlebath and take lodgings in the Paragon. (Bath and the Crescent, as in The Bertrams).

A gloomy story to this point, but it is told with the distant ironic tone that tells the reader that this is a comedy. Margaret visits The Cedars, home of her cousins the Balls, but finding them "very dull," she determines to proceed with the Littlebath plan.

Margaret enters Littlebath society slowly and timidly. We are shown that Littlebath is home to saints and sinners. The sinners go the assembly rooms; the saints go to church—not the high Church of England, but the Low Church. Margaret finds herself too timid to attempt to be a sinner at the assembly rooms; it is easier to go along with the women to tea at the home of a preacher to whom she has been given a letter of introduction. Here she finds a company of benighted souls in thrall to Mrs. Stumfold, wife of the great preacher. Like Mrs. Proudie of the Barsetshire series, Mrs. Stumfold brooks no disorder in the ranks, and we see Margaret stand up for herself when Mrs. Stumfold calls on her to inquire as to her intentions in regard to Mr. Maguire, of the squinting eye, who has been seen paying conspicuous attention to Miss Mackenzie. Short on self-esteem at this point, Margaret is shown to rank high in self-assertiveness. When Mrs. Stumfold tells her that another lady has a prior claim on Mr. Maguire (Mrs. Stumfold has been indulging in a bit of match-making), she insults Miss Mackenzie, informing her that another lady has been before her. "What would you think if you were interfered with, though, perhaps, as you had not your fortune in early life, you may never have known what that was?"

At this, Margaret terminates the interview, sending her to any friend of hers who is behaving badly for the purpose of telling him so, and then telling Mrs. Stumfold that she will hear nothing more about it.

Margaret shakes off three suitors, unworthy souls who merit rejection, though she is so lacking in self-confidence that she gives serious consideration to two of them. Mr. Maguire—the clergyman with the wandering squinting eye—catches her by surprise with his proposal, and she asks for two weeks to think it over. A big mistake—it raises false hopes in Mr. Maguire. She is called away because of her brother's illness before giving the ambitious curate an answer, and she enters the orbit of her cousin John Ball, a widower who had bored her by talking about nothing but money.

The author never refers to John Ball as the hero of the story, and indeed he is not unblemished. But he turns out to be Miss Mackenzie's hero, barely making the cut. He has a house full of children of his own, and though a barrister by profession, he hardly practices law. He is the Victorian equivalent of a day trader, going to town every day to follow the market prices and manage his investments, which seem to yield him barely enough to feed his family. He discusses his investments with his mother every night. When he proposes to Margaret, neither she nor the reader is sure whether it is for love or for money, but whatever, she accepts.

And then Trollope pulls a rabbit out of the hat. In doing research on disposition of the will that had seemed to leave Margaret her fortune, the lawyer determines that the bequest had already been deeded to the Ball family and was therefore not available to be left to Margaret. So now John Ball has it all and Margaret has nothing. And when Mr. Maguire appears and claims that Margaret is his fiancée, John fails the test. He says nothing when it is time for him to reassure Margaret that he believes her, and she immediately returns to the miserable lodgings on the Thames in London. And during the long deliberations about confirming whose money it really is, he says nothing to her. She considers herself bound to him even though he may no longer want her, having the money and not having to bother about the girl. She is still pretty low on the self-esteem scale.

All this makes for an entertaining story. The family history and the mystery of the will are complex enough to keep the reader on the hook. A high-born cousin steps in late in the game to help Miss Mackenzie think a bit more of herself. Mrs. Mackenzie, wife to another cousin who lives far away in Scotland, comes to London for a while and tells Margaret how the cow ate the cabbage. She tells her she is sure that Miss Mackenzie will become Lady Margaret by marrying John Ball, morose though he may be. Her instrument is a muslin flecked with black to replace the mourning that Margaret had been wearing in memory of her brother and then her uncle. A "make-belief mourning bonnet" is tossed in, and these are to be worn to the Negro Soldiers' Orphan Bazaar, at which John Ball sees her in something other than all-black mourning, and both of them get the hint that all need not be dark. This is a little set-piece in which two old favorites appear to play cameo roles: Lady Glencora Palliser, who steps out of the Palliser series, and Lady Hartletop, known to readers of the Barsetshire series as Griselda Grantly.

Lady Hartletop is not referred to by her Christian name, because the name Griselda is already in use in reference to Miss Mackenzie. ("'But you must positively bring Grieselda,' said Lady Glencora Palliser.") Readers of Trollope's day were more aware than those of today that Griselda figured in several folk tales, including Boccaccio's Decameron and Chaucer's "The Clerk's Tale" in The Canterbury Tales, as the personification of patience and obedience. In the former version, a Marquis marries Griselda and tells her that their first two children must be put to death, and then he tells her that he has received papal dispensation to divorce her. She is put away for years, brought back only to witness the wedding of the divorced Marquis. In this ceremony she is told that it is all a joke, and she is restored to her place as wife and mother of the children, who were never killed after all. Some joke; one wonders if her sense of humor is up to it.

Earlier in the book Margaret is referred to as Mariana in the moated grange, who waits vainly for her lover in Tennyson's poem "Mariana":

She only said, 'The night is dreary,
He cometh not,' she said;
She said, 'I am aweary, aweary,
I would that I were dead!'

Another image comes to mind in reading Miss Mackenzie: that of Florence Nightingale, the Lady with the Lamp who revolutionized nursing with her service to the English troops in the Crimea. This revolution was probably still a work in progress when Trollope wrote Miss Mackenzie, describing her resolution to be a hospital nurse as a fall-back option if none of her matrimonial plans worked out. She cared for one brother for fifteen years, and when her brother Tom was on his deathbed, she assumed the role again.

There are women who seem to have an absolute pleasure in fixing themselves for business by the bedside of a sick man. They generally commence their operations by laying aside all fictitious feminine charms, and by arraying themselves with a rigid, unconventional unenticing propriety. Though they are still gentle—perhaps more gentle than ever in their movements—there is a decision in all they do very unlike their usual mode of action.

Miss Mackenzie is an excellent novel. The story moves well in the framework of a Victorian inheritance situation; Miss Mackenzie and John Ball appear as less than perfect but likeable and even admirable figures; those in the supporting cast play their roles well, and through it all the author maintains his deft ironic touch. And for better or worse, the enduring image is that of Rev.

Maguire's squint. "[S]he could not help looking into the horrors of his eye, and thinking that innocent was not the word for him."

THE SCHOOL OF SELF-ASSERTIVENESS
THE BELTON ESTATE

Young people can't be trusted to sort things out for themselves. Sometimes marriages must be arranged. Sometimes they must be rearranged. In The Belton Estate, Clara Amedroz finds herself stuck on high center, engaged for the second time to an immature young man, Captain Frederic Aylmer, who is quite willing to marry her, but who doesn't seem to have his heart in it. Although her cousin Will Belton certainly does have his heart in his unrewarded love for Clara, the stubborn child conceives it to be her duty to marry Captain Aylmer, mainly because she has promised to do so for the second time. Enter the Captain's mother, Lady Aylmer, whose view is that her feckless son must marry money—of which Clara has none. And so Clara is dislodged from high center.

Upon her father's death, Clara has limited options for a place to reside. She has already defied her mother-in-law-elect by refusing to renounce the friendship of a certain Mrs. Askerton, a woman with a checkered past who is considered to be eminently unfit for polite society. Frederic's plea that Clara be given a "second chance" with an invitation to their home is initially refused.

But after "close debate" through Sunday, Monday, and Tuesday, Lady Aylmer recalculates her position, decides not to risk alienating her only son, and assesses her chances: "Not so utterly had victory in such contests deserted her hands, that she need fear to break a lance with Miss Amedroz beneath her own roof, when the occasion was so pressing."

Lady Aylmer's confidence in her own powers is not misplaced. Clara arrives at Aylmer Hall naively expecting to see Lady Aylmer in the hall, not having given sufficient thought to certain "weights and measures":

But Lady Aylmer was too accurately acquainted with the weights and measures of society for any such movement as that. Had her son brought Lady Emily to the house as his future bride, Lady Aylmer would probably have been in the hall when the arrival took place; and had Clara possessed ten thousand pounds of her own, she would probably have been met at the drawing-room door; but as she had neither money nor title—as she in fact brought with her no advantages of any sort—Lady Aylmer was found stitching a bit of worsted, as though she had expected no one to come to her.

Now it so happened that the faithful Will Belton conceived a rather interesting way to express his love for Clara. The heir to the Belton Estate, he had decided that since Clara was the daughter and only remaining child of the late Squire Belton, and since the estate was entailed to him as the eldest male of the family, though only a cousin, he would relinquish the estate to Clara. He already had a farm of his own and had a strong personal interest in Clara's welfare. Clara had absolutely refused, but Frederic had told his mother something of the offer, and this modified somewhat Lady Aylmer's view of Clara—until Clara assured her that she would have nothing to do with the property and would bring no property to her marriage, at which time her Cinderella treatment resumed.

Two interviews take place between Lady Aylmer and Clara. The first is preceded by some softening of Lady Aylmer's manner toward Clara. Unexpectedly, Lady Aylmer selects for Clara a choice piece of hashed fowl at lunch. And though she does not address Clara by her Christian name, she does call her "my dear." And that afternoon Clara finds herself alone with Lady Aylmer for their carriage ride. Frederic's sister Belinda is unaccountably absent—"a little busy, my dear." Lady Aylmer begins her maneuvers with a description of her son's impecunious position, indicating that during her lifetime Frederic will not have enough money to marry. Clara reiterates that she has nothing of her own, but Lady Aylmer hints that there may be some doubt about this.

Clara assures her that she will not accept the Belton estate. Lady Aylmer advises her to put the matter into the hands of Mr. Green, who was her late father's lawyer, but Clara assures her that no lawyer is necessary. Silence. Finally Lady Aylmer ventures that a marriage between Clara and her son cannot be considered—at least for many years. When told by Clara that she will talk to Captain Aylmer about it, Lady Aylmer concedes that he is his own master, but he is also her son.

No more "tit-bits of hashed chicken specially picked out for her by Lady Aylmer's own fork." No more "my dear." Cinderella again.

Captain Aylmer declines Clara's suggestion that he break the engagement. But when asked to set a date, he is "almost aghast," and he returns to London, thus indicating to the reader that he will be no fit helpmate for plucky Clara.

With the matter in this state, and in Frederic's absence, Lady Aylmer decides to bring out the weapon that she has been holding in reserve for so long: Clara's refusal to accede to her command to renounce Mrs. Askerton of the checkered past. The scene of battle is the drawing-room, in the presence of Belinda, Frederic's sister.

This time the silence lasts for a half hour (How many New York minutes are there in a Victorian half hour?) Finally Lady Aylmer mentions the name of the notorious Mrs. Askerton.

Clara draws herself up for battle. "Belinda gave a little spring in her chair, looked intently at her work, and went on stitching faster than before." Clara parries each thrust, saying that what she knows of Mrs. Askerton's past life is in confidence, so that she cannot speak of it. Lady Aylmer says that they must speak of it. "Belinda was stitching very hard, and would not even raise her eyes."

When pressed, Clara states that she was very foolish to come to a house in which she is subjected to such questioning. And when required to promise that the acquaintance not be renewed, she refers to it as an "affectionate friendship" and vows that it will be maintained with all her heart.

Then Clara gives her opponent an opening by observing that they may differ on many subjects, and Lady Aylmer presses to the decisive point, alluding to Clara's hold upon her "unfortunate son." Hereupon Clara declares herself insulted, rises from her chair, and announces that she will inform Captain Aylmer that their engagement is at an end unless she can be reassured that she will never again be subjected to such "unwarrantable insolence" from his mother. Exit Clara.

And with this the course of events is determined; Captain Aylmer and Will Belton play out their roles in the expected fashion. The rest of the book is rather humdrum compared to the prolonged battle between Lady Aylmer and Clara, which is one of the more entertaining of these Trollope set pieces.

A prototype of such contests is the interview between Elizabeth Bennett and Lady Catherine de Bourgh in Jane Austen's Pride and Prejudice. In this classic encounter, Elizabeth defends herself with the understated irony of an Austen heroine when Lady Catherine tells her that the alliance between Elizabeth and Mr. Darcy will be a disgrace and that her name will never even be mentioned by any of the de Bourgh family.

"These are heavy misfortunes," replied Elizabeth. "But the wife of Mr. Darcy must have such extraordinary sources of happiness necessarily attached to her situation, that she could, upon the whole, have no cause to repine."

Trollope demonstrates his skill in presenting the female point of view in his variations on the Cophetua theme, in which the king marries a beggar maid whom he spies from the window of his castle. Lady Lufton, in Framley Parsonage, is not the proud and unbending opponent portrayed in Austen's Lady Catherine de Bourgh or in Lady Aylmer of The Belton Estate.

Lucy Robarts and Clara Amedroz prove themselves to be worthy heroines in the tradition of Elizabeth Bennett as they stand up for themselves. Clara Amedroz's second move in her match with Lady Aylmer is to parry a question with a question:

"I believe it to be an undoubted fact that Mrs. Askerton is—is—is— not at all what she ought to be."

"Which of us is what we ought to be?" said Clara.

Such scenes cry out for television portrayal. Pride and Prejudice is, of course, abundantly portrayed, with Lady Catherine de Bourgh sitting in splendor in her carriage. Wait till BBC asks me for a few suggestions for new shows. The screenwriter would have a bit of work to do with streamlining the plot, but the scenes between Clara and Lady Aylmer are there for the taking.

LOVE CONQUERS ALL, IN THE NINTH INNING
NINA BALATKA

The Story of a Maiden of Prague

How could this short novel fail to delight? A familiar author; his only book about Prague, a city of complexity and charm; and a short novel of only 186 pages, a fourth or a fifth of the usual Trollope novel. So why did I find myself having to force myself to pick it up? It is well written. The heroine is a well rounded Trollope girl, though she is given overmuch to proclaiming that she will stick to her lover no matter what, as many of Trollope's girls do. Perhaps therein lies the seed of dread with which the reader turns its pages. The situation is all foretold in the first sentence of the book: "Nina Balatka was a maiden of Prague, born of Christian parents, and herself a Christian—but she loved a Jew; and this is her story."

Here we go again: the Montagus and the Capulets; star-crossed lovers; nothing good can come of this. This sense of foreboding is built up progressively, with references to the statue of St. John Nepomucene, one of the thirty saints standing watch over the Charles Bridge. As early as the second chapter we are told that this martyr was thrown into the river because he would not betray the secrets of a queen's confession, and that he now keeps the faithful safe from drowning in the river. More and more insistent references to the fear and attraction of the black water appear. Nobody wants Nina to marry Anton; a devious plot is laid to trick

Anton into thinking that she has deceived him about a deed that belongs to Anton but is in the possession of Nina's uncle. Even her faithful servant Souchey is part of the plot, bewitched by Lotta Luxa, the uncle's serving girl. Souchey thinks it's his Christian duty to prevent a marriage that would imperil the soul of his mistress.

Up to the last moment the reader is convinced that this is a tragedy working itself out, and that the dose will be short but bitter. In suspense, the reader reads quickly to the conclusion. Without spelling out the last pages, it can be said that reading the book is liking watching a ball game in which the home team is hopelessly behind for the whole game but mounts a last-gasp effort at the end.

It's a dark book. The motif of the dark waters of the Moldau dominates all others. Nina herself is the brightest spot, forthright and assertive in her love for Anton. Like many Trollope heroines, she is not the most beautiful girl in her story; her rival Rebecca Loth is admitted even by Nina's cousin and suitor, Ziska Zamenoy, to be more striking and beautiful. Yet Nina continues to attract Ziska and Anton even in poverty that is almost starvation. Her circumstances allow little opportunity for humor; and the story pursues its course with no comic relief.

Her lover Anton is a serious and humorless sort, successful as a businessman and ultimately faithful in his love for Nina, though his experience in the business world keeps him from believing fully that Nina, a Christian, is not betraying him. And like so many Victorian men, he insists on the obedience of his intended as a litmus test for her worthiness.

Prague, with its segregated Jewish Quarter, affords an opportunity for exploring the relationship between Jews and Christians. Ziska's foray into the Jewish Quarter is the central dramatization of the distance between them, as he unwittingly arrives there on a Jewish holiday, when the women are dressed for a festival and the men are at worship. Seeking Anton, he is conducted into the synagogue:

The door was very low and narrow, and seemed to be choked by men with short white surplices, but nevertheless he found himself inside, jammed among a crowd of Jews; and a sound of many voices, going together in a singsong wail or dirge, met his ears. His first impulse was to take off his hat, but that was immediately replaced upon his head, he knew not by whom; and then he observed that all within the building were covered. His guide did not follow him, but whispered to someone what it was that the stranger required.

In dreamlike fashion, Ziska is led through the crowd to Anton, who offers to accompany him outside if the business is important. A serious interview ensues, in which Ziska pursues his family's treacherous plot to disrupt the engagement. Here the Jews are presented as a people of dignity and courtesy, long-suffering and patient. Wary of their Christian oppressors, they proceed with caution. In much the same fashion that Shakespeare portrays the Jews in The Merchant of Venice, they are presented with sympathy, even though the usages of the time permit derogatory allusions as a matter of course.

In circumstances such as these, what chance does love have, coming up as a pinch-hitter in the bottom of the ninth inning? Love does have a good at-bat, but the reader is left with the feeling that there will have to be a lot more weddings and a lot more funerals before these issues are resolved.

MORE THAN SOAP OPERA, MORE THAN FAIRY TALE THE CLAVERINGS

This is straight from the noontime soaps. Harry Clavering, the sometimes sheep-like "hero" of The Claverings, rises to challenge his cousin Sir Hugh Clavering, standing toe-to-toe in a hostile verbal encounter, and the younger man (Harry) defies his banishment from his cousin's house. There is some talk of horsewhipping, and Harry walks out, with a cautious look over his shoulder. No violence. We're English (which sometimes helps). But it is soap opera. The Claverings is basically about Harry Clavering and the two women he loves. He proposes to Julia Brabazon and is refused; she marries a wealthy nobleman; Harry falls in love with Florence Burton, the daughter of a hard-working civil engineer; Julia becomes a wealthy widow and reappears. What will Harry do?

It's not so simple. Florence and her family are not to be discounted. Her brother Theodore, committed to building railways and digging tunnels, speaks his piece in Chapter XXVI, "The Man who dusted his Boots with his Handkerchief." (Remember that Mr. Puddicombe, arbiter of proper behavior to his friend Dr. Wortle in Dr. Wortle's School, advised his friend, "When I am taking a walk through the fields and get one of my feet deeper than usual into the mud, I always endeavour to bear it as well as I may before the eyes of those who meet me rather than make futile efforts to get rid of the dirt and look as though nothing had happened. The dirt, when it is rubbed and smudged and scraped, is more palpably dirt than the honest mud.") One of the great questions that arose in the Victorian world was how to identify a gentleman, and although Trollope doesn't spell it out in so many words, it may be taken from this description, and from the drawings of this scene in two different editions, that dusting one's boots is a cardinal sign that one is not a gentleman.

But, gentleman or not, Theodore Burton is one of the two in the story who prove themselves to be men of worth. When Harry is dithering about which woman he will marry (both Lady Ongar and Florence Burton appear willing to accept him), Theodore Burton, who has employed Harry in the engineering office, writes him a letter acknowledging Harry's absence from the office and urging him to come for an interview. After the formalities, Burton comes directly to the point: "Come, Harry, let me tell you all at once like an honest man. I hate subterfuges and secrets. A report has reached the old people at home—not Florence, mind—that you are untrue to Florence, and are passing your time with that lady who is the sister of your cousin's wife." He goes on to urge him to return to Florence and to the Burton family fold. "And this from the man who had dusted his boots with his pocket handkerchief, and whom Harry had regarded as being on that account hardly fit to be his friend!"

The other humble man who proves his worth is Mr. Samuel Saul, the curate for Harry's father Mr. Clavering, a clergyman not given to work of any sort. Mr. Saul is introduced as a serious, conscientious young man who basically does all the work. (This is a mark against any claim that Mr. Saul may have to being a gentlemen. Gentlemen don't work.) Mrs. Clavering later reflects that her son Harry "would never excel greatly in any drudgery that would be necessary for the making of money."

But the humble Mr. Saul aspires to the hand of Harry's sister Fanny. No one in Fanny's family—her father the rector, her mother, or her brother Harry—could even consider such a thing; but Fanny, who initially acknowledges the impossibility of his suit, eventually does begin to consider it, and to consider that the only thing keeping them from being married is that his income as a curate is woefully inadequate. And Fanny rejects any suggestion that Mr. Saul is not a gentleman.

His initial proposal introduces us to him. Trollope specialized in proposals; there seem to be at least two or three in every book. And this one, which occurs in the rain, makes the reader thankful for a warm dry spot where he can only read about the rain. He persists with his statement of purpose in spite of the downpour, and she splashes herself as she forbids him to speak further. "She had her own ideas as to what was loveable in men, and the eager curate, splashing through the rain by her side, by no means came up to her standard of excellence."

But Mr. Saul's powers were not to be underestimated. He later makes another attempt, in which the author dissects Mr. Saul's victory. Fanny does not declare that she does not love him. Mr. Saul's gamesmanship requires a bit of leisurely explanation:

At this moment she forgot that in order to put herself on perfectly firm ground, she should have gone back to the first hypothesis, and assured him that she did not feel any such regard for him. Mr. Saul, whose intellect was more acute, took advantage of her here, and chose to believe that that matter of her affection was now conceded to him. He knew what he was doing well, and is open to a charge of some jesuitry. "Mr. Saul," said Fanny, with grave prudence, "it cannot be right for people to marry when they have nothing to live upon." When she had shown him so plainly that she had no other piece left on the board to play than this, the game may be said to have been won on his side.

Mr. Saul continued to play his hand bravely in his interview with Mr. Clavering, whose strongest card was that Mr. Saul, though a gentleman, was not in his class. And of course the nuances of class were to be of no avail in England in coming decades. Some would persist, but many of these nuances, which were relied upon by those such as Mr. Clavering, who did not work, would fall to the energy of such men as Mr. Burton and Mr. Saul, who did work. In this case, Mr. Clavering bravely declared that Mr. Saul would have to give up his pretensions for Fanny's hand, or leave the parish—which would have left Mr. Clavering without the services of someone to do his work for him. And Mr. Saul called his bluff, declaring that he would leave the parish rather than renounce his claim for Fanny's hand.

As it turned out, all parties stood their ground, and Fanny assumed the role of "a broken-hearted young lady." But this is fairy tale as well as soap opera, and all tears are wiped away in a series of events that open up the position of rector of the parish to the steadfast Mr. Saul, thus removing the last excuse the family had for opposing the union—somewhat to the sacrifice of "cakes and ale in the parish," to Mr. Clavering's regret.

Other less worthy persons claim the reader's attention, two of whom, Archie Clavering and Captain Boodle, provide a welcome bit of comic relief when Mr. Boodle, habitué of the racecourses and "fast friend" of Captain Archie Clavering, the ne'er do well brother of Sir Hugh Clavering, advises Archie about how to advance his courtship of Lady Ongar. Archie knows deep down that he has no chance. "In some inexplicable manner he put himself into the scales and weighed himself, and discovered his own weight with fair accuracy. And he put her into the scales, and he found that she was much the heavier of the two." But Boodle knows too much about horses to allow his friend to shortchange himself in his suit, comparing courtship to riding a trained mare: "I always choose that she shall know that I'm there." Use the spurs if you have to.

Needless to say, Archie's sense of his own weight is a more accurate predictor than Boodle's advice; but Archie and Captain Boodle also attempt to invoke the assistance of Lady Ongar's friend Sophie Gordeloupe, who routs them both. Madame Gordeloupe was a "Franco-Pole," who "spoke English with great fluency, but every word uttered declared her not to be English." In Trollope's English world, she was the classic devious foreigner. Some said that she was a Russian spy. "How could any decent English man or woman wish for the friendship of such a creature as that?"

Archie makes the first visit to the Russian spy, who quickly strips him of the twenty pounds he had tucked into his glove and ridicules him for offering such a paltry sum, demanding fifty pounds as a starter. "Yes, fifty—for another beginning. What; seven thousands of pounds per annum, and make difficulty for fifty pounds! You have a handy way with your glove. Will you come with fifty pounds tomorrow?"

After Archie's second visit succeeds only in Sophie's relieving him of fifty more pounds, Boodle is pressed into service for a third attempt. When Sophie asks him if Boodle is an English name, he replies, "Altogether English, I believe. Our Boodles come out of Warwickshire; small property near Leamington—doosed small, I'm sorry to say." When he utterly fails in his embassy, he feels "quite entitled to twit her with the payment she had taken," and asks about his friend's seventy pounds that she has taken. More ridicule. Boodle is routed. Madame Gordeloupe finds that longer speeches in a tongue not her own are more effective:

"Suppose you go to your friend and tell him from me that he have chose a very bad Mercury in his affairs of love—the worst Mercury I ever see. Perhaps the Warwickshire Mercuries are not very good. Can you tell me, Captain Booddle, how they make love down in Warwickshire?"

The women are strong. Julia Ongar plays her hand well. After terminating her love affair with young Harry Clavering because neither of them has any money, she goes in search of bigger game. "Julia had now lived past her one short spell of poetry, had written her one sonnet, and was prepared for the business of the world." She goes on to win the prize of her widow's bountiful settlement, but she then finds that she is accepted neither by the gentry nor by the servants at Ongar Park when she goes to occupy her new residence. And on learning that she has a losing hand to play against Florence Burton, she plays it with reasonable dignity. She is not, however, above a bit of revenge at the last, taunting Harry that Florence must be very beautiful. Not so beautiful, he says, but very clever.

"Ah—I understand. She reads a great deal, and that sort of thing. Yes; that is very nice. But I shouldn't have thought that that would have taken you. You used not to care much for talent and learning—not in women I mean."

Florence, for her part, is steadfast in her love and prepares to give it up when she senses that she has lost; but the leading lady often has the most stereotyped part to play. Florence's sister-in-law, Cecilia Burton, plays her supporting role well, taking the initiative in confronting Harry when he wavers, and doing it without informing her husband, who might forbid her to do so. The title of Chapter XXVII emphasizes her initiative: "What Cecilia Burton did for her Sister-in-law." And what she did is explained a bit after her effort: "Even Cecilia, with all her partiality for Harry, felt that he was not worth the struggle; but it was for her now to estimate him at the price that Florence might put upon him—not at her own price."

Harry Clavering's reflections on his situation bear the markings of authenticity. Trollope had met his new American friend, Kate Field, about three years earlier, and it is tempting to attribute these comments about how a man can love two women at the same time to his not-entirely-paternal interest in Kate.

Sir Hugh Clavering's death at sea permits the fairy tale ending. Fairy tale, yes; and soap opera plot, yes; but the nuances of Victorian society are exposed with such wit that The Claverings is lifted well above the soap opera mark. It stands as one of my favorites of Trollope's novels, one that could readily be recommended to the reader who is not quite familiar with the author's name.

SEVERAL DEGREES OF STUBBORN LINDA TRESSEL

Be advised and read no further, any to whom it is important that the ending of the book not be known before it is read. Linda Tressel (1867) is one of Trollope's dark books—Sir Harry Hotspur is another—in which the heroine does not fare well after being thwarted in trying to have a life on her own terms.

That a young woman should insist on such conditions in the

nineteenth century would mark this as a work that could be used as a feminist text today; and perhaps it would be so used if it were a little less melodramatic—and if anyone knew anything about it.

Linda is a young woman who shows spunk and determination, but she falls victim to the stubborn steadfastness of purpose of her Aunt Charlotte, shown to be a religious zealot of the evangelical Protestant variety, and Aunt Charlotte's lodger, Peter Steinmarc, a Nuremberger of the slow-witted stubborn sort. Both are so extreme in their positions that they might be taken for caricatures were they not shown in such convincing detail.

The story is that of a motherless child who is taken under the wing of her Aunt Charlotte, a devout woman who "goes far beyond the ordinary amenities of Lutheran teaching." When Linda attains the age of twenty, she learns that Peter Steinmarc has offered to make her his wife. The reader is told that he has previously proposed many times to Charlotte Staubach, who declined the honor and reminded Peter that he would become owner of the house now in Linda's name, if he should become Linda's husband. On being told of his marital intentions by her Aunt Charlotte, Linda immediately refuses, but she becomes "very wretched." A few details tell why:

She told herself that sooner or later her aunt would conquer her, that sooner or later that mean-faced old man, with his snuffy fingers, and his few straggling hairs brushed over his bald pate, with his big shoes spreading here and there because of his corns, and his ugly, loose, square, snuffy coat, and his old hat which he had worn so long that she never liked to touch it, would become her husband, and that it would be her duty to look after his wine, and his old shoes, and his old hat, and to have her own little possessions doled out to her by his penuriousness.

This then is the story, and it plays out with the added complication of Linda's being in love with the young man who lives across the little river behind her house. He is in and out of jail because of his political radicalism, but Linda knows little of this. They attempt an elopement, but it fails when young Ludovic is apprehended by the police at the Augsburg station when their train arrives. Linda had the pluck to run away with Ludovic, and in the end she has the pluck to run away on her own, but though she confronts her aunt several times, she never can bring herself to face her and refute her. When Aunt Charlotte plays the prayer card, Linda never refuses to kneel and listen to the degrading and humiliating prayers offered on her behalf.

The feminist agenda was one that the conservative Trollope never subscribed to, but his stories were too true to life to conceal women's problems. Perhaps his stories got away from him, and the women's stories told themselves. In this one, poor Linda finds herself totally powerless under the domination of her aunt, as no man would be. The world appears to be conspiring to keep her from breaking out of her aunt's smothering sphere. When she leaves the house to go consult an old friend of her late father's, Herr Molk tells her that she should submit herself to her elders and her betters.

Trollope made little secret of his religious tastes—traditional Anglicanism, of the high church sort, but not papist. And he had no patience with any evidence of fanaticism in religion. "But there are women of the class to which Madame Staubach belonged who think that the acerbities of religion are intended altogether for their own sex. That men ought to be grateful to them who will deny?" Poor Linda's final escape is too late to save her; she makes her way to her uncle's house in Cologne, where her Aunt Grüner, a Catholic, tells her that her Aunt Charlotte's mistreatment of her comes of her religion.

"We think differently, my dear. Thank God, we have got somebody to tell us what we ought to do and what we ought not to do." Linda was not strong enough to argue the question, or to remind her aunt that this somebody, too, might possibly be wrong.

Linda's progressive downhill and melodramatic course makes for a rather grim story. Mercifully, it is a short one. The descriptions of Aunt Charlotte and of Peter Steinmarc leave little room for subtlety. However, Aunt Charlotte's breastplate of righteousness was not entirely without a few little chinks, as we see in her last encounter with Linda's wild lover. Trollope's description, I fear, will bring few feminists to his side:

He could get in and out of the roofs of houses, and could carry away with him a young maiden. These are deeds which always excite a certain degree of admiration in the female heart, and Madame Staubach, though she was a Baptist, was still a female. When, therefore, she found herself in the presence of Ludovic, she could not treat him with the indignant scorn with which she would have received him had he intruded upon her premises before her fears of him had been excited.

Like Nina Balatka, Linda Tressel was published as an anonymous work; only later did Trollope declare himself as the author. It has been stated that he wanted to prove that he could write a different kind of novel, set in Europe. Linda Tressel was clearly an effort to take his writing in a different direction. Though it was not a commercial success, it can hardly be dismissed. The story moves inexorably to a tragic ending for the heroine; the author stays on task with the progression of the story, but it is seasoned with bits of irony. The reader begins to suspect that there is heavy weather ahead as the storm clouds gather over the picturesque little red house in Nuremberg; perhaps it is the impact of the inevitable deluge that is so depressing.

THE DOWNSIDE OF CHIVALRY HE KNEW HE WAS RIGHT

Novels rarely have subtitles; Anthony Trollope certainly didn't bother with them. But He Knew He Was Right is a sitting duck for a frivolous little subtitle. How about But He Was Wrong? Or maybe But She Knew He Was Wrong? Or perhaps, But She Wouldn't Pretend That He Was Right? But of course any subtitle would have been redundant. The five-word title tells it all. Of course he wasn't right. But he was stubborn. And she was stubborn. And in this case, it was a case of terminal stubbornness.

The problem with He Knew He Was Right is that the man who knows he is right, Louis Trevelyan, fails to overcome his terminal stubbornness. Or perhaps we should refer to it as a paranoid personality disorder—or maybe as the prevailing diagnosis of the time: madness. Whatever we call it, it isn't pretty, and the story of his progressive delusion is not a pleasant one. Interesting, yes. So is Crime and Punishment. But both stories tell how someone happened to think and do the wrong thing, and these are unpleasant subjects. Both books dilute the dose with little subplots that add humor and diversion. But the main story line is still the main story line. Louis Trevelyan, a young husband, is annoyed by the daily visits to his wife by her godfather, Colonel Osborne, a bachelor with a reputation for pursuing beautiful young married women. He objects, she resents the objection, and both husband and wife shoot past the point of negotiation with their first discussion of the subject. Both are stubborn, things go downhill from there, and in the end Louis Trevelyan goes mad and suffers the consequences.

Trevelyan was set up by circumstances, and to understand some of these circumstances, we must take note of the laws of England at that time. English common law stated that in marriage, two became one, and that one was the husband in the eyes of the law. The husband was indeed the lord and master. In regard to children, John Stuart Mill wrote of the wife's subordination in marriage, "They are by law his children. ... No one act can she do towards or in relation to them, except by delegation from him."

This was part of the system of coverture, in which a married woman surrendered her legal existence, which was suspended during her marriage, "or at least incorporated or consolidated into that of her husband, under whose wing, protection, and cover, she performs everything." [1] The efforts of Victorian feminists, who considered this to be "marital slavery," led to the Married Woman's Property Act of 1882, twenty years after this book was written; but even this was only a partial solution. It was not until 1923 that grounds for divorce were made the same for both sexes, and divorce remained expensive until Legal Aid became available in 1949.

[Footnote 1: Sir William Blackstone's Commentaries on the Laws of England, 1765-1769]

With this as the law of the land, one can begin to see that a young husband, new to the demands of marriage, might feel that his very manhood required that he exercise his authority. (There is a downside to chivalry.)

And on the other side of the equation, we are told that Emily has been brought up away from England, in the Mandarin Islands, where she has developed an independent spirit. Friends of both parties urged them to soften their positions, but both felt that their honor was insulted, and that they could not retreat or compromise.

Today's reader observes pretty quickly in this disaster that such an impasse is less likely to occur these days because women have more rights. And though Trollope never officially endorsed the rights of women, he allowed Emily, and other women in other novels, to be compelling in their arguments. Emily voices these early in our story:

"It is a very poor thing to be a woman," she said to her sister.

"It is perhaps better than being a dog," said Nora; "but, of course, we can't compare ourselves to men."

"It would be better to be a dog. One wouldn't be made to suffer so much. When a puppy is taken away from its mother, she is bad enough for a few days, but she gets over it in a week. ... It is very hard for a woman to know what to do," continued Emily, "but if she is to marry, I think she had better marry a fool. After all, a fool generally knows that he is a fool, and will trust someone, though he may not trust his wife."

"Humankind cannot bear very much reality," and we are mercifully diverted by the subplots, which occupy approximately fifty-four of the ninety-nine chapters of the 823-page book (one of Trollope's longest).

Miss Jemima Stanbury occupies a position of similar prominence among the subplots as she enjoyed in the city of Exeter. This is stated in a single sentence (of some length): "It is to be hoped that no readers of these pages will be so un-English as to be unable to appreciate the difference between county society and town society—the society, that is, of a provincial town, or so ignorant as not to know also that there may be persons so privileged, that although they live distinctly within a provincial town, there is accorded to them, as though by brevet rank, all the merit of living in the county." And Miss Stanbury was universally regarded as "county" rather than "town." "There was not a tradesman in Exeter who was not aware of it, and who did not touch his hat to her accordingly."

Miss Stanbury was rich. She had been engaged to a young banker, Mr. Brooke Burgess, who had jilted her, subsequently died, and left to her "every shilling that he possessed." And she, in her own romantic way, was determined that her inheritance should be hers only for life and that at her death it should revert to the Burgess family and not stay in her own family.

This is the formidable woman who paid for the education of Hugh Stanbury, Louis Trevelyan's best friend, and then cut him off from all support because he abandoned the study of law to write for the "penny press." She then wrote to Hugh's mother asking her to send her younger daughter Dorothy to live with her. "I shall expect her to be regular at meals, to be constant in going to church, and not to read modern novels."

The great problem for Miss Stanbury arose when her beloved niece Dorothy fell in love with and agreed to marry young Brooke Burgess, nephew of Miss Stanbury's late lover. But young Brooke was to inherit the Burgess wealth that Miss Stanbury intended to return to the Burgesses. And if he should marry her niece, it would diminish her posthumous triumph in returning the wealth. So he must not marry her niece. Her niece must marry Mr. Gibson, a young clergyman of Exeter.

Happy endings are permitted in the subplots, and the young people have their way. That is, most of them do. Miss Stanbury comes around with a late night change of heart and grants her blessing to Dorothy's marrying Mr. Burgess. Mr. Gibson receives his just reward. He is claimed by two sisters of the parish, one of whom so terrifies him that he reneges on his engagement to her, escaping her long kitchen knife when a kinsman is summoned to take it away from her, and Mr. Gibson then takes the younger of the two lovely sisters.

There is yet another subplot involving the Rowleys and the Stanburys. Hugh Stanbury, best friend of the unfortunate and stubborn Louis Trevelyan and rejected beneficiary of his Aunt Stanbury, is in love with Nora Rowley, beautiful sister of the also unfortunate and also stubborn Emily Trevelyan. But Nora's parents have their hearts set on her accepting the proposal of one Mr. Glascock, soon to be Lord Peterborough on the death of his father. A handsome and pleasant young man, his proposal comes only after the beautiful Nora has lost her heart to radical young Hugh Stanbury, and Mr. Glascock is refused. We then have the opportunity to follow Mr. Glascock on his journey to Naples to see his dying father, in the course of which he happens to travel with, by great coincidence, Louis Trevelyan himself, and two young Spalding sisters from America. This gives the young Trevelyan, separated from his wife, an opportunity to describe another variety of wives, the American ones, who are "exigeant—and then they are so hard. They want the weakness that a woman ought to have."

We see a good bit more of the Spalding family in Florence, where Mr. Glascock decides that the elder sister Caroline is his favorite, and after a suitable diversion to other subplots, the reader learns that they have become engaged, Caroline having demonstrated her wit with her response to his question about American "institutions:"

"Everything is an institution. Having iced water to drink in every room of the house is an institution. Having hospitals in every town is an institution. Travelling altogether in one class of railway cars is an institution. Saying "sir", is an institution. Teaching all the children mathematics is an institution. Plenty of food is an institution. Getting drunk is an institution in a great many towns. Lecturing is an institution. There are plenty of them, and some are very good—but you wouldn't like it."

Mr. Trollope must have had some unpleasant experiences with one or more American women who served as his model for Caroline Spalding's friend Wallachia Petrie, "the Republican Browning," a "poetess" and a feminist and an outspoken opponent of "European" ways. Inveighing against the "courtiers" of "Europe," Miss Petrie vows that "the courtier shall be cut down together with the withered grasses and thrown into the oven, and there shall be an end of them."

We may hope that the future Lord Peterborough will not be obliged to listen to such speeches at Monkhams, his ancestral home.

But all is not diversion with subplots. The main business at hand is the progressive madness of Louis Trevelyan, who has his young son snatched by his private detective Bozzle (a well-meaning agent who eventually allows his wife to convince him that his own suspicion is correct, and that Trevelyan is mad) and carries him off to Italy. There he becomes progressively weaker, failing to eat, and Emily comes to rescue her son and provide hospice care for her husband. Was he mad? The author answers that he was "neither mad nor sane—not mad, so that all power over his own actions need be taken from him; nor sane, so that he must be held to be accountable for his words and thoughts."

The case of Louis Trevelyan is a tough one. The author, noted for his realistic portrayal of the world, makes a convincing case. And one must remember that Trollope was, after all, a story teller; and the story of a man who went mad because his wife would not accept his authority—because she would not recognize his position as master of his house, where his word was law—was a story worth telling. The subplots and the comedy and the realism are all background, but the strange story is the event in the foreground. The story may have taken its author further than he had intended to go. His own comment on the novel in his autobiography has been often quoted and is worth reviewing:

I do not know that in any literary effort I ever fell more completely short of my own intention than in this story. It was my purpose to create sympathy for the unfortunate man who, while endeavouring to do his duty to all around him, should be led constantly astray by his unwillingness to submit his own judgment to the opinion of others. The man is made to be unfortunate enough, and the evil which he does is apparent. So far I did not fail, but the sympathy has not been created yet. I look upon the story as being nearly altogether bad. It is in part redeemed by certain scenes in the house and vicinity of an old maid in Exeter. But a novel which in its main parts is bad cannot, in truth, be redeemed by the vitality of subordinate characters.

It may well be that Louis and Emily Trevelyan got away from their creator, just as their quarrel took on a life of its own and got out of the control of its two participants. Even with an author who prided himself on discipline in his writing, the pen can sometimes take off with a will of its own. Though the author professed to be displeased with the result, most critics have viewed the result with more favor, and I am inclined to agree with them. As to the strangeness of the story, the more one sees of life, how can anyone say that anything cannot happen? The storyteller's job is to take strange stories and make entertaining stories out of them. When I was in training, one of my chief residents had a comment that he used for strange cases: "You see that sometimes."

He knew he was right, but he was wrong.

THE PRODIGAL DAUGHTER THE VICAR OF BULLHAMPTON

On the day that I finished reading Trollope's The Vicar of Bullhampton, the following appeared in an email from a friend: An Irish daughter had not been home for over 5 years. Upon her return, her father cussed her: "Where have you been all this time, you ingrate!" The girl, crying, replied, "Dad ... I became a prostitute." "What! Out of here, you shameless harlot! ..." "OK, Dad—as you wish. I just came back to give Mom this fur coat and you this new Mercedes Benz. ..." "Now what was it you said you had become?" "A prostitute, Dad" "Oh, you scared me half to death, girl. I thought you said a Protestant."

This is one of the major plot lines of The Vicar of Bullhampton, though not its conclusion. Plots are standard and repetitive. The success of the work relies less on the plot than on its window dressing. Trollope's Carry Brattle has been gone from home, and everyone knows what she has become but delicacy forbids use of the word "whore." Her father forbids her return. Will she come back? How will she be received? This theme apparently was a daring innovation in the mainstream Victorian novel; Mary Magdalene rarely appeared in the printed pages of the nineteenth century.

Sensational as this story line was, the novel appears to move rather slowly. All plot lines revolve around Mister Fenwick, the vicar. He and his wife encourage their house guest, Mary Lowther, to accept the suit of Mr. Fenwick's best friend, Harry Gilmore. She doesn't love him; she refuses him and shortly after falls in love with her cousin Walter Marrable. She accepts his proposal, but they jointly agree to call it off when his prospects in life are ruined by his father's reckless wasting of Walter's inheritance. Against her better judgment she accepts Mr. Gilmore. Then Walter's prospects for an inheritance improve. So she breaks her engagement to Mr. Gilmore and resumes that with Captain Marrable. Like Alice Vavasor in Can You Forgive Her? she becomes a double jilt, and she is roundly criticized by many for such grievous behavior.

Perhaps the most entertaining of the story lines is a church issue reminiscent of the Barsetshire novels. Mister Fenwick is insulted by the great landowner of the county, The Marquis of Trowbridge, and he succeeds in repaying the Marquis with more insults. Here Trollope's familiarity with church sensitivities brings us the Marquis's revenge: he allows a Methodist chapel (not a regular Wesleyan Methodist chapel, but a Primitive Methodist chapel) to be built across the road from the vicarage, where its ugly red bricks and loud discordant bells are a recurring nuisance to the vicar and his wife.

But then: the vicar decides to consider the chapel to be his hair shirt, and he obtains the promise of his wife (who will never open her front door to look at the chapel) not to mention it to him again. The vicar considers the matter closed; but his wife's sister visits with her husband, a distinguished barrister, who volunteers to investigate the matter. He discovers that the land on which the chapel is being built is glebe land! (Glebe land is that which belongs to the vicar for his personal farming or gardening.) And here the vicar refuses to shed his hair shirt.

His clerical mind allows him to demonstrate his virtue by tolerating the chapel, though his poor wife may be obliged to endure the sight and sounds of it without being allowed to complain to him. But the perpetrator of the chapel is not to be spared, and the vicar writes a stinging letter to the marquis, in which he explains the use of very strong words:

He showed the letter to his wife.

"Isn't malice a very strong word?" she said.

"I hope so," answered the vicar.

The pace of the gentle life in Victorian England was surely a leisurely one. This pace is reflected in the whole page that is given to the thoughts of the Marquis of Trowbridge when he receives the insulting letter from Mr. Fenwick; and his reflections are further supplemented by the author's reminding us, if it were not already evident, that the Marquis is an old fool:

His lordship's mind was one utterly incapable of sifting evidence—unable even to understand evidence when it came to him. He was not a bad man. He desired nothing that was not his own, and remitted much that was. He feared God, honoured the Queen, and loved his country. He was not self-indulgent. He did his duties as he knew them. But he was an arrogant old fool, who could not keep himself from mischief—who could only be kept from mischief by the aid of some such master as his son.

Trollope can be more pithy, as when he describes the Marquis's reception and reaction to the letter from the vicar: "His intelligence worked slowly, whereas his wrath worked quickly."

The vicar subsequently feels himself cheated of his revenge after the Marquis's son Lord St. George succeeds in "pouring oil on the waters." But others pursue the matter for him, and in the end the chapel is pulled down.

The vicar is actually rather well portrayed and could stand with his clerical brethren of Barsetshire if he were given six novels in which we could follow his career. He shows himself to be a naive clergyman who thinks he can intervene in the problems of a pretty, banished prostitute without incurring any risk to his reputation. He urges the miller Jacob Brattle to accept his daughter, ignoring the father's refusal to speak to him about Carry. He visits Carry's brother George, urging him and his wife to take her in, facing the wife's wrath after George advises him not to raise the issue with her. He visits Carry's brother-in-law Mr. Jay the ironmonger with similar lack of success. He visits Carry at the small town inn where she is staying and pays for her lodging. Just when the reader begins to wonder whether, in the words of the song in The Music Man, "Hester will win just one more A," the vicar's wife Janet finally persuades him to lower his profile in the matter, but he never seems to understand the damage of gossip.

His instincts are shown to be correct in his championing of Sam Brattle, who is accused of murder but subsequently exonerated, and of Carry Brattle, who returns home and finally regains her father's affection. Carry's return is after setting out on foot, exposing herself to the elements in desperation, half expecting to die of exposure as did Lady Dedlock in Dickens's Bleak House, and as Gerald Crich would do in D. H. Lawrence's Women in Love. Did such a recurrent fictional device reflect an occasional practice of the times?

Trollope is a chatty author. Had he been as reticent as twentieth century practitioners of minimalist fiction, we might not have had spelled out for our curiosity a definition of a gentleman, a recurrent source of fascination for Trollope. Miss Marrable is the author's agent who ponders the matter, concluding that money does not entitle a millionaire to be considered a gentleman. Attorneys don't make the cut by virtue of their profession. A son of a gentleman, however, could maintain his rank by earning his living as a clergyman, a barrister, a soldier, or a sailor. Physicians were not absolutely excluded from the ranks of the gentlemen, but a physician could never participate in the privileges accorded to the Law and the Church. There might be some doubt about the engineering profession, but any man who allowed himself to touch trade or commerce automatically excluded himself. Such men might be ever so respectable, "but brewers, bankers and merchants were not gentlemen, and the world, according to Miss Marrable's theory, was going astray, because people were forgetting their landmarks."

And it goes without mentioning that for Walter Marrable, the option of going to work to make money is never considered. His only recourse is to return to the army.

Obvious generalizations as to class have gone out of style. But Victorian England was a land of class and caste, as shown in this allusion to a hired hand in the mill: "His companion in the mill did not come near them, knowing, as the poor do know on such occasions, there was something going on which would lead them to prefer that he should be absent."

There's also a murder mystery. It occupies several chapters, but at the end it is dismissed with only the limited knowledge of the details told by Carry Brattle and her brother Sam, both witnesses at the trial.

The story of the Mary Magdalene, though innovative, is, after all, sentimental; the love story, perhaps considered essential to sell the book to the public, is tedious; the murder mystery is perfunctory; but I wouldn't miss the story of the Methodist chapel.

A TERMINAL AFFECTION SIR HARRY HOTSPUR OF HUMBLETHWAITE

The beleaguered father of the twenty-first century might at first look with some longing to the mores of the nineteenth century and to Sir Harry Hotspur of Humblethwaite, in a time and place when a father's word was law, and a faithful daughter would not marry without her father's consent. It was not so simple, though, and that's what the book is about. The plot anticipates that of Henry James's Washington Square, written about ten years later about a family in New York.

Trollope presents the story in a short novel of 172 pages, which means there are no subplots. However, the reader is not short-changed by any lack of reflections by and about the characters as each turn of the story unfolds. Whereas James regards his participants in a rather detached fashion, as a puppet master who pulls the strings and watches the unfortunate movements that may result, and with relative economy of words, Trollope regards his characters with as much affection as they deserve, spending paragraphs detailing all aspects of the situation as they may appear to each of them all along the way.

The daughter of a wealthy baronet falls in love with her cousin who is a spendthrift and unworthy of her. We must follow the ground rules of Victorian society—cousins may marry, and a father must decide whether to approve of his daughter's intended husband and is indeed obliged to investigate his character. In this case, we learn that the mortal sin committed by the suitor is that he cheated at cards. Remember T. S. Eliot's line about Macavity the Mystery Cat: "He's outwardly respectable. (They say he cheats at cards.)"

For our later generation, Trollope is a patient instructor: We are reminded that an Englishman's home is his castle. "Nothing on earth should induce Sir Harry to see his cousin anywhere on his own premises."

In a society in which inheritance could be all important, the lover of the fox hunt was beginning to suspect that the laws of inheritance were not universally applicable: "And good blood too will have its effect—physical for the most part—and will produce bottom, lasting courage, that capacity of carrying on through the mud to which Sir Harry was wont to allude; but good blood will bring no man back to honesty."

He gives lessons in the art of negotiation: "Lady Elizabeth had not been instructed to propose a meeting. She had been told rather to avoid it if at all possible. But, like some other undiplomatic ambassadors, in her desire to be civil, she ran at once to the extremity of the permitted concession."

A serious interview ensues when George Hotspur plucks up his courage to ask Sir Harry for Emily Hotspur's hand. Two and a half pages of dialogue follow, during which George pleads his losing case well, leaving Sir Harry to decide: "He sat silent for full five minutes before he spoke again, and then he gave judgment as follows: 'You will go away without seeing her tomorrow.'" Trollope follows the narrative to a point further on, at which, "The process of parental yielding had already commenced."

Ever the patient instructor, he here teaches:

On all such occasions interviews are bad. The teller of this story ventures to take the opportunity of recommending parents in such cases always to refuse interviews, not only between the young lady and the lover who is to be excluded, but also between themselves and the lover. The vacillating tone—even when the resolve to suppress vacillation has been most determined—is perceived and understood.

Not always a dispassionate instructor, the compassionate narrator at one point has tender words for the doomed maiden: "Then he knelt down and prayed ... that he might be as a brand saved from the burning. ... Alas, dearest, no; not so could it be done! Not at thy instance, though thy prayers be as pure as the songs of angels."

The story is built with several materials familiar to Trollope readers: the faithful young woman who can never love another, whatever becomes of the love of her life; the father concerned with the integrity of his estate in generations to come; and the young man who never intends to work and would readily marry for money. Whereas, however, in other novels it all comes out all right (Ayala's Angel, for instance, is a comedy from first to last in which numerous young girls succeed in following their hearts without having to pine away) in this story the chips fall where they may, so the ending is a bit of a downer.

By all accounts Trollope considered himself rather a conservative citizen. But whether consciously or not, he holds up a number of Victorian conventions to the test of reductio ad absurdum and shows their absurdity to a later generation, whatever his contemporary readers may have thought. No feminist, he showed the disadvantaged state of women in novel after novel. And although Father may often know best, his stubborn attempt to prove it might include the risk of disastrous consequences, as shown in Sir Harry Hotspur.

THE HEIR AND THE BASTARD RALPH THE HEIR

There are two Ralph Newtons in Anthony Trollope's Ralph the Heir. One is nephew to the Squire of Newton Priory and is his heir. The other is his illegitimate son. So: why should the title not be Ralph the Bastard? First: this is a Victorian novel; such a title would have been unacceptable to Victorian society. Second: even though the squire's son shows himself to be more worthy than his cousin, the central figure in the story really is Ralph the heir. Trollope merely says that heroes of pure virtue and villains of unalloyed vice are rare.

This is what it is about: There was a complicated inheritance issue—not contested, just complicated. I had to draw a little diagram to get it straight, and I then had to refer to it time after time:

Gregory Newton the Squire, in his youth and before he became the Squire, traveled in Europe and fathered a child (whom he named Ralph, after his father); the mother died before their planned marriage. Outraged at his son's indiscretion, the old Squire then entailed the family estate to the second generation; that is, his son could inherit the estate and use it for life, but he did not have "power of appointment" (a phrase I learned when tracing my father's many trusts to their intended conclusions). That is, he could not pass it on. Unless the first born (Gregory the squire, who had fathered the illegitimate son) should marry and have a legitimate son, the family estate would go to the first born son of his brother Ralph Newton the parson. (We're talking about three Ralphs and two Gregorys in three generations here.) It so happened that Parson Ralph's first born son, Ralph the heir, was a playboy who acquired more debts than he could pay, and he wound up with two choices: marry for money, taking Polly Neefit, daughter of his tailor, who had loaned money to Ralph and would forgive his debts and give him enough money (twenty thousand pounds) to pay his debts and more; or "go to the Jews," that is, put up his birthright as security for a loan to pay his debts.

When Gregory the father of the illegitimate son heard of this (he had now become squire after the death of his father), he saw an opportunity to take the place of the Jews and basically buy the birthright of Ralph the heir, so that he could then pass it on to his own son, Ralph the bastard.

In considering Trollope's John Caldigate, I wondered at the way in which inheritance issues could yield such complicated plots. Obviously there were contested inheritances; today, even without primogeniture, children of a deceased parent often have bitter disputes over the rights to seemingly minor treasures of much greater sentimental than monetary value—not to mention disputes over significant property and money. But did it ever get this complicated? Who knows?

So much for the inheritance issue. There are complicated boy-girl issues also. Ralph the heir becomes the ward of Sir Thomas Underwood, a distinguished but now idle barrister. Sir Thomas has two daughters—Patience, the elder, plain and intelligent; and Clarissa, a beauty. He also has an orphan niece, nineteen years old and "the most lovely young woman he had ever seen," Mary Bonner. So as it starts out: Gregory the parson, brother of Ralph the heir, is in love with Clarissa; Clarissa is in love with Ralph the heir; Ralph the heir kisses Clarissa and tells her he loves her, but when he realizes he needs money he is persuaded by his tailor Mr. Neefit to propose to his daughter Polly. When Mary arrives on the scene he vows to propose to her; Mary keeps her own counsel, but Ralph "not the heir" falls seriously in love with her. Patience may have had some preference of her own but not the looks to express or pursue it.

This tangle of alliances and preferences is a bit like a murder mystery: can the reader guess who will wind up with whom? And in truth, the novel basically stands on its plot. Trollope is sufficiently realistic to show that Ralph never really reforms. One of the most interesting women is Polly Neefit, who is urged by her father the breeches-maker to accept Ralph the heir, after Ralph is persuaded by him to propose. She refuses him twice, first because she doesn't think he loves her, and then, after being somewhat mollified on that score, because he doesn't respect her father and although she could have any one of twenty young men, she has only one father.

Her first refusal is a classic Trollopian dialogue. He swears he can love her, but after a lengthy recitation of probabilities, she concludes: "I ain't come to breaking my heart for you yet, Mr. Newton."

Trollope handles the boy-girl scenes very well. But his forte is politics. He had run for a seat in Parliament once himself, and he had become sufficiently disillusioned to paint the political scene in some raw ways. Here we find Sir Thomas Underwood, who has retired from professional and public life to write the definitive biography of Sir Francis Bacon (but never actually takes pen to paper), deciding to try to re-enter Parliament via the rotten borough of Percycross, on the Conservative ticket. It so happens that one of the other contestants for one of the two Percycross seats is Ontario Moggs, a young radical rebel who preaches the virtues of labor unions and strikes, and who is also an ardent suitor for the hand of Polly Neefit. We follow Ontario to the Cheshire Cheese, the public house where he delivers impassioned orations; and we follow Sir Thomas in his reluctant efforts to canvass the electorate. Sir Thomas and his running mate, the incumbent Conservative candidate, win the election, but there is a petition—a demand for a recount and an investigation into possible improprieties in the election.

In the definitive moment of this story, Sir Thomas learns that his reluctant expenditures for campaign costs were only the first of the demands to be made on his purse. After apparently winning the election, he is persuaded by Mr. Pabsby, the Wesleyan preacher, to make a contribution for a new Wesleyan chapel. (Mr. Pabsby has been shown to us as having a "soft, greasy voice,—a voice made of pretence, politeness, and saliva.") But then Sir Thomas learns from his "supporters" that the election will probably be contested, and that he will need the loyalty of his supporters if he is to prevail. The list of requirements—personal donations for all the schools and all the churches, as well as fifty pounds for the old women of the borough at Christmas—goes on and on. Poor Sir Thomas. To make a long story short, he refuses any further favors, the petition overturns his election, and the investigation discloses that Percycross is such a corrupt borough that it has lost all its representation in Parliament.

Trollope occasionally indulged in dispensing little lessons in the facts of life. Early in the story Sir Thomas goes to Portsmouth to meet his newly orphaned nineteen-year-old niece, whom he has never seen. He has declared that he will serve as her guardian, and as he waits to meet her, he is apprehensive. And now as he observes all the men taking turns to offer her favors, he learns about "priority of service":

There are certain favours in life which are very charming,—but very unjust to others, and which we may perhaps lump under the name of priority of service. Money will hardly buy it. When money does buy it, there is no injustice. When priority of service is had, like a coach-and-four, by the man who can afford to pay for it, industry, which is the source of wealth, receives its fitting reward. ... But priority of service is perhaps more readily accorded to feminine beauty, and especially to unprotected feminine beauty, than to any other form of claim. Whether or no this is ever felt as a grievance, ladies who are not beautiful may perhaps be able to say.

Walt Disney's film makers understood this in producing Mary Poppins, for whom "boxes and trunks seemed to extricate themselves." But even today one can hardly disagree with Trollope that "priority of service is perhaps more readily accorded to feminine beauty" than to any other claim.

It is difficult to dislike a genial friend. And Trollope rewards his readers with his genial approach to his fictional world. In this story Ralph "not the heir" suffers a major reversal of fortune when his father dies before completing the schemes that would have enabled Ralph, the illegitimate son, to inherit the estate and his father's additional fortune. Ralph "not the heir" had resisted ambitions to inherit the family estate. But he had requested permission to propose to the beautiful Mary Bonner when he anticipated some validation of his status. And now it seemed that he would be a "nameless" man without property or hopes of marriage to the woman he loved. At home, his butler continues to be solicitous for his employer's feelings. And the reader feels that the author of his distress has some compassion for the victim. So he does. But the realistic author also adds the butler's observation after finally leaving his young master: "I don't suppose it do come to much mostly when folks go wrong."

But the geniality of the story is shown as the author cruises confidently to his conclusion of the complicated affair, pulling the strings to the satisfaction of as many as possible. Ralph the heir finally receives a reward through the agency of Lady Eardham, mother of three eligible and more or less young daughters. Lady Eardham receives a letter from Polly Neefit's father telling her that Ralph is engaged to marry his daughter Polly. Of course she knows that Mr. Neefit is bluffing, but she shows the letter to Ralph so that he will know she has it. She invites Ralph to call on her the following morning, and when he does, he is toast:

Of course there was nothing done. During the whole interview Lady Eardham continued to press Neefit's letter under her hand upon the table, as though it was of all documents the most precious. ... And, though she spoke no such word, she certainly gave

Ralph to understand that by this letter he, Ralph Newton, was in some mysterious manner so connected with the secrets, and the interests, and the sanctity of the Eardham family, that, whether such connection might be for weal or woe, the Newtons and the Eardhams could never altogether free themselves from the link.

Her husband approves her work. The daughters certainly do not object. "The girls, who knew that they had no fortunes, expected that everything should be done for them, at least during the period of their natural harvest." And Augusta Eardham, the first fruit of this harvest, accepted her lot in life with equanimity. And it worked out all right.

Bickerings there might be, but they would be bickerings without effect; and Ralph Newton, of Newton, would probably so live with this wife of his bosom, that they, too, might lie at last pleasantly together in the family vault, with the record of their homely virtues visible to the survivors of the parish on the same tombstone.

This passage comes thirteen pages before the end of the novel. Had I been the editor, I should have insisted that this coda be placed at the very end.

A HARD CASE THE GOLDEN LION OF GRANPERE

Michel Voss is a hard case. His second wife's niece, Marie, and his son (by his first wife) George want to marry each other. Marie has lived in the Voss household since becoming an orphan at age fifteen, and now at age twenty she is quietly running the family inn, the Lion d'Or at Granpere. But Michel thinks his son, about twenty-five years of age, should prove himself in the world before marrying. "I won't have it, George," he declares, and his word is law. And thereby hangs the tale.

Trollope loved the hard cases. Perhaps none was harder than Louis Trevelyan, whose terminal stubbornness was celebrated in He Knew He was Right. The Last Chronicle of Barset revolves around the celebrated stubbornness of Josiah Crawley, the perpetual curate who walked miles through the mud to face down Bishop Proudie and his wife in a triumphant confrontation. Linda Tressel, in the novel bearing her name, falls victim to her Aunt Charlotte, a religious zealot who insists on a marriage that Linda refuses. Mr. Whittlestaff, in An Old Man's Love, resisted giving up his young fiancée to her young lover for long enough to make a short novel out of it. And there are others—strong characters whose steadfastness of purpose forces everyone else to bend or face a long struggle.

We are told that Michel Voss might have agreed to his son's marriage to his niece if he had been consulted beforehand. As it was, when he hears of it, he immediately determines that it is improper. Considering it his duty to make arrangements for his niece's welfare, he arranges what he thinks to be a suitable match with a prospering—though a bit effeminate—young man who calls at the inn while trading in textiles. M. Urmand suffers in comparison to George in Marie's eyes; to her he is simply a "rich trader," while George is a "real man."

Marie's relation to Michel, the master of the inn, is an interesting one. She supervises all that takes place at the supper table in the inn, "standing now close behind her uncle with both her hands upon his head; and she would often stand so after the supper was commenced, only moving to attend upon him, or to supplement the services of Peter and the maidservant when she perceived that they were becoming for a time inadequate to their duties." When urged by her uncle to sit at table next to Urmand, the anointed suitor, her only response is to gently pull his ears.

This is one of the short novels Trollope set in Europe in an effort to break away from the template of his portrayals of English life. The Golden Lion is in Alsace-Lorraine, and in this memorable image of Marie, Trollope has epitomized the Continental culture, so foreign to the English. Can one imagine a young English woman standing behind her uncle with her hands on his head while supervising his table?

Michel is the character of interest. The others play their parts, with events propelled in large part because of lack of communication. When Marie learns that George is still serious about his love for her, she brings herself to vow that she will never marry M. Urmand; but it apparently does not occur to her that she can marry George without his father's permission. As for Michel himself, he appears to have painted himself into a corner. The Church will certainly be of no assistance to him. The Catholic priest is summoned to consult. "This was very distasteful to Michel Voss, because he was himself a Protestant, and, having lived all his life with a Protestant son and two Roman Catholic women in the house, he had come to feel that Father Gondin's religion was a religion for the weaker sex." He was not troubled by doctrinal differences, nor was he too particular about what betrothal meant. "He hardly knew himself how far that betrothal was a binding ceremony. But he felt strongly that he had committed himself to the marriage; that it did not become him to allow that his son had been right; and also that if Marie would only marry the man, she would find herself quite happy in her new home." Indeed, all Marie's senior advisors—her aunt, her uncle, the priest—fail to give her credit for having a mind, or rights, of her own. After a short time of marriage to her betrothed, she would be perfectly happy with her new domestic arrangements and forget all about the love of her youth.

Trollope does allow the postal service to play its role. When Marie decides to break it off with Urmand, she does so by writing him a letter, and not telling her uncle about it until the letter is safely on its way.

In the end, it's all worked out by the men. The matter is finally settled when M. Urmand comes to the Golden Lion to settle things, is avoided by Marie, and spends his time playing billiards alone. George is also on hand, and he manages to have some long tramps in the fields with his father, mostly discussing business affairs. Michel enjoys the walks with his son, and a satisfactory resolution ensues.

The story is paced with a light and masterful touch. A climactic scene between Marie and Urmand is followed by stepping away from Marie's little room to a long range view in the first line of the next chapter: "The people of Colmar think Colmar to be a considerable place, and far be it from us to hint that it is not so. It is—or was in the days when Alsace was French—the chief town of the department of the Haut Rhine." It is in this perspective that Michel rests from his decision-making labors to return to his genius for making plans, announcing his plan for a picnic the next day. It's too cold for a picnic, but all go. Urmand is shown to be a friend of the family, speeches are made, and toasts are drunk. All is well.

The Golden Lion of Granpere is a short, straightforward little love story. It gets deeply enough into the details of running a rural inn in Alsace Lorraine to be entertaining. As is usual with Trollope, a number of lengthy paragraphs give the reader no excuse for not knowing exactly what each character is, or is not, thinking. Trollope the traveler learned enough about Europe for a few little short novels. Perhaps they afforded him the breaks he needed between the three-volume English blockbusters.

HOW TO BECOME A LADY LADY ANNA

One doesn't discuss titles and honors much these days. We may even pretend that they don't matter much, and that in these days of democracy and equality we have no ambition for such frills. My wife and I recently spent half a day with a friend of two of our friends, and we were told before the meeting that he was the "Right Honorable" and had recently been made a Knight Companion in the New Zealand Order of Merit after a distinguished political career. Of course this was nothing that I would have mentioned to him; he dismissed very quickly even a comment of recognition I made on seeing his portrait over his staircase. But the title is out there, and I will be hard pressed to report our visit to any of our friends without making some offhand reference to the "Right Honorable."

We tend to smile at the emphasis placed on hereditary and acquired titles in Victorian England. They still exist, however, and the reader can hardly dismiss as completely dated the central role that the issue of a hereditary title plays in Anthony Trollope's Lady Anna. As the title of the novel indicates, the heroine is not just "Anna Murray"; she is "Lady Anna," and the story moves about the efforts of her mother to establish the legitimacy of the title. The plot is an ingenious, if improbable, one:

The unscrupulous Earl Lovel has married a commoner, but shortly after the marriage he informs her that he has previously married a woman in Italy, and that their marriage is not valid. This means that she is not his Countess, and their unborn child will not be legitimate. Needless to say, she does not take this well, and she spends the rest of her life fighting for her title and for that of her daughter. In almost fairy tale fashion, an humble tailor helps her in her struggle, providing encouragement and significant loans of money. In the fullness of time the tailor's young son and the Countess's young daughter move from being childhood friends to sweethearts, and they vow to marry each other. The tailor's son, Daniel Thwaite, becomes a radical advocate of equality for all and abolition of nobility.

The countess becomes obsessed with the defense of her title, and so vehemently does she oppose her daughter's preference for a commoner that she threatens violence and forcibly keeps her daughter sequestered from the young radical.

The late cunning Earl had so arranged his affairs that though his land and title would devolve upon his nephew, his immense wealth was in personal property—stocks and other investments that would go to the Countess and Lady Anna if his previous marriage to an Italian wife were not verified.

A young Earl Lovel appears, heir to the title and perhaps to the late Earl's wealth; whatever had happened in Italy is a great mystery, and the lawyers for the Countess and for the Lovel family fail to find any evidence that they consider strong enough to convince an English jury that an Italian woman should hold an English title. Facing a lengthy dispute, the lawyers for both sides of the family decide among themselves (!) that a compromise should be reached, and that it could best be accomplished by a marriage between the two sides of the family: the young Earl and Lady Anna.

The young Earl is agreeable to this, and he woos and proposes to Anna. All involved parties, most notably Lady Anna's mother, urge the match; but Anna and Daniel the tailor resist all these efforts.

In the presence of such fairy tale elements, the American reader might expect that the author's sympathies would lie with the young lovers, and their fate would constitute either a pathetic failure, or a true fairy tale ending with justice emerging triumphant, with a rousing authorial chorus. But the warring parties are a bit more complex. Daniel Thwaite is initially presented as "a thoughtful man who had read many books." But we are also told that Daniel Thwaite was a man of a certain power. "Men are persuasive, and imperious withal, who are unconscious that they use burning words to others, whose words to them are never even warm. So it was with this man."

And though Trollope had a predilection for the woman who has but one heart to give and never looks back, and though Lady Anna is stated to be one of this sorority—"She had given her heart to Daniel Thwaite, and she had but one heart to give"—it is at least granted to Lady Anna to have some daydreams: "She already began to have feelings about the family to which she had been a stranger before she had come among the Lovels. And if it really would make him happy, this Phoebus, how glorious would that be!"

Trollope was never one to use the blue pencil over passages that spelled out how his characters felt. Not for him the implications and brevity of a later day. We see Daniel Thwaite not as a pure young idealist, but as one with a flip side:

Sir William Patterson had given him credit for some honesty, but even he had not perceived,—had no opportunity of perceiving,—the staunch uprightness which was, as it were, a backbone to the man in all his doings. He was ambitious, discontented, sullen, and tyrannical. ... Gentlemen, so called, were to him as savages, which had to be cleared away in order that that perfection might come at last which the course of nature was to produce in obedience to the ordinances of the Creator.

Development of this story provides no reassurance that Anna will escape from her troubles; after all, a significant mortality risk does accompany certain Victorian novels. As it turns out, her rescue does require a bit of stage business with the desperate countess attempting to use a pistol properly. But the story does evolve with credible development of character: Anna is indeed tempted to throw over her original lover and opt for the life of ease among the nobility. And the author does tell us, in one of his authorial asides, that if the countess and the lawyers had played their cards more skillfully, they might have persuaded Anna to give up Daniel Thwaite if they had given him his due for integrity and virtue instead of trying to persuade Anna of his greed for her money. However, their efforts to blacken him in her eyes only increased her determination to stick by the humble tailor no matter what.

Thwaite is shown to be corrupted to the extent that he will listen to Sir William Patterson, the Solicitor General, the lawyer for the Lovel family, when he explains things to him at the end. Sir William is shown to be the deus ex machina who had also persuaded the Lovel family that there should be some accommodation with the Countess and her daughter Lady Anna. It is true that he had advocated a marriage of convenience, but as this became less likely, he still arranged a compromise between the Lovels and the Countess in court, conceding that the widowed countess's marriage was a legal and binding one. And he did this over the objections of members of the family—chiefly "Uncle Charles," the rector of Yoxham.

And so the "great decider of all things" comes to Daniel in the end and congratulates him on his success, and we find that Daniel likes and respects Sir William, though he attempts to maintain his total opposition to nobility in general and the Lovels in particular. This conversation is presented with skill and humor as the author takes the reader into his confidence, revealing what the story is all about. Here are Sir William's comments on the great theory of equality: "The energetic, the talented, the honest, and the unselfish will always be moving towards an aristocratic side of society, because their virtues will beget esteem, and esteem will beget wealth,—and wealth gives power for good offices."

The eloquence of the urbane lawyer is not lost on Daniel Thwaite. The reader comes to believe that Anna and Daniel have responded to circumstances and modified their views of the world somewhat. Not so the Countess. Determined to do anything to make a wealthy and respectable Lady of her daughter, the Countess disgraces herself and disappears.

One of the byproducts of the story is another of Trollope's portraits of the warts and all of the clergy, in the person of the rector of Yoxham, who never wavers in his opposition to the legitimacy of Lady Anna. This results in an entertaining example of how certain words could and could not be used in Victorian print:

"——— Sir William!" muttered the rector between his teeth, as he turned away in his disgust. What had been the first word of that minatory speech Lord Lovel did not clearly hear. He had been brought up as a boy by his uncle, and had never known his uncle to offend by swearing. No one in Yoxham would have believed it possible that the parson of the parish should have done so. … But his nephew in his heart of hearts believed that the rector of Yoxham had damned the Solicitor-General.

Lady Anna is a fairy tale, as are many of the best stories. One can hardly do much better than to use a good fairy tale as a framework for entertainment, if the elements of originality are grafted onto the framework. In this case genial humor in the face of looming tragedy, and credible character development, allow the appreciative reader to go along for the ride, and the moments of pleasure justify the occasional tedium along the way.

TERRITORY FOLKS SHOULD STICK TOGETHER
HARRY HEATHCOTE OF GANGOIL

It was sheer coincidence that I happened to be reading Trollope's only Christmas novel—Harry Heathcote of Gangoil—on Christmas day. A Christmas story had been requested for the Graphic, and the resulting novel, which was Trollope's shortest, appeared in the 1873 Christmas issue of the magazine. To mark it as a Christmas story, it duly began, "Just a fortnight before Christmas, 1871, a young man, twenty-four years of age, returned home to his dinner about eight o'clock in the evening."

The author had just returned from a year's visit to his son, who was a sheep herder in Australia, and the character of Harry Heathcote was acknowledged to be based on his son. Australia was England's Wild West, and this story is a Western, with its issues resolved by a no-holds-barred fight between the good guys and the bad guys.

"Territory folks should stick together,/Territory folks should all be pals," is the teaching of the square dancers in Rodgers and Hammerstein's Oklahoma, but Harry Heathcote has not learned this bit of wisdom when he becomes suspicious that his neighbor Mr. Medlicot might even be involved in starting the fires that threaten his sheep, their pastures, and the fences that enclose the paddocks where they graze. Mr. Medlicot is a free-selector, one who purchases a relatively small piece of land and farms it, in this case raising sugar cane on 200 acres. Harry Heathcote, on the other hand, runs his sheep over a vast area, some 120,000 acres—"almost an English county"—but he doesn't own the land. He rents it from the English Crown, at so much per sheep, and he fears the encroachment on his acreage by the free-selectors.

Arson was a capital offense in Australia at this time, and Harry Heathcote pushes himself to exhaustion in the summer heat, riding out at night to look for mischief. His brusque manners have not won him many friends, and some disgruntled ranch workers are indeed setting fires. In the heat of the struggle he does finally learn that it helps to have a friend or two. Mr. Medlicot provides assistance, incurring a broken collar bone in the ensuing melee, and the alliance of English aristocrats is cemented by the betrothal of Mr. Medlicot to Harry Heathcote's sister-in-law.

The bad guys are sent packing, Harry learns a lesson, and the lovers join hands. "'That's what I call a happy Christmas,' said Harry, as the party finally parted for the night." Zane Grey could hardly have scripted it better.

Trollope appeared to relish his versatility as a story teller, and though he is often identified with the English settings of the Barsetshire and Palliser series, his travels and his novels ranged all over the world. He used his first hand knowledge of Australia to good advantage in Harry Heathcote, his only novel to be set entirely in this English colony. It's a short, well-constructed story, and after working through the introductory chapters, the reader is rewarded with a quickly told romance, a rousing bush fight, and a happy ending, all wrapped up as a Christmas story.

THE WAY THEY LIVED THEN THE WAY WE LIVE NOW

It seemed that there was but one virtue in the world, commercial enterprise—and that Melmotte was its prophet.

Sometimes a fictional character can take on a life of his own during the writing of a story, and even after publication, capturing the imagination of the author and thereafter of the public. Sherlock Holmes, Scrooge and Tiny Tim, Hamlet, and Uncle Tom have all become iconic in our popular culture. [2] I doubt that any of Trollope's characters make any of the "Top 100" lists; that's part of the Trollope problem: he's just not that well known. But if he were, who would make the list? Mrs. Proudie, Obadiah Slope, Lady Glencora, Mr. Crawley, Plantagenet Palliser perhaps—all these are from the Palliser and Barsetshire collections. And from the other novels—the "singletons"—Augustus Melmotte would certainly take his place. In this century he would be assisted by the strong portrayal by David Suchet in the 2003 BBC production, in which he is described as "this huge monster, Melmotte, sitting like a fat spider, drawing all the other characters into his great scheme."

[Footnote 2: Lucy Pollard-Gott, who has launched a website fictional100.com, lists her top ten: Hamlet, Odysseus, Don Quixote, Eve, Genji, Oedipus, Don Juan, Chia Pia-Yu, Sherlock Holmes, and Arjuna.]

The Way We Live Now has been described as a work of bitterness and disillusionment, but the tone of the book is not one of bitterness. It is certainly satirical; but one could believe that the character of Melmotte stepped in and ran away with the story, just as he swept through London society in 1873 (the year it was written—remember "Now" in the title). One would be hard pressed to say that The Way We Live Now heralded a precipitous darkening of Trollope's view of the world. He did continue to explore the folly of mankind in the novels that followed—The Prime Minister, with the appearance of Ferdinand Lopez, an ambitious, unscrupulous foreigner like Melmotte; Is He Popenjoy? featuring the arch villain the Marquis of Brotherton; The American Senator; The Duke's Children; and John Caldigate. The more Trollope experienced the world, the more targets for his satirical pen appeared.

The Way We Live Now is replete with such targets. Likeable characters are lacking. Two exceptions are Mr. Brehgert, the Jew who tolerates the frank anti-Semitism of Victorian England with saintly perseverance; and John Crumb, "the dealer in meal and pollard at Bungay," who loves Ruby Ruggles and thrashes the useless young Sir Felix Carbury when he assaults her. (Pollard is a fine protein-rich feed supplement for farm animals; it is a byproduct from the milling of wheat for flour.)

Melmotte is introduced as a foreign element that intrudes on English society in the fourth chapter, in which we learn that he is the giver of a great ball. Having just arrived in London from Paris about two years earlier, he admitted that his wife was a foreigner—"an admission that was necessary as she spoke very little English." Though Augustus Melmotte, Esq., spoke his "native" language fluently, he had "an accent which betrayed at least a long expatriation." His daughter Marie "spoke English well, but as a foreigner," and had been born "out of England"—perhaps in New York or Paris.

Only a foreigner could have done what Melmotte did. It is likely that Trollope, who amused himself and us with his observations of the English "as they lived then," did not think that a native-born Englishman could have disrupted society in such a way. This foreigner came in with an ambivalent attitude toward the English. He thought they were gullible enough to buy his schemes, but an essential part of his ambition was his desire to obtain a position of great prominence in English society. He would buy a country place, Pickering, from Adolphus Longstaffe, the squire of Caversham in Suffolk, and he would remodel it so that he could be a country gentleman. He would get himself elected to the House of Commons. He would obtain a noble title—perhaps a baronetcy. His daughter would marry Lord Nidderdale. His wealth and his connections would bring all these things.

The traditional English life that Trollope so revered was crumbling. Adolphus Longstaffe cannot afford to maintain the social schedule that his wife and children enjoy, and the sale of family property offers an expedient solution. Sir Roger Carbury strives to maintain his country place, but he finds himself powerless to marry and carry on his family line. He has set his heart on marrying his cousin Hetta Carbury when she comes of age, but the young girl has little interest in marrying an older man. Hetta's mother, Lady Carbury, attempts to charm editors and other writers into praising and publishing her books so that she can save herself and her worthless son, Sir Felix Carbury, from financial ruin.

Which of these can the reader like? None of the above. And there are more. Paul Montague is a young man who has had to leave Oxford because of some unfortunate rows, and he has spent three years in California, losing his fortune in unsuccessful business ventures and becoming engaged to a woman who may or may not have shot her husband in Oregon. He thinks he can escape her by returning to England, but she pursues him. Like Pinocchio, he falls into bad company (the Beargarden Club in London). Hetta Carbury (to whom Sir Roger has unsuccessfully proposed marriage) falls in love with the young man, little more than a hobbledehoy who consistently gets in over his head, whatever the venture. Yet it is Paul who is the only one to attempt to ask questions at the board meetings of the South Central Pacific and Mexican Railway, and he is the first to discover that Melmotte had been diverting its funds to such personal uses as rebuilding the Longstaffe house in the country.

Such is The Way We Live Now. The country is going to the dogs, led by a foreign Pied Piper with a strange accent. Here is his introductory description:

Mr. Melmotte was a big man with large whiskers, rough hair, and with an expression of mental power on a harsh vulgar face. He was certainly a man to repel you by his presence unless attracted to him by some internal consideration. He was magnificent in his expenditure, powerful in his doings, successful in his business, and the world around him therefore was not repelled.

It appears that had not Melmotte appeared, someone in London would have invented him. As it happened, his great project was actually invented by Hamilton K. Fisker, the young American who had met Paul Montague in California and made a partnership with him. It was Fisker who concocted the idea of the South Central Pacific and Mexican Railway and sold the idea to Melmotte. The presentation was brief. Melmotte and Fisker understood each other. The documents referred not at all to future profits to the railway or to its benefit to society; they emphasized rather the appeal of such stock to the "speculating world."

Melmotte undertook the chairmanship of the Board of Directors in England, and he very quickly found willing buyers of shares, hopes, and dreams. Like Professor Harold Hill in The Music Man, "When he dances, the piper pays him." But when he makes his speech to his directors, it is one that would not do for BBC. In its production, David Suchet is Melmotte larger than life, full of vitality, projecting himself with a powerful personality. Trollope's text would not have been such good theater; in it we see a man who is not eloquent, mostly looking at his plate. His eager audience, however, cheers him "to the echo."

The way we live now is portrayed not as a society that is sold a bill of goods by a huckster, but as one that carried the huckster out over his head even further than he might have ventured on his own. "It can hardly be said of him that he had intended to play so high a game, but the game that he had intended to play had become thus high of its own accord. A man cannot always restrain his own doings and keep them within the limits which he had himself planned for them."

Fisker is the little tugboat that nudges the mighty Melmotte out into the deep. "He had sprung out of some Californian gully, was perhaps ignorant of his own father and mother, and had tumbled up in the world on the strength of his own audacity. But, such as he was, he had sufficed to give the necessary impetus for rolling Augustus Melmotte onwards into almost unprecedented commercial greatness."

What Melmotte does understand is "credit." In attempting to

browbeat Paul Montague, Melmotte rages, "Gentlemen who don't know the nature of credit, how strong it is—as the air—to buoy you up; how slight it is—as a mere vapour—when roughly touched, can do an amount of mischief of which they themselves don't in the least understand the extent!"

Melmotte does of course come to grief, from having forged the signature of Dolly Longstaffe, feckless son of Adolphus Longstaffe, authorizing transfer of the title deed for the house to Melmotte. He also forged his daughter's signature and his secretary Croll's signature to a document giving him access to his daughter Marie's money. Elected to Parliament at about this time, the rumors of the forgery cause his stock prices to collapse. Melmotte's final performance is to go drunk to the House, attempt a speech, fall to the floor, go home and commit suicide with prussic acid.

Set against these affairs of such great pith and moment, the story of Winifred Hurtle is a welcome relief. She was the American woman (another foreigner in England) who pursued Paul Montague to England, where she asserts her rights as an engaged woman, threatening legal action if Paul should break their engagement, and presumably spending several nights with him, according to a narrative a bit skimpy in such details.

The memorable climax of the story is the suicide of Melmotte; but Trollope lets the dark side die with the great financier. There are a few marriages. And the share prices of the South Central Pacific and Mexican Railway begin to rise again as Fisker gets back to work on selling shares in America. What went up came down; and it came back up a little.

We follow the fates of a large cast of characters. Perhaps we don't see that much into the soul of Melmotte. His actions and words speak for him. For once, Trollope doesn't take us into the head of a character who plays such a pivotal role. But we follow the meditations of Paul Montague, Hetta Carbury, and others in the usual detail. Not such a likeable lot, but their stories hang together and justify claims that this is among Trollope's greatest novels, if not the greatest. It was Trollope's longest novel, and perhaps its greatest accomplishment is that the reader is entertained by the light touch that keeps such a dreary story of human stupidity from being abandoned after a few chapters.

WHAT'S A POOR GIRL TO DO? THE AMERICAN SENATOR

Elias Gotobed is the American senator in Trollope's novel of the same name. And in the last chapter the author reveals that Larry Twentyman, a rising young yeoman farmer, "has in truth been our hero." But more memorable than either of these is Arabella Trefoil, the husband hunter. Life was not easy for ambitious Victorian women. Success might have been achieved, with great difficulty, in several different endeavors, but the only path that really led a woman to a high place in society was through birth or marriage. And to this end Arabella aspired.

She herself did not care much for pleasure. But she did care to be a great lady—one who would be allowed to swim out of rooms before others, one who could snub others, one who could show real diamonds when others wore paste, one who might be sure to be asked everywhere, even by the people who hated her. She rather liked being hated by women and did not want any man to be in love with her—except as far as might be sufficient for the purpose of marriage.

Her great sin is that she pursues Lord Rufford, a more eligible catch, while still engaged to John Morton, squire of Bragton. And in introducing her, the author does tell us, "She had had many lovers, and had been engaged to not a few." No one pretends that Trollope was an advocate of feminism. And she hardly emerges as a heroine. And yet a sympathetic reader of the present day can see her as a victim of her times. What, indeed, was a poor girl to do?

Poor, yes, but not without some family connections—enough to put her on the bubble of society—enough, perhaps, to make her feel obliged to reach for success. Her father was the younger brother of a duke. Her other assets were strength and determination, beauty, wit, and enough freedom from scruples to lead her into trouble. "As for caring about him, Mamma," she had once said of a suitor, "of course I don't. He is nasty and odious in every way. But I have got to do the best I can, and what is the use of talking about such trash as that?"

If Arabella is the memorable character, her memorable scene is the one in the postchaise after a hunt when she succeeds in drawing from Lord Rufford a positive response that he loves her—but nothing more. At this point she knows that he will go no further, but she resolves to use what she has gained to try to bring him to the altar, fainting helplessly upon his shoulder. As it happens, Lord Ruffton calls her bluff and escapes. Can you blame a girl for trying?

What of the American senator? In Elias Gotobed we find the prototype of the Ugly American, described in the novel that gave the phrase to our political vocabulary, as pretentious, loud, and ostentatious—changed, in some way, when they leave their native land. Senator Gotobed's sins in England are a bit different. Loud, yes. Lacking in tact, yes. Convinced of the superiority of American ways, yes. But unlike the Ugly American in Vietnam, Mr. Gotobed was not required to expose his bad manners to a third world country; his opportunity was to go to the mother country and demonstrate how a rebellious child behaved toward the parent.

We are introduced to Mr. Gotobed as he meets his host John Morton, the absentee squire, and views Bragton Hall—"quite a pile," he declares.

Mr. Gotobed is diligent in his research and amasses enough data to prepare a lecture for the edification of the English public. He accurately identifies some English ways, such as primogeniture, voting restrictions, and inappropriate clerical wealth, which would not much longer survive the scrutiny of the masses. One suspects that Trollope was using this as another means of exposing these little ways for the entertainment of his readers, and he was able to use a broader brush for this purpose than he used in his own depictions of these same institutions. As an American, I find Mr. Gotobed a rather tiresome caricature of the nineteenth century American. But his likeness resembles a number of others so closely that I fear I might have found some of the real Americans of the time rather tiresome.

The virtues of the English way of life are not lost on Mr. Gotobed. He concedes in his letters to his friend in the USA that the English gentleman is indeed charming, even though idle; pleasant and able to discuss almost any subject, even though he may know very little about it; and hospitable. In addition to these gratuitous observations, he does insert himself into the activities of the community by supporting the cause of Mr. Dan Goarly, accused of poisoning Lord Rufford's foxes.

And here we have the mystery of the red herrings. In an earlier incarnation of the battle between fox hunters and those who considered it a barbaric sport, the animal rights advocates sometimes left red herrings in a fox's path, obscuring the scent so that the hounds were unable to stay on the right trail. Hence our term that applies to a diversion that takes one off the correct pathway to solving a problem. And in this case it was worse. It was suspected that the herrings were laced with strychnine to poison the hounds. Mr. Gotobed, ardent in his opposition to the absurd sport of hunting and killing foxes, defies the conventional wisdom of the village that knows Goarly to be a scoundrel, because he thinks any sabotage of a fox hunt is worthy of support. In this effort he fails.

An ardent devotee of fox hunting, Trollope often used the hunt as a piece of the plot in his stories, and his descriptions of the sport convey the authenticity of the literate sportsman. Each of my two paperback editions of The American Senator show hunt scenes on the cover. And in this novel the hunt shows us Senator Gotobed in his quixotic defense of sabotaging the sport, and Arabella Trefoil on the hunt for Lord Rufford.

The world of the English gentry of which Trollope wrote was not such a large one that prominent characters from other stories might not sometimes make their appearance; and the faithful Trollope reader will smile to get a glimpse of Lady Chiltern and the Duchess of Omnium, old friends from the world of the Palliser series, as they visit the home of the Duke of Mistletoe, Arabella Trefoil's uncle.

And one last bit of trivia: When Senator Gotobed presents his lecture enumerating the follies of the English, he is shouted down and some cry, "Buncombe!" Also spelled bunkum and sometimes shortened to bunk, this term for nonsense traveled across the Atlantic as the legacy of a congressman from North Carolina, whose district included Buncombe County, after he felt obliged to "make a speech for Buncombe" in Congress.

The main plot is complicated and a bit commonplace, introduced in the first chapters that require the reader to go through with a marking pencil to identify the players, their generations, and their family relationships. The requisite dues having been paid, the reader may then go on with the story, but one is still obliged to return to these chapters for reference. Less patient generations of readers have limited tolerance of such introductions, even though some of the author's capsule comments can be quite quotable, as in this observation in describing Lawrence Twentyman: "And his farming was well done; for though he was, out-and-out, a gentleman-farmer, he knew how to get the full worth in work done for the fourteen shillings a week that he paid to his labourers—a deficiency in which knowledge is the cause why gentlemen in general find farming so very expensive an amusement."

If Lawrence Twentyman is the real hero of the story, he is a frustrated hero, unsuccessful from start to end in his courtship of Mary Masters, threatening to sell his farm and emigrate to New Zealand when he fails to win her. He loses Mary, daughter of the lawyer whose family has handled the Morton family business for generations, to Reginald Morton, some fifteen years their senior and heir to the property. Reginald's cousin, John Morton, is the squire of Bragton until his untimely death of "gastric fever." (What was "gastric fever?" Did he have typhoid fever? Or just a convenient diagnosis in the "chapter of accidents" that a novelist must resort to?) John is a victim of Arabella's scheming, introduced as her fiancé in a match with no outward signs of affection. He is employed in the foreign office, is assigned to the United States, is known by his colleagues as "The Paragon," and is later assigned to Patagonia, a remote outpost of the foreign service. John's grandmother dreams up schemes that require closer attention to family feuds than the casual reader will be willing to undertake; Reginald's great-aunt Lady Ushant is the good gentlewoman who is Reginald's champion, and she also befriends Mary Masters. Mary is constantly harassed by her wicked stepmother who urges her to accept Larry Twentyman and avoid the temptation to associate with the gentry. In particular, Mary is urged not to go "Ushanting" by visiting kind Lady Ushant.

This is all well and good, and it's enough to keep the story going; but it's pretty predictable Trollope fare. Arabella, the American Senator, and the poisoned red herrings are the spice to the story.

LESSER BARCHESTER IS HE POPENJOY?

Is He Popenjoy? puts us in familiar Trollope territory: the cathedral and close, and the manor house. We have a lord of the manor, the Marquis of Brotherton, who exercises his rights with such persistent rudeness that one is hard pressed to think of any redeeming virtues; and from there the cast of characters is a familiar one: his younger brother, Lord George, a lesser Plantagenet Palliser, a dull fellow who marries a true heroine, Mary Lovelace, and proves that he hardly deserves her when he allows himself to get his fingers burned by his first lover, Adelaide Houghton, because he can't figure out how to avoid it. Mary's father, the Dean of Brotherton, is a lesser Archdeacon Grantly, rich enough to provide money for his impoverished son-in-law, and too ambitious and proud to keep from offending Lord George with his largesse. Lord George has four ugly sisters, close to a straight copy from Cinderella's stepsisters, who intimidate poor Mary with their family position and their good works for the poor. One of them, Lady Susanna, is worse than the others and at one time visits Mary as an unwelcome duenna. The eldest, Lady Sarah, is better than the others and sometimes sees the light.

Essentially a comic novel, it is almost a farce. The curious interrogatory title (a bit clumsy, like Can You Forgive Her?) is finally elucidated after about a hundred pages when it is learned that the hated Marquis, who has left England to live in Italy, has (perhaps) married an Italian countess and has had a son, Lord Popenjoy. But no Englishman can trust the Italian institutions. Is he really married? Is the child legitimate? "Lord Popenjoy" is the title of the heir to the Marquis. Is he really Popenjoy?

The Dean doubts it, for if the Marquis has no legitimate son, the title will pass to his brother Lord George at his death; and then the Dean's grandson, should he have one, will be next in line. The Marquis's sibs are all skeptical, but they are hesitant to offend their brother. The Dean does not hesitate.

The story proceeds as the Marquis advances from villainy to villainy; he writes to announce the birth of his son and that he will return home. His mother, four sisters, and brother are all to be turned out and obliged to move far away from the family estate. He finally makes his appearance, one third of the way into the book, and insults them all, saving his most cutting sarcasm for the dean, whom he refers to as "that stable boy."

Mary is a credible heroine. She likes to have fun, and she is a bit indiscreet with her friend Jack de Baron, whom she unwittingly encourages to the point that he falls in love with her after she has become Lady George. And the author, who tells us a lot, never tells us so in so many words, but she surely loves him. But the author does tell us that she succeeds in her effort to come to love her husband. Halfway through the book, "She was ever trying to be in love with him, but had never yet succeeded in telling even herself that she had succeeded." But in the process of fighting off a rival—Adelaide Houghton, whom she never forgives—she becomes pregnant, and enduring a separation related to her husband's resentment of his father-in-law's interference in family affairs, she finally convinces herself that she has succeeded in learning to love her husband.

Among the Victorian customs that jar the current reader, that of the wife's duty to obedience is a note that clangs: "The husband would of course be indignant at his wife's disobedience in not having left London when ordered by him to do so."

The author indulges in some sideswipes at the movement for the rights of women. The German advocate is shown to be a money-grubber, and the American expert with the nasal twang, Dr. Olivia Q. Fleabody, "made a rapid fortune out of the proceeds of the hall." Women came twice a week to hear her preach that "a glorious era was at hand in which women would be chosen by constituencies, would wag their heads in courts of law, would buy and sell in Capel Court, and have balances at their bankers."

A woman's duty was to find a husband, and the man's duty was to make it difficult for her. All this sounds as though P. G. Wodehouse had read Trollope and had taken it a bit farther.

He did not mean to marry Guss Mildmay. He did not suppose that she thought he meant to marry her. He did not love her, and he did not believe very much in her love for him. But ... [he] had run his bark on to the rock, which it had been the whole study of his navigation to avoid. He had committed the one sin which he had always declared to himself that he never would commit. This made him unhappy.

Mr. Groschut, the dean's secretary, plays Mr. Slope to the bishop. His letter to the rude Marquis is the only flattering or kind letter the Marquis receives. (The family tries to be nice to the Marquis, but they don't flatter like Mr. Groschut does.) And in the end Mr. Groschut is banished, honored only by being the subject of the book's last paragraph: "Of Mr. Groschut it is only necessary to say that he is still at Pugsty, vexing the souls of his parishioners by sabbatical denunciations."

This book could be legitimately recommended in a paraphrase of the familiar line: "If you loved Barchester Towers, you'll like Is He Popenjoy?" No, that's not strong enough. If you loved Barchester Towers, you'll really like Is He Popenjoy?.

TOO NEAR THE PRECIPICE AN EYE FOR AN EYE

The Cliffs of Moher, now among the sites being considered for an upcoming list of the Seven Wonders of the World, have become the most visited tourist attraction in Ireland. However, there were only a few other visitors when our own little family of five, mist swirling in our faces, paid our respects in 1974. These sheer precipices, facing the Atlantic from the western coast of Ireland, had shed their cloud cover; and our primary concern was to keep the children away from the edge.

Young Frederick Neville, the new Earl of Scroope after his uncle's death, gave no thought to how close he was to the brink as he stood there with Mrs. O'Hara while her daughter Kate, pregnant with the young Earl's child, waited in the cottage. That was the problem, of course: the young Earl paid little heed as to how near he might come to any precipice—hence the liaison with Kate O'Hara, a beautiful Irish lass whose cottage was not so far from his regimental quarters as to prevent his frequent visits. This connection, so offensive to his family at Scroope Manor in Dorsetshire, is the story of An Eye for an Eye, written by Anthony Trollope in 1870.

This short novel is set both in Ireland and in England. After setting his first two novels in Ireland, Trollope later returned to the Irish countryside for Castle Richmond and, some ten years later, An Eye for an Eye, which he wrote shortly after a return visit to Ireland. The towering physical feature of the story is the collection of cliffs. The towering social institution is the order of the nobility of England. Like other institutions, practices, and ideas that appear to be threatened by common sense, this one required vigilant defense and faithful observance of its demands. In this story we find young Frederick Neville called, somewhat to his surprise, by his uncle the Earl of Scroope to be his heir. It would be inconvenient for Frederick to become the Earl. A handsome young man in the process of sowing his wild oats, he had a few more to sow.

And so he does. Frederick returns to his regiment in Ireland and pursues his infatuation with Kate O'Hara of the lonely Ardkill cottage, knowing as he does so that whatever her personal attractions and gifts, he lacks the courage to present her in Dorsetshire as Countess of Scroope. The Earl, before his unexpected death, insists that Fred abandon his Irish conquest and marry the fair and well-born Sophie Mellerby.

The women weigh in pretty heavily on the issue. Kate's mother, we learn, has been married to a Captain O'Hara, presumed to have died after misadventures. We see her walking beneath the cliffs, where she would remain for hours, "with her hat in her hand and her hair drenched."

In this she anticipated the memorable Sarah Woodruff, played by Meryl Streep in the film adaptation of John Fowles's novel The French Lieutenant's Woman, hooded and patient, looking out at the storm from the end of the Cobb in Lyme Regis. In each case, the impression is the same: don't trifle with this woman.

But the drumbeat of the story has begun. Mrs. O'Hara reflects as she observes the development of love between Frederick Neville and her daughter: "Men are wolves to women, and utterly merciless when feeding high on their lust."

After the Earl dies, Frederick must decide. Although his brother Jack advises him to marry the Irish lass and bring her home and be done with it, Frederick is swayed by the advice of his aunt, the late Earl's widow. Lady Scroope, in turn, relies on information from her friend Lady Mary Quin, who sends her regular letters with the gossip from Ireland. Lady Mary entertained no qualms as to the young Earl's duty: he must marry Sophie Wellerby. "There are women, who in regard to such troubles as now existed at Ardkill cottage, always think that the woman should be punished as the sinner and that the man should be assisted to escape."

The die is cast. Although Frederick, as the new Earl, attempts to have it both ways and pull a Duke of Windsor (in a century before Wally Simpson's disruption of the monarchy), his proposal to leave the property to his brother and take Kate to Europe and marry her there is scorned by his brother and by the priest who advises Kate and her mother.

And so the young Earl finds himself on the cliffs of Moher, near the edge and confronted by the mother of the woman he has deflowered and deceived.

Trollope framed his story by introducing us to a madwoman in a private asylum in western England, who cornered everyone she met with her mantra, "An eye for an eye, and a tooth for a tooth." The narrator then reassures the reader that there will be no more of the asylum story, but there will be the story of how the woman happened to come there; and the reader thus knows in advance that this will be a story with a violent ending.

It's a relatively short (160 pages) novel with a single thread that leads the players to their fate. They are not presented as bad people. The reader can have some sympathy for each of them as they make their way along, overmatched and overshadowed by the overwhelming Cliffs of Moher and the binding institutions of the time.

WHAT HAPPENS IN AUSTRALIA … JOHN CALDIGATE

Anthony Trollope sailed to Australia in 1871 to visit his son Fred. (He wrote one novel, Lady Anna, during eight weeks of the voyage out.) While visiting a goldfield in Currajong, New South Wales, he met one of his son's school mates who had visited in the Trollope home. As he described it in Australia and New Zealand (1876):

I saw him in front of his little tent, which he occupied in partnership with an experienced working miner, eating a beefsteak out of his frying-pan with his claspknife. … He had no friend near him but his mining friend,—or mate, as he called him. … He had been softly nurtured, well educated, and was a handsome fellow to boot; and there he was eating a nauseous lump of beef out of a greasy frying-pan with his pocketknife, just in front of the contiguous blankets stretched on the ground, which constituted the beds of himself and his companion. It may be that he will strike gold, and make a fortune.

And so John Caldigate was born. It is the story of a young man who amasses more gambling debts than he can pay while a student at Cambridge and subsequently forsakes his inheritance of the family estate and strikes out for Australia. He falls in love with a local girl, Hester Bolton, after only seeing her once before he leaves, but on the ship he has an encounter with "Mrs. Smith," also in the second class section, and they talk about marriage. We then follow John Caldigate to the goldfields, where his experiences are basically those described above. And then we fast forward some four or five years and see him returning home a wealthy man. But what about the woman from the ship—who became known in Australia as Mademoiselle Cettini, singer and dancer? The text is silent.

Armed with maturity and money, John patches up his relationship with his strict father and becomes reinstated as the heir of the family estate in the fens near Cambridge. Despite misgivings by her family, Hester, the young girl of his dreams, agrees to marry him, and the young hero appears to be triumphant in all. But the reader is less than halfway through the book, and it's too early for a happy ending.

And now we begin to learn more about the woman from the ship. After John and Hester are married and have a child, he receives a telegram from his mining partner in Australia, asking for a large sum of money. He then receives a letter from the woman, signed, "Euphemia Caldigate," in which she says she will return their marriage certificate to him if he pays the money to Tom Crinkett, his former partner; and then she will marry Crinkett and make no further claim on him. Otherwise "the law must take its course."

So what did happen in Australia? Caldigate immediately goes to Hester's brother, a lawyer in Cambridge, and shows him the letter. In response to hostile questioning from Robert Bolton, he states that it is all true except that he was never married to her. He concedes that he was "very intimate with her," and that she lived with him as his wife. When a Wesleyan minister called on her to upbraid her, she said that John had promised to marry her, and John did not deny it. When Bolton asks him if she used his name there, he replies, "It was a wild kind of life up there, Robert, and this was apparent in nothing more than in the names people used. I daresay some of the people did call her Mrs. Caldigate. But they knew she was not my wife."

Oh, these Victorians! "It was a wild kind of life up there." How does this play in England? Answer: Not well. Caldigate is believed by his father, his priest, and, most importantly, by his wife. It soon becomes apparent that Hester has developed from a quiet maiden lass sitting in the corner, into an assertive wife and mother, willing to defy her mother, father, and brothers in defense of her husband and herself. And here we meet one of the blackest villains Trollope has given us: Mrs. Bolton, mother of Hester and second wife of her husband. Mrs. Bolton was a zealot of the low church (which provided Trollope with several of his villains), and her daughter's suitor never convinced her by his attendance at Sunday services that he was anything other than a "lost sinner." His father did not attend church, and despite John's efforts to keep up appearances, he did not have a history of perfect attendance at divine services. And there were even rumors of a relationship with a Mademoiselle Cettini in Australia. John made an explanation to Hester, which she accepted. But Mrs. Bolton never gave her blessing to the match, and although her daughter finally persuaded her to attend the wedding, she only did so as a heavily veiled spectator from a back pew.

And then it becomes known that he has been accused of having had a wife in Australia! With the consent of her stepsons and the grudging consent of her husband, Mrs. Bolton lures her daughter to Puritan Grange, the Bolton home. In a great scene of conflict, she makes her a prisoner there. We have come to learn by this time that Hester is endowed with all her mother's determination and stubbornness. When Hester finds the doors locked against her, she seats herself in the hall with her baby in her arms, opposite her mother, seated in another chair. Hester spends the night stretched out on the floor. Although Mr. Bolton pleads with his wife to let her go, she is more concerned with the salvation of her daughter's soul than with such earthly consequences as murder. "Oh, He knows! He knows! And if He knows, what matters what men say that I have done to her." (Mrs. Bolton shares this concern for the welfare of the soul, at the expense of the body, with another of Trollope's zealous villains, Aunt Charlotte in Linda Tressel.)

In the end Hester's half brothers decide that she must be allowed to leave, and after a three-day standoff the gates are unlocked, and she bids goodbye to her parents and leaves.

In this scene Mrs. Bolton had outdone even the wife of Bishop Proudie in the Barsetshire novels. Mrs. Proudie stands as a comic figure in comic novels, but there is little comedy about Mrs. Bolton. Her sin is the same as Mrs. Proudie's—an excess of zeal in the cause of religion—but here there is little to laugh at.

After this climax, the story plays itself out, but it is clear that Hester will not be defeated. John Caldigate is tried and convicted of bigamy. Prior to the trial he even finds himself conscience-bound to pay twenty thousand pounds (he had received from his Australia ventures some sixty thousand pounds) to Tom Clinkett, Mrs. Smith-Cettini, and their two conspirators, who had not been so fortunate as he with their market timing. (Trollope's visit to the gold mines had convinced him that the gold seeking was all a gamble.) At this point this reader lost patience with John Caldigate, and it is said that his editor did, too, but Trollope refused to change the story, saying that it was essential to the plot.

While John Caldigate is languishing in prison, further evidence in the case is uncovered. Ever the postal service man, Trollope gives us a detailed look at how close inspection of postmarks and stamps helps determine whether an important envelope addressed to "Mrs. John Caldigate" in John's hand was stamped before or after it was alleged to have been sent.

The attitudes toward John Caldigate's wild oats are interesting. His wife's family is horrified, as are some others who feel personally involved. But the consensus of (male) public opinion in Cambridge was that what happens in Australia stays in Australia. "It was a wild kind of life up there." From what we know of the double standards in Victorian morality, it's of interest that a popular novel dared to present a hero with a history of such indiscretion.

This is a good Trollope novel. The plot is an ingenious one. The long paragraphs in which the details of the characters' thoughts are teased out and dissected can be scanned or simply skipped by the modern reader. Some people really are as earnest and naive as John Caldigate. I doubt that very many readers have swallowed the twenty thousand pound gift as a plausible one, but given Caldigate's character it's at least possible—though, in my estimation, unlikely. I had to set the book aside a couple of times when I thought the author was sailing into rougher seas than I cared to navigate. (Trollope could not be relied upon to avoid maudlin unhappy endings at times.) But in the end the reader has had a visit to the Australian gold fields, has gone through a trial for bigamy, and has been well entertained.

A GIFTED CHILD AYALA'S ANGEL

Gifted children are a blessing to society, but they can pose their little challenges along the way. Such a gifted child is Ayala Dormer. Quick and witty, and pretty when she smiles, Ayala receives offers of marriage in rather quick succession from a number of men, eligible and ineligible, and she refuses them all, more than once, for a reason she cannot disclose: she is waiting for the appearance of the Angel of Light, the perfect knight: "How could she make her aunt understand that there could be no place in her heart for Tom Tringle seeing that it was to be kept in reserve for some angel of light who would surely make his appearance in due season,—but who must still be there, present to her as her angel of light, even should he never show himself in the flesh."

In her adherence to this belief she shows herself to be one of Trollope's Constant Heroines, though surely an outlier among the lot. Others remained constant to better men, some being rewarded in this life, some not. But Ayala's adherence is to her own ideal, thus causing a great deal of trouble to those around her, and, I fear, to a number of readers.

This sometimes tedious story is made palatable by Ayala herself, who is as capable of charming the reader as she is of winning the love and loyalty of many of those around her. Her sister's lover Isadore Hamel captures with a vivid simile her bursts of energy, recalling to the reader of Tolstoy the similar sudden rays of sunshine that charmed those who knew Natasha, the heroine of War and Peace:

"I remember her almost as a child, when she would remain perfectly still for a quarter of an hour, and then would be up and about the house everywhere, glancing about like a ray of the sun reflected from a mirror as you move it in your hand."

Ayala and her sister Lucy have been left as senior orphans (a young Victorian woman could not live alone or move about in society unaccompanied) who are taken in by their late mother's brother and sister: one sister to each. Although this becomes a bit complicated when Ayala becomes unsuitable to the aunt who has chosen her and the girls change places, Ayala wins the love of the uncle in each of the two households. In doing so she presents a bit of a problem to each of the aunts—to one because she is a bit poky in assuming the household duties required of a woman in an impecunious household, and to the other because she outshines her aunt's own two daughters.

Providing some relief from Ayala's quest for her angel are the subplots that constitute the comedy of manners in which Trollope excels. These little subplots are so entertaining, why bother with a serious major plot? It takes an uncommonly skillful genius to satisfy the reader with nothing but pies and cakes. Barchester Towers, one of the earlier Trollope novels, came close; it contains only enough serious plot to serve as a scaffolding for the satire of the clerical community of Barchester. And Thackeray's Vanity Fair comes to mind as a long novel of the same period designed to demonstrate what fools mortals be. In Ayala's case, fools disport themselves around her while she is waiting patiently for her knight.

First among these is Tom Tringle, even though the author's sympathy for him tells us that his foolishness is temporary, and he is destined to grow up, though not necessarily within the confines of the present novel. Tom is a hobbledehoy, and one suspects that the author may be recalling his own youth when he reminds us that though a young man and woman may be about the same age, the young woman is often more advanced in her knowledge and understanding of the world and of how to comport herself. Tom suffers from this truth, showing himself to be one who may yet prove himself to be a late bloomer, but too late to be a successful suitor for such a prize as Ayala.

But though women often outshine and outperform the men in their lives, they suffer the restrictions of Victorian society. Living in a later age in which women have won the right to assert themselves more successfully, the differences between men and women still provide the basis for novels, short stories, and drama. Today a woman may knock on the door of a man who does not return her text messages, but men may still be boys while the girls in their lives are women. No Victorian woman novelist knew this better than Anthony Trollope, who described the world as he found it; and the circumstances spoke for themselves.

And here lies the comedy of manners, presented on the stage of the household of Sir Thomas Tringle, a wealthy man of business. Sir Thomas is vexed by his son-in-law Septimus Traffick, a man of birth and a Member of Parliament, but also devoid of fortune or income and sufficiently thick of skin to ignore all Sir Thomas's efforts to dislodge him and his wife Augusta from the Tringle home, whether in town or country.

Augusta, the elder of the two Tringle daughters, is sufficiently haughty to provoke Ayala, in one of the pivotal moments in the story, to ask Augusta to run upstairs and fetch a scrapbook for her. Such effrontery cannot be forgiven. Now more than ever, Augusta often finds it necessary to remind both her family and the poor Ayala that she is married to one of the most important men in the country.

The younger sister pushes herself into the comedy by asserting that she too must be blessed with dowry and husband, and in her sequential pursuit of two ineligible young men, she invites each in his turn to elope with her to Ostend.

The unfortunate Tom Tringle, son and heir to Sir Thomas Tringle, may be the biggest fool of all, betraying himself by his dress as he adorns himself with gaudy jewels and ornate finery when he comes to see Ayala. His offer to fight a duel with his rival Colonel Jonathan Stubbs provides the same mockery of the code of honor as does a similar offer in The Macdermotts of Ballycloran. However, the author finally confesses to the reader that Tom Tringle is the real hero of the novel. His folly is that of youth, and his devotion to his ideal is his redeeming quality. Tom and Ayala share a determination to adhere to the highest standard in pursuit of a mate, and it may be that this youthful idealism and perseverance cause them to be the author's declared hero and heroine.

Another variant of the relation between the sexes appears in the on-again, off-again romance between Frank Houston and Imogene Docimer. Lacking the means to support themselves in the manner to which Frank has become accustomed, they have already broken off an engagement when the reader meets them. Frank, who declares frankly that he has no intention of working for a living, becomes the first of two suitors for the hand of Gertrude Tringle and the handsome dowry she is expected to bring with her. In this suit he finds Gertrude more than willing to accept him and assume the same elevated status of a married lady that her sister has already attained.

Already vexed by the reluctance of his newly acquired son-in-law Septimus Traffick to vacate the premises and establish a home of his own, Sir Thomas refuses to promise any dowry at all to Gertrude if she marries another potential parasite upon his resources. Frank wavers between one young woman (Imogene) who would accept him in spite of his poverty because she loves him, and another young woman (Gertrude) who would accompany him, or almost any Tom, Dick, or Harry, to Ostend, the favored destination of eloping English couples.

Sir Thomas follows the foolishness of the Tringle family with despair. His trenchant observations provide the voice of reason in assessing the motives and machinations of the members of his household who concern themselves with how best to capitalize on the wealth his business affairs have brought them.

The problems of the poor are less farcical. Imogene waits to see what the fates will have in store for her as her true and less than worthy lover pursues the Tringle prize. Ayala's sister Lucy and her poor but proud lover Isadore Hamel push themselves along by fits and starts to their goal of matrimony.

And in the midst of this beehive of activity sits Ayala, stuck on high center in her reluctance to commit herself to any suitor who does not meet her impossible standards. Time after time she refuses a perfectly suitable lover, Colonel Jonathan Stubbs. Here the author repeats for the long-suffering reader her reason:

He was not the Angel of Light,—could never be the Angel of Light. There was nothing there of the azure wing upon which should soar the all but celestial being to whom she could condescend to give herself and her love. He was pleasant, good, friend-ly, kind-hearted,—all that a friend or a brother should be; but he was not the Angel of Light. She was sure of that.

Friends and family make certain allowances for gifted children, and Ayala's friends and family entertain the reader with scheme after scheme for leading her to the light, if not to her own precon-ception of her Angel of Light. Angels are in Heaven; men of flesh and blood walk the earth, and it takes Ayala a long time to figure this out. And as she does so, the patient reader is diverted by the folly of those on this earth who are far less than angels.

And finally, another compensation for the reader is the author's indulgence in presenting old favorites from a previous novel, The American Senator, written three years before Ayala's Angel. (Both were products of his later years—The American Senator in 1875 and Ayala's Angel in 1878. Trollope's stroke and his death were in late 1882.) He named Larry Twentyman as the hero of The Amer-ican Senator in its last pages, but Larry did not win the hand of Mary Masters, who married Reginald Morton. Hopes for a match between Larry and Mary's younger sister Kate are mentioned in the conclusion of that novel, but "Kate is still too young and childish to justify any prediction in that quarter." Larry's modest reward at the end of The American Senator is that Mary gets him to swear that he will be her friend.

But in one of the fox hunting scenes in Ayala's Angel, who should appear as one of the popular habitués of the hunt but Larry Twentyman, married less than a year to Mary's sister Kate. Lord Rufford, "now the happy father of half-a-dozen babies," can no longer jump a fence. Her ladyship is always telling him not to jump over anything he can avoid, and he acknowledges that he does "pretty much what her ladyship tells me." And we are told further, "No doubt she generally was right in any assertion she made as to her husband's affairs."

Trollope took care of his heroes. Had he lived long enough, sure-ly Tom Tringle would have reappeared at a later stage in his life with some of the success that the author predicted for him.

KEEPING THE OLD ACREAGE TOGETHER
COUSIN HENRY

"Cousin Henry is an original novel," Anthony Trollope wrote his publisher, "but it is not for me to say so." I think Trollope's pride in his accomplishment is justified. It's a short novel (280 pages), and it follows with few distractions the thought processes of a weak and indecisive young man who is summoned to his uncle's large estate in Wales and told that since he is the only male descendent, he will inherit it, "unless you show yourself to be unworthy." Henry's cousin Isabel Brodrick has been living with her uncle, and he would prefer to leave it to her, since it is not entailed and he has the right to do so. The uncle soon deems Henry to be unworthy, but the uncle soon dies, and the will leaves the property to Henry. But Henry knows there was a later will changed to leave it all to Isabel. Only he knows where it is. What is he to do? This is what Trollope considered to be his original contribution: he follows the nephew's vacillating attempts to resolve his dilemma so that not only does the author consider his portrayal of these mental agonies to be plausible, he arranges for the family lawyer, Mr. Apjohn, to guess exactly what the young man has thought and what he plans to do.

Does he convince the reader? Yes, I'll accept it. The author holds all the cards, of course, but I find it believable that a young man could be this indecisive. He wants the farm, but he doesn't want to commit a crime to get it and keep it. Everyone knows that Henry is concealing something, and this is perceived through nonverbal communication. The housekeeper and Isabel notice how pale, wan, and spiritless he has become.

Isabel has a suitor, the Reverend William Owen, and they both show themselves to be proud and stubborn lovers similar to such other Trollope couples as Caroline Waddington and George Bertram in The Bertrams. Mr. Owen withdraws his suit when he learns that Isabel is to be an heiress (by an even earlier will) because he considers himself too poor to press his suit on a wealthy woman. Then when Isabel appears to be disinherited, he makes his proposal, but Isabel refuses him because she considers herself so poor that she would drag him into poverty. However, the author has mercy on them. After Henry is found out by the wily Mr. Apjohn, Isabel boldly goes to her lover's house, steps close to him and urges him to kiss her. (Here the reticent Victorian novelist indulges in a bit of sensuality.) Then she tells him that he could never hold his head up again if he should refuse to marry her after "that."

"And I beg, Mr. Owen, that for the future you will come to me, and not make me come to you." This she said as she was taking her leave. "It was very disagreeable, and very wrong, and will be talked about ever so much. Nothing but my determination to have my own way could have made me do it."

Perhaps it would be going too far to say that all Trollope's women outclassed the men, but the women's victories far outnumbered those of the men.

Mr. Apjohn, the Jones family lawyer, believes that Cousin Henry has cheated Isabel out of her inheritance by concealing or destroying the final will, and he bullies Henry into an effort to clear his name in public by bringing suit for libel against the local newspaper, which has taken great interest in the suspicion of tampering with a will. Mr. Apjohn then deprives us of a courtroom drama when he correctly interprets Henry's body language and solves the mystery. But we do encounter the dreaded Mr. Cheekey of the Old Bailey, perhaps a slightly less unscrupulous and unsavory barrister than the infamous Mr. Chaffanbrass of several earlier novels, but one who still "would make his teeth felt worse than any terrier."

Only a glimpse of a vast English country estate is sufficient to make quite clear the importance of inheritance in the English scheme of things. The oldest male heir gets it all. The other sibs get nothing, unless the father or the firstborn son is gracious enough to make some provision for them. Trollope explored variations on this theme in Is He Popenjoy? and Orley Farm, among others. In Cousin Henry, the entire community plays the role of the Greek chorus and condemns the suspected crime. But the tenants of the estate and the servants are all convinced that Cousin Henry is not the true heir. They don't like him, and the servants all give notice of resigning their posts. Trollope allows the victorious Mr. Apjohn to summarize his thoughts about primogeniture. Here is the unabridged sermon:

"A man, if an estate belong to himself personally, can do what he likes with it, as he can with half-crowns in his pocket; but where land is concerned, feelings grow up which should not be treated rudely. In one sense Llanfeare belonged to your uncle to do what he liked with it, but in another sense he shared it only with those around him; and when he was induced by a theory which he did not himself quite understand to bring your cousin down among these people, he outraged their best convictions."

"He meant to do his duty, Mr. Apjohn."

"Certainly; but he mistook it. He did not understand the root of that idea of a male heir. The object has been to keep the old family, and the old adherences, and the old acres together. England owes much to the manner in which this has been done, and the custom as to a male heir has availed much in the doing of it. But in this case, in sticking to the custom, he would have lost the spirit, and as far as he was concerned, would have gone against the practice which he wished to perpetuate. There, my dear, is a sermon for you, of which, I dare say, you do not understand a word."

"I understand every syllable of it, Mr. Apjohn," she answered.

One last detail: The landed estate appeared to confer a personal name with it, which took precedence over a wife's using her husband's surname. The legal maneuvers required by this requirement were quite complicated, but after a detailed explanation by Mr. Apjohn, the result was that when Isabel bore William a son, it is reported that "Llanfeare was entailed upon him and his son, and … he was so christened as to have his somewhat grandiloquent name inscribed as William Apjohn Owen Indefer Jones."

There was always some question as to how Mr. Apjohn should be recompensed for his work as Cousin Henry's "advocate." One would guess that he was rewarded in more ways than one. Among other compensations, he is recognized as the genius who solved the mystery in an early example of the psychological crime study, one that manages to hold the reader's interest through speculative passages about how a man's mind may work under certain circumstances.

WHAT TO DO ABOUT MUDDY BOOTS DR. WORTLE'S SCHOOL

Although Anthony Trollope traveled to North America five times and wrote a two-volume travel book, North America, about his second trip, only one of his novels, Dr. Wortle's School, includes any scenes on American soil. It's a relatively short book, 199 pages, and only two of its twenty-four chapters are set in the United States. But it's a robust story, emphasizing action over reflection, certainly in the two American chapters.

Dr. Wortle is a clergyman with a parish that occupies relatively little of his time—time mainly devoted to his boarding school that prepares boys for Eton. To this school comes an "usher" (a subordinate or an assistant teacher at a school) who seems for Dr. Wortle's purposes to be too good to be true. And indeed the mystery that surrounds this overqualified teacher, a fellow of Oxford, and his American wife, who seems equally overqualified for cleaning up after unruly school boys, confirms that they bring with them baggage that threatens the continued existence of the school itself. The author unburdens himself of this mystery at the first opportunity, with a lengthy "O kind-hearted reader" paragraph that explains his intention of putting the "horse of my romance before the cart" by revealing the mystery "in the next paragraph—in the next half-dozen words. Mr. and Mrs. Peacocke were not man and wife."

Mr. Peacocke had gone to St. Louis and become Vice-President of the College at Missouri, where he had met Mrs. Ferdinand Lefroy, whose appearance—dark brown complexion, with hair dark and very glossy, "tall for a woman, but without any of that look of length under which female altitude sometimes suffers"—suggests that she must have been a Creole, even though she was the daughter of a Louisiana planter ruined by the Civil War. Colonel Ferdinand Lefroy had gone to Mexico to seek his fortune, was reported to have been killed there, and Mrs. Lefroy had then married Mr. Peacocke. When her supposedly dead husband reappeared and again disappeared, Mr. Peacocke and Mrs. Lefroy went to England as man and wife.

So here is a secret in an unstable state. The Peacockes' behavior is so guarded—they accept no invitations, say nothing of their history—that a secret is suspected, and when Ferdinand Lefroy's brother suddenly appears and attempts to blackmail the Peacockes, the fat is in the fire. Dr. Wortle remains loyal to his faithful usher, but the hounds of gossip are hot on the scent, and a number of students are withdrawn from the school, threatening its viability.

The unkindest cut of all is a paragraph in a London gossip sheet, "Everybody's Business," alluding to Dr. Wortle's visits to Mrs. Peacocke in the absence of her husband, who has gone to America to seek out the truth about the status, living or dead, of Ferdinand Lefroy.

"It must be admitted," said the writer, "that the Doctor has the best of it. While one gentleman is gouging the other—as cannot but be expected—the Doctor will be at any rate in security, enjoying the smiles of beauty under his own fig-tree at Bowick. After a hot morning with "τυπτω" [3] in the school, there will be "amo" in the cool of the evening."

[Footnote 3: Τυπτω—to "thump", that is, cudgel or pummel by repeated blows; by implication to punish]

How to respond? Here is the crux of the story. There are, to be sure, interviews between Dr. Wortle and his bishop, and Dr. Wortle seriously contemplates a suit for libel against the gossip sheet, which will bring the bishop into court. But perhaps the most pertinent interviews are those between Dr. Wortle and the colleague whom he selects as his confidante and advisor, Mr. Puddicombe, rector of a neighboring parish. Mr. Puddicombe effectively plays the role of Jiminy Cricket, the conscience of Dr. Wortle. In Chapter XIII, "Mr. Puddicombe's Boot," Dr. Wortle first goes to Mr. Puddicombe with his resolution to reply to the "Broughton Gazette," which has written, "Parents, if they feel themselves to be aggrieved, can remedy the evil by withdrawing their sons."

Mr. Puddicombe tells Dr. Wortle that he has fallen into a misfortune and advises restraint:

"It was a misfortune, that this lady whom you had taken into your establishment should have proved not to be the gentleman's wife. When I am taking a walk through the fields and get one of my feet deeper than usual into the mud, I always endeavour to bear it as well as I may before the eyes of those who meet me rather than make futile efforts to get rid of the dirt and look as though nothing had happened. The dirt, when it is rubbed and smudged and scraped, is more palpably dirt than the honest mud."

Would that each of us had a Mr. Puddicombe to keep us out of trouble!

There is an obligatory little romantic subplot, with a romance between Dr. Wortle's seventeen year old daughter Mary and a noble young boarding student, Lord Carstairs, age eighteen years. Are they too young for an engagement before he even enrolls at Oxford? Will the young lord's father Lord Bracy accept the daughter of a clergyman into his family? After a moderate amount of reflection, these issues sort themselves out.

Mr. Peacocke's journey to America to seek the grave or the person of Ferdinand Lefroy occupies the two American chapters. Peacocke goes in the company of Ferdinand's brother Robert, an unscrupulous but ingenious scoundrel whose inventions are matched by the determination and bravery of the intrepid Mr. Peacocke. These adventures provide an opportunity for Trollope to vent some of his observations about American manners:

He found his wife's brother-in-law seated in the bar of the public house—that everlasting resort for American loungers—with a cigar as usual stuck in his mouth, loafing away his time as only American frequenters of such establishments know how to do. In England such a man would probably be found in such a place with a glass of some alcoholic mixture beside him, but such is never the case with an American. If he wants a drink he goes to the bar and takes it standing—will perhaps take two or three, one after another; but when he has settled himself down to loaf, he satisfies himself with chewing a cigar, and covering a circle around him with the results. With this amusement he will remain contented hour after hour—nay, throughout the entire day if no harder work be demanded of him.

This is one of those Fantastic Premise books, in which a credible story is built around the Fantastic Premise—in this case, the Enoch Arden story of the man who goes off to fight, is presumed dead, and returns home to find his wife married to someone else. Not so fantastic, perhaps; considering the time, distance, and inadequate communication techniques of the period, it is only surprising that such occurrences did not take place more often. The story carries itself along with a good pace; but the greatest reason to read the book is to follow the struggles of Dr. Wortle, sucked into challenges to his pride, wrestling with how to dig himself out.

And for readers who like to close a book with a take-home lesson, one could do worse than to remember what to do and what not to do with muddy boots.

THE CURSE OF CONSUMPTION MARION FAY

I was six years old when I met Tommy Wallace. He spent a good bit of time with his Aunt Rushie, who lived two doors down from us, while his mother spent a year at the Booneville Sanatorium with tuberculosis. We still see an occasional patient with tuberculosis nowadays, but the sanatoriums are all closed or used for other purposes. However, it still causes 1.5 million deaths worldwide each year, trailing only respiratory diseases, AIDS, and diarrheal diseases as the leading infectious killers.

Tuberculosis, known back then as consumption, was widespread in the nineteenth century, causing one out of four deaths in England in 1815. It only began to subside between 1850 and 1950, when deaths due to tuberculosis decreased tenfold, from 500 per 100,000 population in 1850 to 50 per 100,000 population in 1950. Improvements in public health reduced the incidence of tuberculosis even before the advent of antibiotics in 1946 with the introduction of streptomycin. Poor living conditions and the development of resistance to antibiotics have contributed to its resurgence and worldwide threat.

Before the discovery of the tubercle bacillus in 1882, the common understanding of consumption was that it was a constitutional disorder with a strong hereditary element, giving a pale, even "haunted" look to the sufferer. As such, it played a prominent role in literature and the other arts. John Keats, Frederic Chopin, and Franz Kafka died of consumption, as did Edgar Allen Poe's wife, Virginia. Among the familiar victims in our collective consciousness are Mimi in Puccini's La Boheme, Violetta in Verdi's La Traviata, and Camille, played by Greta Garbo in the MGM film of 1936. Doc Holliday died of tuberculosis in 1887, and his bloody cough figured prominently in the 1993 film Tombstone. Consumption claimed a number of characters in Dickens's novels: Little Nell in The Old Curiosity Shop, Nell's friend Kit, Nicholas Nickleby's faithful companion Smike, and both Richard Carstone and the boy Jo in Bleak House. Thomas Mann's The Magic Mountain portrays a sanatorium in the Swiss Alps. Other victims include Ralph Touchett in Henry James's A Portrait of a Lady; Edmund Tyrone in Eugene O'Neill's Long Day's Journey into Night; Fantin in Hugo's Les Miserables; Dostoevsky's Katerina Ivanovna in Crime and Punishment and Kirillov in The Possessed; and Jane Eyre's best friend in Charlotte Bronte's novel.

Anthony Trollope's two sisters and two of his three brothers died at a young age with consumption, an "established sorrow" described in his autobiography as the horrid word, Consumption. With this experience, it is no surprise that Trollope should write a novel, Marion Fay, about a young woman with consumption. The wonder is that it took him so long to write it; it was more than thirty years after his first novel that he wrote Marion Fay, which was finished in 1879.

Marion Fay's story is a sad one. A Quaker's daughter and the eldest son of a marquis meet and fall in love with each other. She refuses to marry Lord Hampstead, however, pleading first that it would be an unequal match for him, but finally admitting she has a strong family history of early death and does not expect to have a long life. Hampstead's emotional reactions are described in great detail, and much of their story is told from his point of view. She is determined from the first that she will not marry, and there is little more to think or say about it. She gradually becomes more open with him as her illness progresses, writing frequent letters from her seaside location. Most of the agonies belong to him, while she appears relatively tranquil, though she does indulge in a Trollopian flop onto the sofa to bury her tearful face in a cushion.

The reader is shielded from some of the details. For one thing, the descriptions emphasize the mental processes. There are no bloody scenes. The color would sometimes rise to Marion's cheeks, and those in the room would hear only a preparation for a cough, not the cough itself. This preparatory sound, the author tells us, is the one so familiar to those obliged to follow the downward course of someone dear to them. And that's it. Marion's illness is said to be a description of the course of Trollope's sister Emily, and she is said to have had a quiet and peaceful course and death. Apparently, if she had a hacking cough or brought up bright red blood, Anthony missed it. In any event, the reader is spared.

As Marion becomes more ill, a frustrated Hampstead, who has fallen under the Victorian illusion that a woman is obliged to obey the man she loves, fails to understand how he cannot control the situation. He has difficulty accepting the inevitable fate she has predicted. A woman has no right to accept such a fate.

Such things must be left to "Providence, or Chance, or Fate, as you may call it."

On the other hand, Marion's friend Mrs. Roden confirms her understanding and acceptance, and she marvels that Marion can soar above weakness and temptation. This angelic portrayal is surely influenced by Trollope's recollection of his sister Emily.

Two chapters of comic relief follow the end of Marion's tragedy, and the author's ironic touch is shown in his summation of the Civil Service, which had figured in the novel's subplots and was personified by Lord Persiflage: "Everybody knew that Lord Persiflage understood the Civil Service of his country perfectly. He was a man who never worked very hard himself or expected those under him to do so; but he liked common sense, and hated scruples, and he considered it to be a man's duty to take care of himself,—of himself first of all, and then, perhaps, afterwards, of the Service."

Interestingly, the word "consumption" is never mentioned. Trollope had written about Henry and Emily's illness in his autobiography, saying that though she was doomed and he knew it, the word was never spoken.

The edition published by the University of Michigan Press in 1982 features the original illustrations of William Small, in which we see the Marquis of Kingsbury (father of Lord Hampstead) looking remarkably like the author, who was used as the model for the Marquis.

No one can begrudge Trollope his novel about consumption. His brothers and sisters died from it, and he used his observations of his sisters to create Marion Fay. The tragedy of the fatal familial curse is presented, and, though it is quite sentimental, it is not badly done. The artist in Trollope knew that he had to leave 'em laughing, and he backed away from the central sadness of the story to return to his objects of fun. Good. He was better at comedy than he was at tragedy.

THE DOG THAT WOULDN'T STAY UNDER THE BED KEPT IN THE DARK

"Secret" is a powerful word—secret police, the Secret Service, The Secret Garden, a secret passage, family secrets, trade secrets, secret recipes, "The Secret Life of Walter Mitty." And secrets are sometimes too good to keep—"That dog won't stay under the bed." Such a secret is the subject of one of Trollope's last novels,

Kept in the Dark, written in 1880. Relatively simple and short, the story is a cautionary tale, one of those that could be recommended as a lesson in life.

A man tells a new female acquaintance about a recently terminated engagement, and the young woman, who has also terminated an engagement recently, fails to respond with an immediate, "Oh, really! Why, that's just happened to me!" And then she feels that she doesn't want to take anything away from his story by sharing her own. And later he proposes to her, and for some reason she postpones making the full disclosure that she knows she must make. And then circumstances fail to provide her with a good enough opportunity; they part, to meet again only shortly before the wedding, and it gets harder and harder for her to tell her story.

Why doesn't she tell, the reader keeps wondering; and the reader is told, in great detail, why she dithers, and of the great pride of the new husband, whose wrath will now be terrible when he is told.

The frustrated reader is now diverted a bit by the closest thing to a subplot in this short and straightforward story line: the young bride (Cecilia Holt) has a friend, Miss Francesca Altifiorla, who is sufficiently bored with the advantages of the single life that she has been espousing to Cecilia, that it becomes clear that the great secret, which of course is known to everyone except the happiest of men (Mr. George Western) is not safe. Miss Altifiorla is not proof against the wicked plans for revenge being plotted by Cecilia's first fiancé, Sir Francis Geraldine, who is smarting from having been jilted with good cause. (Instead of continuing to court his prospective bride after the engagement was made known, he took himself off to the races at New Market, saying that he would be back in a few weeks in time for the wedding, thinking that his title and relative wealth gave him such privileges. Cecilia, with more spunk than either title or wealth, thought otherwise, summarily dismissed him, and then refused to tell her friends who had jilted whom, considering it to be a private matter.)

But the mischievous Miss Altifiorla succeeds in bumping into the recently liberated Sir Francis at the railroad station and subsequently sharing a compartment sitting opposite him on the way to London. From this point, things are foreordained. In the course of giving Sir Francis an opportunity of seeking revenge by letting Mr. Western know of his previous engagement, Miss Altifiorla even has a moment of glory as a temporary fiancée of Sir Francis in her own right.

Their short-lived engagement is the entertainment highlight of the book. Miss Altifiorla sets her trap in the railroad carriage with care and skill. "You know," she said, "that Cecilia Holt was my dearest friend, and I cannot bear to hear her abused." Sir Francis squeezes her hand as they part at Waterloo, and he proceeds to write his poison pen letter to Mr. Western. Considering Miss Altifiorla to be a broadminded woman, likely to tolerate his little ways, and as likely as any to serve his eventual need for a wife, he writes a much more cautious last paragraph in a letter to her: "Don't you think that you and I know each other well enough to make a match of it? There is a question for you to answer on your own behalf, instead of blowing me up for any cruelty to Cecilia Holt. Yours ever, F. G."

Here the clever Miss Altifiorla allows herself to be faked out, and she overplays her hand. Soon, "The milliners, the haberdashers, the furriers and the bootmakers of Exeter received her communication and her orders with pleased alacrity." Unfortunately for her, Sir Francis has already become a bit bored with the wit in her frequent and lengthy love letters; he seizes upon a gossipy mention of his projected marriage in the Exeter newspaper, protests in a follow-up letter to her that he may have expressed himself so badly in his previous letter that she may have understood more than he meant; and then he leaves for the United States.

But as for the husband who has been kept in the dark, and the wife who allowed such a thing to happen: we are given such detailed insights into their backgrounds, personalities, and thoughts that such an improbable understanding begins to seem credible. He takes himself off to Dresden in a huff. (One would think that there must have been a fraternity of fictional English exiles in Dresden, the apparent destination of choice for the disaffected.) He shows all the signs of terminal stubbornness, nursing his wounded pride and making generous provisions for his disgraced wife, who, in her own pride and stubbornness, refuses all such provisions. It becomes apparent that an intervention will be required to break the stalemate, and I had wondered if Sir Francis's disenchanted friend, Dick Ross, who told Sir Francis that he was doing an evil thing, thus giving up his friendship and patronage, would be the agent of reconciliation; but it turned out to be Mr. Western's sister, Bertha Grant, who left her husband and children to make the pilgrimage to Dresden to bring her brother to his senses so he could make the right decision.

It's a short book that tells its story in 176 pages, much less space than was devoted to the similar story of mutual pride and misunderstanding in He Knew He Was Right. Both are intimate stories of marital relationships. Cecilia Holt may be a little less headstrong than Emily Rowley, but Cecilia's pride is brought out by the mischievous letter of her "most affectionate friend, Francesca Altifiorla": "What has Mr. Western said as to the story of Sir Francis Geraldine? Of course you have told him the whole, and I presume that he has pardoned that episode."

The ploy worked. On reading it, Miss Holt's immediate reaction was that she had done "nothing for which pardon had been necessary."

Cecilia's lengthy reflections go further, of course; the more she procrastinates, the more she dreads the unveiling of the secret. Nothing is off the record, as celebrities and others have demonstrated many times. The more she dithers, the more, heaven help me, I sympathize with her husband. He deserved better. But he did overreact a bit. A little toot would have been in order. Victorian to the core, he indulged in a big toot.

Trollope excelled in the nuances of familiarity between man and woman. This comes across as another variation on the theme of poor communications; "secret" is not one of the better policies.

THE ADVANCE DIRECTIVE THE FIXED PERIOD

Dr. William Osler, upon his retirement as head of Medicine at Johns Hopkins Medical School in 1905, delivered a speech, entitled "The Fixed Period," in which he alluded to Trollope's 1881 novel of the same name with comments which, to his astonishment and dismay, brought down a storm of journalistic and popular fury and mockery on his head. Sharing wry and politically incorrect observations which might better have been reserved for private conversation, Osler described two "fixed ideas well known to my friends": the comparative uselessness of men above forty years of age, and the complete uselessness of men over sixty. (Osler was sixty himself at the time.) He went on to describe the plot, which "hinges upon the admirable scheme of a college into which at sixty men retired for a year of contemplation before a peaceful departure by chloroform." The comments were made in an ironic and self-deprecatory mode, and Osler's colleagues congratulated him. Journalists, however, knew a good story when they found one, and Osler, who was leaving the United States to become Regius Professor of Medicine at Oxford, was made miserable by the exaggerations of mischievous newspaper reporters and the outrage of simple souls to whom it was not funny. "Oslerization" entered the language and was listed in some dictionaries as a synonym for euthanasia. [4]

[Footnote 4: Bliss, Michael: William Osler: A Life in Medicine, Oxford University Press, 1999]

And what was the fate of the author of the novel that Osler imperfectly recalled? (The planned technique was the letting of blood from the jugular vein, not chloroform. And it was done at age sixty-eight, not sixty.) Anthony Trollope was sixty-six when he wrote The Fixed Period. He described himself as an old man, and indeed he died of a stroke two years later, before publication of the novel in book form. Osler was one of the few who could appreciate its ambiguity and irony. The book sold only 877 copies, and the publishers lost money. [5]

[Footnote 5: Terry, R. C., editor: Oxford Reader's Companion to Trollope, Oxford University Press, 1999]

It's a rather clumsy bit of science fiction, set in 1980, a hundred years ahead of its time. The location, Brittanula, is a small island about two hundred miles from New Zealand. (If the readers could imagine New Zealand, why not Brittanula?) Rapid transit is by steam tricycle. Under the leadership of the aptly named John Neverbend, the Parliament has decreed that each citizen is to be "deposited" in a College in a place called Necropolis at age sixty-seven, there to wait in contemplation until the end of the "Fixed Period" one year later.

Though the reviews of The Fixed Period showed little appreciation for Trollope's whimsy, he was spared the violent reaction that Osler suffered. The serial magazine publication was anonymous, and the subsequent book publication was after Trollope's death. Even John Neverbend, the fictitious narrator of the tale, endured none of the ridicule heaped upon Osler. So popular and respected was Mr. Neverbend, President of Brittannula, that he was courteously and quietly, though firmly, whisked on board a steamship and deported to England.

Neverbend finally acknowledges that mankind was not yet prepared, even in 1980, for the obvious advantages of the "Fixed Period." Public works could be funded without debt if the cost of caring for the aged were eliminated. As an inducement to accepting the proposal, the "College" would be an approximation of some conceptions of Heaven on Earth. "There are twenty acres of pleasure ground for you to wander over." Interestingly, the honoree did not see his family. Neverbend, true to his name, never forsook his conviction; on board the English ship transporting him back to England, however, he did realize "how potent was that love of life which had been evinced in the city when the hour for deposition had become nigh."

Events on the island give Neverbend every opportunity to change his mind. His closest friend and colleague, Gabriel Crassweller, is several years older and is scheduled to be the first to be deposited. Even though Neverbend himself offers to do all the honors for his dear friend, Crassweller finds himself reluctant as the time approaches. Neverbend's son is in love with Crassweller's beautiful daughter Eva, and she seems more nearly able than anyone else to dissuade the old President from his fixed purpose. But she can't. The power of the English navy, with its 250-ton steam-swiveller gun, is required. Would this terrible weapon have really been used to level the city? "I don't know, Sir. There are some things so terrible that if you will only create a belief in them, that will suffice without anything else."

Reading the story more than a century after its appearance, the reader is brought up short by mention of the chimneys of the College and how they disturbed the neighbors—perhaps more than did those that later actually appeared at Auschhwitz. Eugenics, ethnic cleansing, and the Holocaust were far in the future in 1880. And current outcries about rationing of care and "death panels" indicate how sensitive the public can be about issues of "life and death" that may not be well understood.

The Fixed Period is a clever joke that gets old pretty quickly. People have strong feelings about the sanctity of human life, especially when the issue becomes personal. There is a place for black humor, but it must be sought with great care. The appreciative target audience for Trollope's venture into such waters turns out to have been pretty small. Alas, this small audience happened to include a departing great physician.

DETAILS ABOUT ENTAILS MR. SCARBOROUGH'S FAMILY

Our attorney smiled when he came to the passage, "heirs of his body," in going through our family legal documents, explaining that it was an archaic usage derived from old English law. The term, as used in a deed, creates a "fee tail," so that the property in question goes to the recipient and the heirs begotten by the landowner himself. (On the other hand, "fee simple" allows the property to be passed on to the property owner's heirs, whatever their parentage.) Land under these conditions was thus in tail, or entailed.

The law of entail, which was a prominent feature of Victorian English society, is the basis of the plot of Mr. Scarborough's Family. Entail was created in England in 1285 and was useful to feudal lords in keeping property in the family and undivided, with all the real estate going to the oldest son. Landed gentry tended to favor this arrangement, which promoted stability in feudal society; it was not favored by the monarchy or the merchants. Entail was abolished in England in 1925; in the United States, only four states still recognize entail. Similar goals may be achieved, these days, with trusts.

Mr. Scarborough, however, succeeds in overcoming the limitations of the entail. His property is entailed to his oldest son; since he can't do anything about that, he changes his oldest son. When Mountjoy Scarborough, his firstborn, demonstrates an addiction to gambling, Mr. Scarborough declares that Mountjoy is illegitimate, and he produces marriage documents from a marriage to Mountjoy's mother after Mountjoy was born, thus making the gambling addict illegitimate. The second son, Augustus, becomes the eldest legitimate son. No one has any proof of an earlier marriage, and Mr. Scarborough has his way.

Since this was a "three-volume novel" (Trollope's last of this length), another plot was required, and it too involves an entail. Harry Annesley, declared in Chapter III to be "the hero of this story," is the recognized heir to the estate of his uncle, Peter Prosper, who is fifty years of age and has never married. Mr. Prosper, however, becomes cross with his heir, who has failed to show sufficient respect on his visits in his youth, and he begins to consider marriage to a forty year old woman in an effort to "beget issue," an heir of his own. This was a legal and accepted method of attempting to circumvent a burdensome entail, as opposed to Mr. Scarborough's iniquitous method of branding his eldest son as a bastard.

Lawyers are of course involved in Mr. Scarborough's attempt to circumvent the law, and the family lawyer is Mr. Grey. Trollope required many lawyers in his stories, but they generally are presented as two-dimensional role players. Mr. Chaffanbrass, perhaps the best known of Trollope's lawyers, exemplifies the doctrine that his duty is to his client. Defending Lady Mason in Orley Farm, "To him it was a matter of course that Lady Mason should be guilty. Had she not been guilty, he, Mr. Chaffanbrass would not have been required. Mr. Chaffanbrass well understood that the defence of injured innocence was no part of his mission." Mr. Camperdown, in The Eustace Diamonds, is a bird dog determined to solve the mystery of the diamonds, and he does so. Mr. Furnival, in Orley Farm, proves himself to be all too human in allowing himself to be diverted by the charms of Lady Mason. Sir William Patterson, the Solicitor-General in Lady Anna, is a powerful person, a deus ex machina who forms his own opinion of how affairs should be arranged and attempts to order them so, with little regard for Mr. Chaffanbrass's scruples about limiting his efforts to the pursuit of his client's interests.

But we see Mr. Grey as we see none of Trollope's other lawyers because of his daughter Miss Dorothy ("Dolly") Grey, "motherless, brotherless, and sisterless," about thirty years of age, whom he sometimes calls into his bedroom in the middle of the night to discuss his cases. They also have more formal conversations, as in this discussion of the effort made by Mr. Scarborough and his younger son Augustus to settle Mountjoy's gambling debts. Here she tells her father that he should lay down the law to Mr. Scarborough:

"The law is the law," said her father.

"I don't mean the law in that sense. I should tell him firmly what I advised, and should then make him understand that if he did not follow my advice I must withdraw. If his son is willing to pay these moneylenders what sums they have actually advanced; and if by any effort on his part the money can be raised, let it be done. … Go there prepared with your opinion. But if either father or son will not accept it, then depart, and shake the dust from your feet."

I can't think of another such father-daughter relationship in any of Trollope's works. The above speech so reeks of wisdom that one suspects the author is merely using Dorothy as a mouthpiece for his own editorial comments on the affairs of his story.

Dorothy herself is one of Trollope's finest female characters. The one o'clock conversations, when she is summoned to her father's room by the "well-known knock" and "usual invitation," afford us an intimate understanding of them both. Unencumbered by devotion to a lover, she goes about her duties with a peculiar devotion that her father only begins to understand after he retires from his practice. She visits her aunt's family every day, though she does not care for them, turning "old dresses into new frocks." She has her own innings, in a sense, when her father presents his junior partner Mr. Barry as a suitor. She reads Mr. Barry's character better than her father has done, and she knows better than to accept his offer.

The woman in the story who is encumbered by devotion to a lover is Florence Mountjoy, who has fallen in love with Harry Annesley and has pledged herself to him by a nod of her head. "A man's heart can be changed, but not a woman's. His love is but one thing among many," she declares to Mountjoy Scarborough in declining his repeated proposal, affirming the doctrine to which so many of Trollope's heroines adhered. Florence shows spunk and determination, standing her ground against her mother, uncle and aunt in the British legation house in Brussels to which she has been brought to clear her head and heart of Harry Annesley.

Trollope was sixty-six years old when he wrote Mr. Scarborough's Family. He completed a short novel and almost completed another before dying of a stroke at age sixty-seven. His skills were undiminished. His overall themes and views were familiar ones; he was now looking at life, if not through a rear view mirror, at least with a bit more detachment and irony than in earlier decades. He was still able to generate and maintain detailed story lines, and he continued his mastery of showing many facets of his characters and events, mostly through revealing the inner thoughts of several characters.

Memorable characters continued to appear in his landscapes. Besides Dorothy Grey and her father, there is the old rascal, Mr. Scarborough himself. The others all marvel at successive revelations of his deviousness, and their assessments show us both him and them. All "London had declared that so wicked and dishonest an old gentleman had never lived." Mr. Barry, after traveling to Germany to unearth the documentation of his first marriage to the same woman, in an obscure village, concluded, "In my mind he has been so clever that he ought to be forgiven all his rascality." And now, "Everyone concerned in the matter seemed to admire Mr. Scarborough, except Mr. Grey, whose anger, either with himself or his client, became the stronger, the louder grew the admiration of the world." Mr. Merton, the medical apprentice who stayed with him the last three months of his life, concluded, "One cannot make an apology for him without being ready to throw all truth and all morality to the dogs. But if you can imagine for yourself a state of things in which neither truth nor morality shall be thought essential, then old Mr. Scarborough would be your hero. He was the bravest man I ever knew."

No Trollope novel is complete without several proposals of marriage, and this story includes four to Florence Mountjoy, some of them repeated; but the scene between Squire Prosper and Miss Thoroughbung, in which Mr. Prosper pursues his purpose of getting an heir to disinherit Harry Annesley, must rank near the top of all Trollope's proposals. Miss Thoroughbung is the sister of a brewer and has money of her own; she also has her own agenda, as Mr. Prosper learns. Her encouragement leads him to the point, and he recites one of the sentences he had composed for the occasion: "In beholding Miss Thoroughbung I behold her on whom I hope I may depend for all the future happiness of my life."

The engagement does not last; it falls afoul of the Victorian equivalent of the pre-nup, in which the would-be bride insists on bringing with her a pair of ponies and her friend Miss Tickle. Other financial considerations were negotiable, but the match founders on Miss Tickle and the ponies.

The visitor from the twenty-first century is allowed a few peeks into the world of the nineteenth: A visitor to Mr. Prosper's country place declines to stay for the night, pleading that he has neglected to bring a dress coat. "Mr. Prosper did not care to sit down to dinner with guests who did not bring their dress coats." And courtship follows its own protocols. Harry Annesley goes to Tretton Park when Florence Mountjoy is there, and he

endeavoured to plead his own cause after his own fashion. This he had done after the good old English plan which is said to be somewhat loutish, but is not without its efficacy. He had looked at her, and danced with her, and done the best with his gloves and cravat, and had let her see by twenty unmistakable signs that in order to be perfectly happy he must be near her. ... But he had never as yet actually asked her to love him. But she was so quick a linguist that she had understood down to the last letter what all these tokens had meant.

And there was a Victorian equivalent of Las Vegas, where the best entertainment can be enjoyed for the most reasonable prices, because a gambling house is a profitable business, and the entertainment is a "loss leader:"

Who does not know the outside hall of the magnificent gambling house at Monte Carlo, with all the golden splendour of its music-room within? Who does not know the lofty roof and lounging seats, with all its luxuries of liveried servants, its wealth of newspapers, and every appanage of costly comfort which can be added to it? ... [At] Monte Carlo you walk in with your wife in her morning costume, and seating yourself luxuriously in one of those soft stalls which are there prepared for you, you give yourself up with perfect ease to absolute enjoyment. For two hours the concert lasts, and all around is perfection and gilding. ... Nothing can be more perfect than the concert-room at Monte Carlo, and nothing more charming; and for all this there is nothing whatever to pay.

Rather a leisurely survey of one aspect of the Victorian scene. And as the author brings the story to a close, some of the characters are rewarded with their own chapters, in order to make their exits. Of these, that of Mr. Grey shows us the destiny of the lawyer who tried to be good and to do good. Disillusioned with how the world has changed under his feet, feeling guilty and inadequate after having had the wool pulled over his eyes by Mr. Scarborough, and uncomfortable with his junior partner's more lenient views of professional ethics, he retires and vows to do good deeds, starting with his sister's family of a drunkard husband and five daughters in need of husbands. He rings their doorbell and is met by Mr. Matterson, a widowed clergyman with five children who has offered to marry Amelia, the eldest. He then learns from

Amelia that she has no reservations about leaving Papa, who "is getting to be quite unbearable," and marrying the clergyman.

Poor Mr. Grey, when his niece turned and went back home, thought that, as far as the girl was concerned, or her future household, there would be very little room for employment for him. Mr. Matterson wanted an upper servant who, instead of demanding wages, would bring a little money with her, and he could not but feel that the poor clergyman would find that he had taken into his house a bad and expensive upper servant.

"Never mind, Papa," said Dolly; "we will go on and persevere, and, if we intend to do good, good will certainly come of it."

And we devoutly hope so. There are two more chapters to tie up some loose ends. But this pretty much wraps it up. Is this what comes from a lawyer trying to be good and to do good?

PROMISES, PROMISES AN OLD MAN'S LOVE

Some children discovered the first diamond in South Africa in 1867, an event described by Anthony Trollope in "The Diamond Fields of South Africa," [6] upon visiting the area during the last six months of 1877. The rush for diamonds then duly turned up five years later in a novel, An Old Man's Love, completed just six months before his death. John Gordon is the adventurer in the story; he goes away to make his fortune in diamonds when he is told that he cannot marry his beloved Mary Lawrie because he is a pauper—even though they have never spoken to each other of their love. He returns three years later as a rich man, only to find that Mary has promised, only a half hour earlier, to marry someone else—Mr. William Whittlestaff, who at fifty years of age is the "old man" of the title.

[Footnote 6: South Africa, Vol. 2, chapter VIII, 1878]

No matter that she told Mr. Whittlestaff, who took her into his house when her stepmother died, that she loved Mr. Gordon and would always think of him. A promise is a promise, not to be given or broken lightly. Though she would not allow the "old man" to kiss her, she would not break her promise. Bad timing. The diamonds don't seem to make much difference.

They certainly don't make much difference to Mrs. Baggett, the woman who rules Croker's Hall as Mr. Whittlestaff's housekeeper. She puts no trust in diamonds—"only in the funds, which is reg'lar." She has her own concerns; she is incensed that Mr. Gordon would even presume to come speak to the young woman in her master's house, and she sternly tells Mary that her duty is to see to it that the master has his way.

Mrs. Baggett has her principles. Though she urges Mary to accept Mr. Whittlestaff in the first place, and to keep her promise when the matter appears to be in doubt, yet she maintains that she will not stay to serve under another woman who is mistress of Croker's Hall. Not only will she not stay, she will go to Portsmouth to take care of her drunken one-legged husband. Mr. Whittlestaff cannot shake her from this resolve, and she tells him he must not abandon his engagement: "It's weak, and nobody wouldn't think a straw of you for doing it."

The author reaches into his bag of churchmen to produce Reverend Montagu Blake, who is addressed appropriately by his fiancée when she says, "Don't be a fool, Montagu." We see the young curate celebrate his good fortune at the death of Rev. Harbottle, freeing his pulpit for Mr. Blake, and also permitting him to marry Kattie Forrester. "But now that old Harbottle has gone, I'll get the day fixed; you see if I don't."

What of the "old man?" Mr. Whittlestaff listens to his housekeeper's stern counsel to be a man and keep what is his. Then he retreats to a secluded hillside to consult his well-worn copy of Horace (the Victorian gentlemen knew their classics) in an effort to identify the wisdom of the ages. And finally he asks himself whether Mrs. Baggett's lessons correspond to those of Jesus Christ. In these ruminations he is shown as a man who rises above the cardboard cutout of a selfish old country squire in love with his young ward. His deliberations with himself are lengthy; though he consults his volume of Horace, he finds that he remembers Horace's counsel well enough to weigh it without looking; and he finds it wanting.

His moment of critical decision involves a short serious interview with his young fiancée—an unusually tender Trollopian interview—as he prepares to go to London to see John Gordon and offer Mary to him. She puts her arm upon him and entreats him not to go, telling him that he his entitled to have "whatever it is that you may want, though it is but such a trifle."

Mr. Whittlestaff finally settles the issue when she announces that she will burn the letter he had written to Mr. Gordon arranging to meet him; he calls for a sandwich and a glass of wine, swearing that he will start in an hour.

The reader must remember that her original agreement to marry Mr. Whittlestaff was verbal, not physical; she did not allow him to kiss her; nor did she go beyond putting her arm on him and looking into his face on this occasion. Though this modest gesture is sufficient to mark it as a tender interview, one cannot help concluding that this young Victorian woman fought the battle with one arm behind her back.

Mr. Whittlestaff shows that he understands this by the completion of his mission. The subsequent interview with Mr. Gordon in Green Park is hardly a tender one; indeed, it becomes a bit testy on both sides; but the mission is accomplished.

"The most important part of our narrative" is compressed into the last page of the book. Youth is served; but so well has the groundwork been laid in the relatively few pages of this short novel, that the reader closes the book feeling that it has all been a bit more than just a fairy tale.

This was Trollope's last novel to be completed. He was in the middle of writing The Landleaguers when he had a stroke and died. An Old Man's Love was published posthumously in 1884.

RUNNING IN FULL STRIDE AT THE END THE LANDLEAGUERS

The sense of urgency that ordinarily attends the last few pages of a novel is absent as one approaches the end—but not the conclusion—of The Landleaguers, knowing that the story is to be terminated at the place where Anthony Trollope had the stroke that ended his writing career and, a month later, his life. The reader, instead of racing to the conclusion, tends to linger, watching for any clue as to the impending blow, dreading the moment when the storyteller closes the book for an unexpected interruption, never to return. At least the stroke did not occur during the writing, with the pen dropping from his hand in midsentence. He actually dictated these pages to his son Harry on the morning of November 3, 1882; on that evening he suddenly fell silent while everyone else was laughing at the reading of a comic novel after dinner in the home of his friend John Tilley, and it was apparent that he had had a stroke, leaving him with paralysis of his right side and inability to speak.

Trollope made two trips to Ireland during his last year to familiarize himself with the efforts at land reform and the accompanying violence that he depicted in The Landleaguers; he returned for a second visit after he had already begun writing it. This was the most topical of his novels, and he interviewed several government officials and other knowledgeable Irishmen, but not any of the Landleaguers—those who advocated reform measures that would infringe on the rights of property. Indeed, he interrupted his story of "our three heroines," declaring it necessary to describe the "political circumstances of the day" with an entire chapter. Although Trollope had personal affection for Ireland as the place where he had spent eighteen years and had begun his writing, he was a son of England first and foremost. He had no sympathy for rebellion.

Events on the ground in 1882 marched right through his story, including a reference to the murder of Lord Frederick Cavendish on his first day on the job as Chief Secretary for Ireland, and of his Under Secretary T. H. Burke, in May, eleven days before Trollope arrived to begin his research. And in August, five members of a Joyce family were murdered—a tragedy he incorporated into his story.

Ordinarily, an unfinished work is not to be judged, but knowing what we know about Trollope's writing patterns, it seems unlikely that any major revisions would have occurred in what he had already written. We do have forty-eight of the planned sixty chapters, with a short note by Harry Trollope to confirm what any experienced Trollope reader would suspect as to who married whom and who was to be hanged in the end. And as we follow the misfortunes of the Jones family members who occupied Morony Castle, we see the effects of a campaign of terror in a quiet green countryside. Outside agitators, surely from America, have come among the "generous, kindly, impulsive, and docile" country Irish folk, leading them to believe that one man is as good as another (nothing said about the women, of course), and that those who rent land don't really have to pay their full rent to the lord of the manor. Farmers in America don't pay rent to a landlord, they are told. Each man has his own (small) farm. If the lands of America were there to be taken from the Indians, why should not the Irish farmers take it from the greedy landlords?

Mr. Jones's problems at Morony Castle begin when his sluice gates are opened, flooding eighty acres of good bottom land. His ten-year old son Florian, who happened to witness the event, is terrified into silence by his father's discontented renter who makes him swear not to tell, invoking the Catholic religion that the lad had innocently adopted as a bit of filial rebellion. After months of pressure and wheedling by his sisters, who guess correctly that he knows, young Florian finally names Pat Carroll as the culprit. On his way to the courthouse with his father to give testimony, he is shot through the head and killed by a double barrel rifle poked through a hole in a stone wall along the road.

This reign of terror happened to occur in rural Ireland; it could have been the Taliban in Afghanistan, the mafia in Sicily, the mob in Chicago, or the Ku Klux Klan in the Jim Crow South. But here in County Galway the usual ingredients were to be found: inadequate law enforcement, young men with more testosterone than employment, and a fearful populace.

Less violent but more widespread rebellion had already appeared in the disruption of a fox hunt. The author had learned fox hunting in Ireland, and many of the momentous events in his novels take place at fox hunts. On this occasion, whenever the hunters arrive at a gorse covert, they find the local farmers already there, having beaten the area so that no fox would have remained for the chase.

And the Jones family finds itself the victim of a boycott, a term that had only come into use two years earlier when Captain Charles Boycott, land agent of an absentee landlord in County Mayo in Ireland, had attempted to evict eleven tenants who refused to pay their full rent. Charles Parnell, the champion of Irish nationalism and a land reform agitator, had already recommended that an offending landowner might be ostracized. Captain Boycott then found himself victim of the process that later bore his name. And in The Landleaguers all the servants but one leave the Jones household. The family is unable to buy anything in town, and no one in the town will buy from the farm. The daughters come to enjoy, in a way, household duties such as cooking, making beds, and churning butter. The family, though, is devastated.

And the women pay a surcharge. As we see Mr. Jones carving the mutton and serving a male visitor first, the author explains: "In a boycotted house you will always find that the gentlemen are helped before the ladies. It is a part of the principle of boycotting that women shall subject themselves."

As the nonviolent civil disobedience changes to murder, the story takes on the dimensions of a western movie when the heralded lawman comes to town to institute law and order and set things straight. This was Captain Yorke Clayton, possessed of two attributes that would lead any man to fame: recklessness and light blue eyes. With these attributes he wins the hearts of both Jones sisters, Ada and Edith. Edith, the younger and brighter of the two, tells herself and everyone else that he will prefer Ada, the elder and the more beautiful. By the time he declares himself to be in love with Edith, she has such a difficult time getting rid of her story that the issue is not resolved within forty-eight chapters. After Florian is killed, Captain Clayton becomes obsessed with the identification of his killer. The villain is assumed to be Terry Lax, an agitator from another county who is guilty of murdering the other witness who was prepared to identify the opener of the sluice gate. This was done in a crowded courtroom with the pistol at the victim's head, and no one could be found who would say he had seen who did it. The author did not live to unravel the murder for us and wrap up all the loose ends; we are assured by Trollope's son Harry, however, that the Captain did marry Edith and that the infamous Mr. Lax was hanged by the neck until he was dead.

Besides all this there is the subplot, a story that moviegoers in the following century would recognize as show-biz melodrama. Young Frank Jones, son of the lord of Morony Castle, is in love with Rachel O'Mahony, whose beautiful singing voice on stage is her meal ticket. "We may best describe her by saying that she was an American and an actress," the author tells us. Rachel came to Ireland with her father, who had "probably" been born in America, though the family was Irish. She is accompanied by her manager, referred to by her as the "greasy Jew" Mahomet M. Moses, who also wants to marry her. Rachel, a tiny thing, holds out against him, but then she receives attention from Lord Castlewell, forty years old, eldest son of the Marquis of Beaulieu, with lots of money and a fondness for young ladies of the theater. Frank has not the money to support her, refuses to be supported by her, and, in short, she accepts Lord Castlewell's proposal—only to change her mind after she becomes ill and loses her singing voice. Harry tells us that Frank was to marry Rachel in the end.

And so Anthony Trollope began and ended his writing career with a novel about Ireland. He didn't live long enough to play this one out, but we're fortunate to have the first forty-eight chapters and his son's assurance of how it was to have ended in the last twelve. His last work was one that reprised some of his favorite themes—the fox hunt, a murder mystery, a young American woman with a smart mouth, a stubborn young woman reluctant to accept a suitor whom she loves, and the ways of the simple folk of Ireland. He was running in full stride when he fell.

ACKNOWLEDGMENTS

One hesitates to implicate others in a private madness. A project such as this one requires a certain bit of monomania. However, there are a few who cannot escape complicity.

Chip Paris of Williams/Crawford & Associates has added great value to this and a previous book with graphic design of the cover. Amanda Holland's creativity has allowed The Way They Lived Then to present itself to the reader in a fashion that has been pleasing to me and all who have been asked to comment. Kay Aclin, two of whose paintings hang in our house, provided valuable last minute advice on the color scheme of the cover. Chip's father Charles Paris is an old friend who provided the photograph of the author.

Todd Stewart and I share a few eccentricities, but he is far ahead of me in understanding how to prepare and publish a manuscript. I don't want to know how many hours he has devoted to promoting this and our other joint ventures.

Professor Rebecca Resinski of the Classics Department of Hendrix College maintains a web site for classical allusions in Trollope, www.trollope-apollo.com, which has been a handy way to try to keep up with Trollope's training in Greek and Latin. More important has been her personal encouragement.

My wife Mary read all these reviews, and nothing went out of the house, nor did I ever dare punch "Send," without her ok.

Taylor Prewitt grew up in McGehee, Arkansas and received his BA in English from the University of Arkansas and his MD from Washington University. His training in internal medicine and cardiology was at North Carolina Memorial Hospital in Chapel Hill. He practiced cardiology at Cooper Clinic in Fort Smith, Arkansas, from 1969 to 2003, interrupted only by spending the year 1974 as a Senior Fellow in Cardiology at the Brompton Hospital in London.

He has been reading the novels of Anthony Trollope for some forty years. He is the author of Reciting Robert Frost in the ICU: Essays in the Literature of Medicine and several other collections of book reviews.